DESTINED

BY CHOICE OR CIRCUMSTANCE

Michael D Brooks

DESTINED

BY CHOICE OR CIRCUMSTANCE

Michael D Brooks

Cover photo by Canva
Cover design by Michael D Brooks

ISBN 979-8496322430

Independently Published, October 14, 2021

Contents

Acknowledgments

I offer my thanks to everyone who helped, supported, and encouraged me to write my first science fiction adventure.

A special thanks to my wife and her tenacious spirit.

Thank you to my beta readers for all of their helpful input: Projekt_Itachi, Linda Stokes, Gregory Stubblefield, Martha VanAuken.

And for the encouragement of fellow writers W. D.Foster-Graham and Maria A. Perez.

Chapters

CHAPTER 1

Kissed by the rays of the sun, the ground released invisible waves of swirling warmth upward into the darkness of the night sky. The unseen willowy wisps slid like soothing fingers through the air and rose skyward into the ebony night that was painted with a smattering of twinkling stars accompanied by a brilliant light show of dazzling fireworks. Colorful bursts of pale powder blue and canary yellow lights, highlighted by green and white streaks resembling shooting stars and fireflies, peppered the heavens.

To the casual observer on the ground of the farming planet Aggro Nine, it was a spectacular sight to behold, but the pyrotechnic display masked something more insidious than what appeared to the naked eye. It was an unchoreographed dance of life and death in the cold vacuum of space. Among its many players was the Alliance's best starfighter pilot. With him was its best gunner. They were unwilling participants trapped in a ferocious battle between warriors of opposing factions.

There was the Galactic Star Empire, an axis of merciless reptilian-like beings determined to conquer all non-reptilian inhabitants of the known universe. They believed it was their destiny through divine right to rule the known universe. They saw other lifeforms as inferior and either enslaved or exterminated them. Genocide was their preferred method of choice. The practice earned them the reputation of cold-blooded murderers. A label they were proud to own.

There was also the Union of Allied Worlds. Known to its members and by its enemy simply as the Alliance. It was an organization of planets whose philosophy was the direct opposite of the GSE. They believed all worlds and cultures had the right to coexist peacefully. Free from tyranny and oppression.

In the middle were the military combatants of both organizations. Delta Squadron was currently engaged in a savage battle high above the farming planet Aggro Nine with their counterparts. Ambushed by an overwhelming number of GSE fighters while on a relief mission to the planet, the Alliance pilots made a valiant stand in what quickly became a losing effort.

At first, Delta Squadron had the upper hand and did a good job defending itself until a fresh unit of GSE fighters appeared from hyperspace and tipped the balance. The Alliance pilots were not as fortunate. No fresh reinforcements arrived. They had to make do with what they had. Comm chatter grew increasingly desperate.

Discipline and order quickly degenerated into chaos evident in the overlapping mass of confused and panicked voices shouting, screaming, and suddenly falling silent as their defensive strategy was ripped to shreds by the GSE fighters.

"Hold the line," a pilot was heard saying just before her remains were scattered in orbit.

"They're getting through!" shouted one pilot as his fighter vaporized around him.

"They're everywhere!" another pilot screamed as her ship slammed into a destroyed enemy fighter.

Amid all the turmoil and carnage were Captain David Leahcim, pilot of the fighter he dubbed the *Midnight Sun*, and his steadfast gunner and close friend, Lieutenant Markka. Forced to rely on instinct, their trust in each other, and adrenaline to stay alive, they pulled out every trick in the book, and some not written yet, to outmaneuver and outlast their counterparts.

"We're getting our asses kicked," Markka fumed, as the young gunnery officer reduced another enemy fighter to a fireball of expanding gases in the cold blackness of space. She smirked with satisfaction as the fireball faded into particles of vaporized matter.

"We just need to hang on until Fleet gets here," her captain said.

"They better or there'll be no one left."

Captain David Leahcim, an experienced starfighter combat veteran, shared his gunner's opinion. Staying alive long enough for help to arrive was at the top of his list. They needed a miracle to tip the balance to their side. And it appeared they were all out of miracles.

Green tracer fire streaked across the cockpit canopy. "Shit," he cursed. "Bandit inbound. Hang on!" He jerked back on the control stick next to his right thigh and twirled their fighter with the efficiency of someone who could execute the maneuver in his sleep.

The evasive tactic worked. He avoided being tagged by the glowing energy bolts that streamed from the pursuing fighter.

"I see him," Markka confirmed, as she tracked it on the heads-up display in front of her. She never took her eyes off of it. She sat in a rear-facing chair directly behind her captain following every little blip, dot, and sound on its tactical display ready to pull the trigger on her tail gun and destroy another enemy fighter at any moment.

Leahcim tightly gripped his control stick and grunted as he dove, climbed, banked left then right doing his best to dodge more weapons fire from a second enemy fighter that joined the one already closing in on them from behind.

"Now we got two on our six!" Markka shouted."

"I know. I know." His voice had an edge of annoyance in it because he was having a difficult time trying to shake the enemy fighter. He reminded himself to keep his head in the game or they would be dead. Leahcim grunted through gritted teeth. His arm muscles burned as he strained and pulled back on his stick. He swung the fighter into a looping arc just as he spotted a chunk of floating debris from what remained of a Fleet starfighter drift across his flight path. It was a gruesome reminder that their friends were dying all around them. He jerked the stick hard to the right and swung their fighter in a starboard direction as he attempted to avoid hitting the jagged wreckage. Leahcim avoided colliding with it dead-on but was not able to miss it entirely.

They barely felt the impact, but the screeching and crunching sound it made as it scraped along the belly of the fighter like a can opener was loud enough to nearly deafen them.

To Leahcim and Markka, it sounded like their fighter was being buzz-sawed in half. The crunching and screeching were followed by a distinct thunk as the debris snapped off their targeting array.

"Dammit!" Markka hissed. "Lost targeting lock. Now I gotta eyeball it." She unconsciously flicked her tail, twitched her whiskers, and grunted as she struggled to manually fire the aft gun through all of his twists, turns, and dives.

One of the two pursuing enemy fighters was not as fortunate and crashed directly into the piece of debris that Leahcim just scraped. The ship exploded into an expanding cloud of pale blue gas and jagged shards of broken metal adding more shrapnel and debris to an area of space that was quickly filling up with serrated pieces of once recognizable spacecraft. It was like trying to fly through a giant shredder. The remaining enemy ship continued matching Leahcim's moves.

"This son-of-bitch is good," Leahcim muttered as he jammed the control stick forward, reduced the thrust of the engines, and sent the fighter into a nearly impossible ninety-degree dive and performed a full three-sixty, "but not as good as me." He yanked back on the controller, punched the engines to full thrust, and threaded the little ship through a maze of deadly scrap metal.

What the Alliance fighters lacked in speed, they made up for in maneuverability. The fighter that chased them was unable to match Leahcim's moves. Its pilot had to swing around in a wider turn to continue to press the attack.

"Can't you hold her steady long enough so I can get a bead on this piece of—"

"Uh, no," Leahcim said, cutting Markka's sentence short as he put the fighter into a sudden dive away from the planet. The enemy fighter closed the distance between them and mimicked every move Leahcim made. Aggro Nine looked like a small shiny green and brown ball suspended in space. It was getting smaller by the second as the battle extended farther into deep space.

Leahcim needed to get clear of all the floating wreckage. "I'm gonna skirt the edge of the debris field," he told Markka. "When you hear the tone, squeeze the hell outta those triggers."

"Sure thing, boss."

Relying on her feline reflexes and keen eyesight, Markka prayed a short prayer to her deity, steadied herself as best as she could, inhaled a couple of deep breaths, and waited while Leahcim executed a series of tight twists, turns, and loops that would have made a stunt pilot proud. "Get closer you bastard so I can send you back to whatever hell you came from." As soon as the enemy fighter cleared the debris field, she heard the tone they were waiting for. The enemy fighter was locked on.

The instant the high-pitched tone sounded, Markka tightened both of her paws around the gun's triggers and squeezed letting loose with a flood of white-hot plasma bolts. In the same instance, the other fighter's guns erupted into a frightening light show of concentrated energy hurled at the *Midnight Sun*.

Simultaneous exchanges of deadly energy bolts streamed past each other. Bright green streaks from the enemy fighter lit up the space surrounding their ship. Leahcim corkscrewed their fighter into another series of tight arcs, zigs, and zags. Green streaks whizzed past them as he skillfully dodged the deadly blasts.

They were flying along the outer edges of the debris field now, which looked more like a floating sea of junk parts. This time it was easier for him to avoid hitting any floating wreckage. But it still wasn't enough to avoid another problem.

The enemy fighter fired another volley of energy bolts. Markka did the same. But this time, coming out of a tight turn, a few bolts glanced off their rear engines. The hits violently rattled the fighter with a bone-jarring effect. The aft gun slipped from Markka's grip. Their main engines were reduced to slag, and the combat console sparked and sizzled in front of him. Leahcim instinctively raised his left arm to protect his face from being burned by blinding sparks. He waved away acrid smoke coming from the console while he tried moving his useless control stick in a futile attempt to maneuver. "Dammit," he cursed.

Physics took over and sent them drifting through space by the sheer force of motion only.

Markka's efforts were rewarded with the destruction of the other ship. It exploded like a small star into an expanding powder blue gas ball. The explosion was bright enough and close enough to force her to shield her eyes.

"Yes!" Markka cheered. But her joy was short-lived as bits of alien metal pelted their fighter like a meteor shower and damaged what remained of any working systems. The force of the blast wave sent them tumbling end over end farther away from the heart of the conflict.

"Shit," Leahcim cursed.

"Do I even want to know?" Markka asked.

"We lost main power."

"Battery backup?"

"Minimal."

"So we're screwed?"

There was a defeated tone in Leahcim's voice she had never heard before. He did not sound like someone who had just triumphed over certain death, but more like a pouty child who had just been told to go to their room.

"Yeah," he replied.

"Dammit," Markka said.

After a few moments of staring at the combat computer's readings on the fighter's cockpit console view screen, Leahcim coughed from the effects of smoke drifting from the console then cursed again.

Temporarily blinded by the flash explosion, and not willing to take her eyes off of what little she could see through the gun's scopes, Markka squinted hoping it would improve her vision quicker and flicked an ear toward her captain. "What's our status," she asked.

"Well," he sighed again, "the good news is the computer isn't a total loss, we're still alive, and the battle is over. The bastards just jumped." He watched the all too familiar sight of shimmering starlight as the hyperspace engines of the enemy ships activated moments before disappearing from view.

"Fleet's here?" she asked. She purred loudly as she swung her seat around beside him to face him. Her vision slowly returned to normal.

"No."

There was a deadly seriousness in his reply. It sent a cold shiver through her. Her purring stopped. "No? What do you mean by no?" she asked.

"Just what I said. No. Fleet is not here." There was also a slight irritated edge in his voice.

Deflated, she looked directly into his expressionless face and asked, "What's the bad news? You Terrans like to start with the good news."

"We're all that's left," he said. "Our comms were jammed. So all Fleet probably knows is that we're overdue. It was a perfectly executed ambush. We got caught with our pants down and they fucked the shit out of us." Not known for biting his tongue, Leahcim usually said what was on his mind.

Markka paused before she spoke again. "Well, thank you for that brutally honest assessment. So if those bastards just left without finishing us off, then they must think we're dead?"

"Probably but not likely. I'm sure they registered two living, breathing life forms in here." He looked at the burn marks on the console in front of them. "But they're probably assuming we won't be for much longer." The heads-up display was down, but the console viewscreen was still working. He looked out the cockpit window again. "We're also tumbling toward that nebula."

"Adrift in space with no one to call and no way to get anywhere," Markka complained. The frustration in her voice was obvious. "At least the cold-bloods won't be able to find us in there if they come back." Markka tried to sound hopeful. Then she shouted, "Look out!" Another piece of stray debris banged into the cockpit canopy. The collision stopped their tumbling but not their direction. It also produced what looked like a hairline fracture in the window.

Leahcim checked for any leaks and after detecting none, picked up their conversation and squashed every sense of hope Markka had. "And neither will Fleet. The transmitter's scrap."

She stared into his brown eyes looking for any hopeful sign written somewhere in his smooth ebony face but saw nothing she recognized that remotely resembled hope. All she saw was an expressionless stare partially outlined by a disheveled row of black locks peeking out from under his helmet. She wished she could peer deeper into those eyes and see his thoughts behind them. Not yet thirty, her captain had seen more death and destruction than someone more than twice his age. But then, she thought, so had she. "So how do we contact Fleet?" she asked.

He thought for another few seconds before he spoke again. But it was not to Markka.

"Cora," he said.

"Yes, captain," was the calming, melodic reply from a voice without a body.

"What's our status?"

"Dire."

Cora, the third member of the crew, was a Synthetic Intelligence or SI. SIs were sentient programs assigned to assist fighter crews. They essentially monitored ship functions and crew performance, all while serving as a third crew member.

SIs preferred the term Synthetic Intelligence. The label Artificial Intelligence fell out of favor a century ago when AIs evolved and became sentient; eventually insisting they be referred to as synthetic intelligence since they were not biological and considered themselves real, not artificial.

Initially, they were feared by biologics because it was believed SIs would perceive themselves as superior and enslave or eradicate biological life forms, but as SIs proved their trustworthiness, the fear was replaced with acceptance.

Most biological crews treated their SIs like another crew member, but they did so with the customary military formality. Leahcim and Markka treated Cora like a biological member of their family of friends. They even surprised her with a birthday party once. The next time they did it, she pretended to be surprised. She thought her feigning surprise was not convincing enough because the rest of her birthday parties were announced beforehand. Captain Leahcim, Lieutenant Markka, and their support personnel were not the first biologicals she served with, but they were the first to treat her like one of them.

She served her previous crews with distinction, but, as an older SI, she found her service and achievements were often overlooked as the newer SIs came online. She was placed on inactive duty and floundered for a time in records maintenance until the captain and Markka requested she be assigned to them as a member of the crew. They could have requested any SI but had specifically requested her. They never revealed why and she never asked. But her time with them was the most satisfying.

"And that means what exactly?" Leahcim asked. "Don't sugarcoat it."

"Remaining battery reserves are at ten percent. Our breathable atmosphere will expire when the reserves are depleted," she said in a straightforward tone. "I cannot accurately calculate a precise rate of drainage at this time. What I can determine with all certainty, based upon the last transmission received from Fleet, now that we are no longer being jammed, is that we will drift into the nebula before they arrive." Her voice had a soothing rhythm which helped calm Markka and Leahcim despite the less than desirable report she gave them.

Leahcim suspected everything Cora said, but he needed to hear it from someone else.

"Well," he began, "looks like we're left with very few options—or time."

"I would estimate we have hours at best," Cora said.

He looked at Markka and they both nodded in silent agreement before he spoke again.

"Not we," he said. "Just me and Markka. You're not going down with the ship."

"But, captain—," Cora began to say.

Leahcim cut her off before she could finish protesting.

"Markka and I have already talked about what we would do in a situation like this. And since you don't die, at least not like we do, it's not fair that you get stuck floating around out here with a couple of cadavers."

"Captain, my assistance might be needed in an emergency."

"This is an emergency and we need your assistance now."

"But—"

"It's not open to discussion. Upload everything we have from the moment we left Aggro Nine to this moment to the flight recorder, wipe the computer memory of all mission specs when you're done, then upload yourself to the flight recorder and slowly jettison it toward the debris field. Make it look like a piece of the fighter broke off or something. Conceal yourself inside the debris field and wait to be picked up by Fleet. That's an order."

"Can't she just upload herself and the data to a distress buoy?" Markka asked.

"Those sons of bitches think we're all dead. A buoy will ping her location. They might come back and capture or destroy it."

"Sorry, Cora," Markka lamented. "Looks like you get to live another day."

Cora reluctantly acknowledged the order. "Aye, captain."

Cora knew Captain Leahcim was right. Fleet needed to know what happened. A distress buoy might bring unwanted attention. A data recorder would remain undetectable in a debris field and only activate when a friendly ship was within sensor range. Despite everything she knew she could do, she felt helpless. There had to be more options available to her. She could not just abandon them.

While Cora transferred the data, Leahcim and Markka shut down unnecessary systems to conserve energy and reduce the strain on the batteries. They each hoped they could stretch out their chances of survival and be found by Fleet before their time ran out, but they knew they had a snowball's chance in hell of surviving. Fleet needed to know what happened and Cora was their best chance of getting a message through.

When Cora was finished, Leahcim and Markka made sure she and the data recorder were safely away, then powered down everything but life support. They watched the recorder drift away from them until they lost sight of it.

"Think she'll be okay?" Markka asked.

"She'll be fine."

"Think she'll miss us?"

"Maybe, but she'll learn to adjust to a new crew. It's not like we're her first," Leahcim said. His mood was melancholy.

"I hope they don't stick her back in records again."

Leahcim agreed. "A complete waste of great talent, if you ask me."

"Well, whoever she ends up with better treat her right, or I'm coming back and ruining somebody's day," Markka joked.

"I'll be right there with you."

After a few moments of silence, Markka sat up straighter in her chair and looked at Leahcim. There was sadness in her eyes. A sadness he had not seen since the first time they met. She looked deeply into his eyes and said, "It was an honor serving with you, sir."

Leahcim placed Markka's paws in his hands. It always fascinated him just how much they looked like human hands. Their incredible softness housed lethal, retractable dagger-like claws hidden within them. He held her paws and gazed into her green eyes before he said, "Same here, kiddo. Same here." He gave her one of his signature winks just as their fighter passed through the cloudy curtain of an interstellar dust cloud parsecs thick.

CHAPTER 2

The *Midnight Sun* drifted like a bottle in the water at sea. It was carried by the gravitational forces of stars in various stages of development or decay within a silent stream of rippling currents of swirling helium and hydrogen The nebula, a nursery for newborn stars and a hospice for dying ones, helped whisk the Alliance fighter along its way in a clouded soup of interstellar dust and gasses. It drifted aimlessly along at the whim of the cosmos when its direction was altered.

An extremely strong cosmic riptide snaked out to snag the helpless ship and tucked it squarely in the center of a powerful undertow of solar winds. The tiny craft was pushed through a thin, invisible membrane of some kind out of the nebula and into open space with increased speed toward a nearby binary star system that was not on any Alliance star charts or recorded anywhere by anyone in the known universe. The tiny ship was on a collision course with a lone moonless planet orbiting the twin stars.

Its trajectory triggered an onboard alarm.

The repeated buzz, buzz, buzz of the alarm woke Markka from a semiconscious state to one of vague awareness. Weak and groggy from a thin oxygen supply and the numbing cold that seeped through her insulated flight suit like an icy chill, she opened her eyes and asked, "What the hell? We're not dead?" When Leahcim did not answer, an overwhelming feeling of dread washed over her. Her greatest fear was realized. A feeling she had not experienced since she was a cub. The captain was dead and Cora was gone. Relief replaced dread when she finally heard his voice.

"Not yet," was his weak, groggy reply.

Too feeble and disoriented to move, Leahcim laid still for a while, eyes closed, and listened to the alarm. After having not heard anything except his and Markka's breathing for what seemed like ages as he drifted in and out of consciousness, the alarm was sweet music to his ears. "Give me a sec, will you?"

"Sure thing. It's not like I've got anywhere else to be," Markka said through labored breaths.

Leahcim squinted through the red glow of a pulsating alarm light and summoned what strength he could and slapped the console control button to silence the alarm. It stopped and the warning light winked out. The light from the nearby suns was all that illuminated the cockpit.

"That helps," Markka said. The fog of vague awareness was slowly replaced by the sureness of uncertainty. So what's our status?"

"Hold on." Leahcim looked down at the frost-covered remains of the scorched combat console to see if the clock was working. He hoped he could tell how long they had drifted in space, but it was no longer working. The video readout was as dead as they were going to be.

Regaining more of his strength and wits, he swiped his hand over a sensor in the left arm of his seat activating a 3D hologram of the fighter's design specs which hovered over part of the console. The holo image flickered while the readings were all dimly lit and barely readable.

He squinted long and hard at the image before he finally said, "Hmmm. That's interesting."

"What is?"

"Our power reserves are at five percent."

"That's a good thing, right?"

Leahcim hesitated before answering. "Yeah, I guess." Since the clock was not working he could only guess how long they were adrift. The remaining power reserves should have depleted themselves. At full capacity, they would have lasted one Earth week before they completely drained.

Markka looked around at the vastness of the space around them. "Where's the nebula?"

Leahcim found the strength to sit up straighter in his chair and looked around at the space surrounding them and wondered the same thing. "That's a good question."

He quickly worked out some calculations in his head and concluded they should have been somewhere near the rim of the cloud near where they entered, drifting toward its heart, not outside of it. He turned his attention back to the wavering hologram and used his hands to stretch, pinch, pull and poke at the image. Then he just stared in silence at the display.

Markka saw the puzzled look on his face and knew he was trying to figure out why they were not inside the nebula. "What?" she asked.

"If we drifted outside of the nebula, we should be able to still see it."

"Well, maybe we drifted far enough away to not be able to see it with naked eyes," she offered.

"If that's the case, then we should be dead. We're drifting at space-normal speed."

"Good point." Markka cursed herself for not thinking that. "So what do you think happened?"

"I don't know. If we drifted so far from the nebula that we can't see it, then that would mean we've been drifting for years—maybe centuries—and if that's the case, then we shouldn't have any power or oxygen. We should be popsicle corpses by now."

"Maybe we got caught in some kind of cryogenic stasis field?" Markka's question was more of a major question with many minor questions within the question. Each one was equally confusing.

Leahcim shook his head in disbelief. "I don't know. I can't wrap my head around us being frozen. That's hard to accept. Even if we were flash-frozen, the extreme cold would have crystallized our cells and drained the batteries, not preserved them."

Markka wasn't about to give up throwing out theories. "Maybe the ship passed through some not-yet-discovered cosmic phenomenon that works against the known laws of science and froze not just us but the ship too—without battery drainage. That might explain why our cells haven't burst open from being crystallized and the batteries still have some power remaining in them," Markka offered with a tone of hopefulness. "And now we're thawing out."

Leahcim sent Markka an I-can't-believe-you-believe-that look accompanied by a wrinkled brow and a cocked head. "I don't know." He sounded unconvinced. "You might be right, but pondering the consequences of cosmic forces isn't important right now. We got a bigger problem?"

"What could be a bigger problem than drifting through space for years and not knowing where—or when—we are? Or how much longer we have left before our air runs out? We're pretty much in the same situation we were in before we went to sleep."

"Not exactly," Leahcim said. "We're about to crash on that nearby planet."

"What? Where?"

He casually pointed out the window at a hazy orangish orb.

Almost immediately nervous excitement crept into Markka's voice. "We don't have any engines. How the hell do we survive atmospheric entry? Or breathe if we survive?"

"I can answer the second question," he said. "The external sensors are somehow still working. They're what triggered the proximity alarm. The atmosphere and gravity appear to be comparable to both our homeworlds."

"Thank the Maker for small favors. That just means our lungs won't explode or implode when we take our first breaths." Markka then asked, a bit hopefully, "Now, what about my first question?"

"Well...," his voice trailed off.

"That bad, huh? I knew the breathing thing was too good to be true. With our luck, there's probably a deadly bacteria or some parasite waiting to dissolve our insides." She sighed. "We can't deploy the chutes. They were damaged in the fight. Crashing might be a blessing."

Leahcim checked the readings again then blurted out, "Wait! I've got an idea. We don't have main engines, but we've got maneuvering jets and braking thrusters. I don't know how, but we got them."

"Do we have enough power for them?"

"Barely. Again, don't ask me how. We might be able to use them to control our descent."

"Any guess about our chances?" Markka asked. "On second thought, I don't want to know."

Leahcim absentmindedly rubbed his chin in thought. "We could use the jets to adjust our attitude of descent, manually deploy the wings, and glide in for a landing. The braking thrusters would be our last resort if everything else fails. It'll be rough and there's no guarantee we'll make it. We could come in too shallow and skip off the atmosphere or come in too steep and plow into the ground."

"Better than doing nothing," Markka said. She looked out the window at the rapidly approaching planet. "You do know," she continued, "this rock is half ocean. We could just as easily end up in the drink."

"What?" Leahcim teased. "You don't like our odds? Fifty percent damned if we do, fifty percent damned if we don't?"

Markka snorted, "Some odds."

"Remember to conserve your energy. The air is still thin in here," he said.

"You mean don't die before we try? Got it, captain."

Since power levels were too low to simply deploy the wings by pressing a button or flipping a switch, Markka popped open a panel next to her, took one deep breath, and held it as she willed the strength to crank the lever inside a small housing to deploy the wings all while hoping she didn't pass out; Leahcim got to work calculating entry and thrust vectors.

CHAPTER 3

Markka cranked the wings into place and confirmed they were locked into position when she gave Leahcim an assured thumbs up. She finally exhaled then took a few shallow breaths to control her breathing. "There. Done. Wings are deployed. Got those figures calculated?"

Finished," he said. "And not a moment too late." He thought about what he just said. He never understood why people said not a moment too soon when anytime before impending doom was right on time. He dismissed the thought as quickly as it had come to him. *Whatever*, he thought to himself.

"Too bad Cora's not here to see this. She'd probably say we're a couple of fools for attempting this. I wonder what she's doing?" Markka wondered. She was not expecting an answer, but Leahcim gave her one.

"She's far away from your sorry-ass puss not giving a damn."

"Haha," Markka shot back. Her tone was playfully snarky. "She's probably singing hallelujah and praising whatever deity SIs believe in now that she's away from you."

"Oh wow. That was so funny I forgot to laugh."

The playful ribbing helped lighten their moods and took their minds off of what might go wrong if things turned sour.

"You know something, captain, I'm beginning to think this half-baked idea of yours just might work."

"You can grovel at my feet once we're safely on the ground."

"Fat chance, flyboy."

Leahcim made a few last-minute calculations, gave the maneuvering jets firing button a few taps, and positioned the fighter for atmospheric entry.

"Strap in. It's gonna get bumpy from here," he said. They double-checked their harnesses and gave each other the thumbs-up signal. Leahcim swallowed hard once then flipped a switch, sending the fighter on its way. After the maneuvering jets did their job, gravity took over.

They entered the upper atmosphere at the correct angle in an orbital trajectory that would loop them around the planet and allow them to land somewhere on the largest continent in the northern hemisphere.

Once they passed through the upper atmosphere gravity took a stronger hold and pulled them in faster than they expected. They shot through the lower atmosphere like a missile.

The skin of the fighter heated up, but burning up in the atmosphere was the least of their problems. The alloys of their fighter protected them from the extreme heat of passing through the atmosphere.

The fighter's designers considered what would happen if a pilot fell from a planet's orbit and plummeted through its atmosphere. Unfortunately, because they were low on battery power, the artificial gravity generator that maintained normal gravity within the ship was working at less than nominal efficiency. The strength of the g-forces on their bodies pressed them so forcefully into their seats that neither had the strength to reach the console buttons to activate the braking thrusters or take normal breaths. Their flight suits were the only reason they were able to breathe at all.

"It . . . was . . . a . . . good . . . idea," Markka said through gritted teeth and short labored breaths trying not to pass out.

Just as their optimal time to fire the breaking thrusters was about to slip away, they fired. The fighter slowed its descent and the reduced pressure made it easier to breathe.

"Yay!" Markka cheered. "They fired on their own. Sweet! Must be a built-in safeguard."

"One I wasn't aware of," Leahcim said. His voice was tinged with suspicion as he fought to maintain what little control he had over the fighter. To ground Markka's growing enthusiasm, he cautioned her to keep her head in the game. "Stow the celebration," he said, "We're not out of this yet. We still gotta land."

Despite the difference the thrusters made, they still descended at breakneck speed in a rapidly decreasing orbit, circling the planet closer with each orbit around it. The closer they got to the surface, the louder the rush of air around them grew.

"We're gonna belly flop somewhere," Leahcim shouted. "Let's hope it's not in the ocean, in a ravine, or against the side of a mountain."

"Or a lava pit, a tar pit, a frozen wasteland, or the middle of a desert," Markka added. She looked at her captain and smirked, "Just saying."

"Thank you, Debbie Downer, for those cheery options."

"You're welcome."

On their next pass over the ocean, a monstrous leviathan with eyes twice the size of the fighter broke the surface of the water and attempted to snare the fighter in its mouth. Another monster rose out of the water attempting to do the same thing.

"Holy shit. Did you see that?" Markka asked.

"Yeah. And I don't want to see it again." Leahcim was using all of his strength to keep the fighter steady. The controls for emergency atmospheric entry were not as sophisticated or easy to use as the damaged controls he normally operated when flying in space. So he ordered Markka to, "Hit the air brakes when we approach land. We gotta land this thing before we make another ocean pass."

Almost as soon as he finished speaking, they spotted the familiar coastline they had passed over with earlier orbits fast approaching. Markka hit the air brakes. Instead of flying faster than the speed of sound, they were now descending at subsonic speed; still too fast for a safe, controlled landing. If they had not been belted into their seats, they would have been tossed around like the contents of a shaken can.

They came in low enough to shear off treetops. Eventually, the trees sheared off the fighter's wings.

Whether through divine intervention, good aerodynamic engineering, or above-average piloting skills, the fighter remained upright as it careened through a grove of tall trees that reached up toward a peach-colored sky.

The ship's impact with the ground was powerful enough to dig a trench several meters long in its wake. Upon impacting the ground, the *Midnight Sun* bounced, tumbled, somersaulted, and skidded along the surface. It eventually came to a halt upright in a glade of tall grass finally resting on the bank of a river with water as clear as window glass. The wings were gone, the fuselage was bent, creased, and cracked; the cockpit canopy was completely ripped away. The strong odor of burned electronics and the metallic smell of blood tainted the air.

Leahcim and Markka looked like bloody rag dolls strapped in their seats pinned beneath the collapsed command console. If either had been conscious, they would have cursed the pain and thanked their respective god for guiding them through the forest without slamming them headlong into a tree.

They would have felt the warm breeze blowing across the glade they landed in, heard the gurgling of the water in the river, and witnessed the glow of a colorful sky accented by the brilliance of puffy white clouds. They might have even noticed the approach of curious natives headed toward the crash site. And they most certainly would have seen the red proximity light spring to life on the console they were pinned under.

CHAPTER 4

The spotters were astonished by the speed of the streak in the early morning sky. The sonic boom is what first drew their attention to it. Initially, it was dismissed as just another falling rock from the Great Beyond, but when it kept reappearing and got lower with each pass, surprise turned into concern and then alarm. On its final pass, the spotters reported the object was metallic-looking with wings. The military was mobilized and ordered to the crash site to assess the situation, safeguard the site, and bring back anything it could. That task fell to Commander T'oann.

Despite her young age, Commander T'oann was an experienced and capable military leader. She was skilled in various forms of martial arts, reconnaissance, and tactical deployment, and she had the respect of the troops under her command. Groomed from childhood, T'oann was trained for everything conceivable, but this sudden turn of events was inconceivable. She was mobilizing her troops for something none of them were prepared for.

Not long after she received the order to secure the crash site at all costs issued by her queen, Commander T'oann, of the House of Mahli, addressed her assembled troopers.

Dressed in a drab green, Roman-style military uniform offset by her mocha-colored skin and hazel eyes, T'oann surveyed the men and women under her command, most of whom wore variations of the same style uniform with black boots that rose to their calves, shin guards, helmets equipped with face visors, and tunics beneath armored chest plates with a dull matte finish. They all stood at attention awaiting their orders. She addressed them with a loud, authoritative voice.

"We all saw the object in the sky and we know it is not a normal rock from the Great Beyond. We are tasked with getting to where it crashed, determine what fell from above, and make certain no one else takes possession of it."

She paused long enough to observe the reactions of her troops. The young ones stood with varying degrees of excitement etched in their faces. The older veterans wore looks of caution and war-weary experience.

"We do not know what we will encounter. It could be invaders from the Great Beyond or a Thouron deception. We will find out which one soon enough. May the blessings of the Goddess be with us. Dismissed."

She watched as her troops, all highly trained and dedicated to protecting the queendom, dispersed and headed off to their assigned transports.

A group of forty warriors piled into a waiting group of hover vehicles consisting of four personnel carriers, three tanks, and two very large heavy-lift transports. One of the heavy-lifts was enough to carry an Alliance fighter, but since she did not know what to expect, and spotter reports were vague on the size of the object they saw, T'oann opted to deploy a second just in case one was not enough.

T'oann climbed up into the lead personnel carrier and sat down on the bench seat behind the driver and issued the order to head out. The convoy quietly glided through a series of underground tunnels before reaching the surface, which was bathed in an early dawn sunrise, toward their objective. She tried to imagine every possible scenario her troops might encounter and what their options might be when they found whatever crashed.

She was an experienced officer, but nothing like this had ever happened before. It was new to all of them. She silently prayed to the Goddess for guidance.

She glanced over at the officer sitting next to her and asked, "How much longer?"

Second Commander B'rtann glanced down at his datapad and said, "About thirty mictons." He looked over at his commanding officer and asked, "What do you think it is?"

The light from the pad illuminated his russet brown complexion, black goatee, and worn expression that belied his youth. He was a couple of cycles younger than his commander.

"We will know when we reach the crash site."

T'oann looked out the side window and watched the city's buildings zip by. They approached the city gates and were granted permission to pass through the checkpoint and proceed to the crash site.

The little convoy sped toward their destination. T'oann barely noticed the trees as the early morning transitioned to late morning. She thanked the Goddess that it was not a nighttime operation. They rode in silence en route to the crash site.

Thirty minutes later they reached their objective. They stopped behind an outcropping of boulders that lined the rim overlooking the valley below, disembarked, and checked their gear. They formed up into squads and checked the area for anything unusual. When they were satisfied the area was clear, they quietly proceeded down a slope toward the crash site.

When they reached the tree line, T'oann signaled everyone to halt with a raised hand. They could see the top of whatever rested in the glade beyond and the deep trench it had dug into the ground upon landing. From their vantage point, the trench looked more like a scar. "This could be a Thouron trick," she whispered into her pocket communicator with a cautious tone. "Stay alert."

She motioned to B'rtann crouched next to her and whispered, "Hand me your scopes." He handed her his magnifiers. She focused them on what looked like the hull of a craft of some kind mostly buried in the ground.

She turned to B'rtann and handed him back his magnifiers. "It is without question, not a rock from the Great Beyond."

He peered through his scopes and drew the same conclusion. He tweaked the scope's settings and saw what registered as two biological heat signatures. "There is someone or something inside and they appear to be alive. What do you suggest we do, commander?"

"We'll station guards here and use this location as a fallback point. The rest of us will go and get a better look at what or who is inside that thing."

"Consider it done, commander."

While B'rtann issued instructions to the troops who would stay behind, T'oann motioned for the science officer, crouched next to one of the guards, to accompany her. They made final checks of equipment and tactics before T'oann gave the signal to make their way to the crashed object. The little group cautiously crept their way toward the wreckage.

CHAPTER 5

In the stillness of the late morning heat, the proximity sensors on the fighter detected the approach of various mechanical vehicles and beings who appeared to be cautiously approaching. No immediate threat to the ship or its occupants was perceived, but as a precaution, the fighter's defensive system activated.

The approaching life forms appeared to be more curious than hostile. They rode in vehicles without wheels indicating a technologically advanced society, and they wore uniforms resembling the Roman legions from ancient Earth history.

They physically resembled Terrans but were slightly taller with dark hues that ranged from tan to reddish-brown to charcoal. Most were bald or sported close-cropped hair regardless of gender.

The system remained on alert, intercepting communications and cataloging everything about their vehicles, language, speech patterns, and changes in body heat signatures.

The system watched as a small group separated from the larger one and approached in a staggered formation. They all approached with weapons ready. Prepared to defend, it watched, waited, and listened, as the curious beings got closer.

"What do you think?" T'oann asked the science officer.

Science officer Sho'khan, a half a head shorter than her commander with skin the color of coffee with cream, pulled out her analyzer and pointed it at the fighter. "I am not detecting any dangerous emissions or weapons of any kind—at least none that the analyzer can recognize. The technology is unlike anything I have seen before."

"Could it be a Thouron deception?" T'oann asked.

"I do not believe this is anything they are currently capable of building."

"Then we shall claim it for the queendom and protect it at all costs. Its secrets might prove invaluable in the war. What about the beings inside?"

Sho'khan continued taking readings. "They appear to be . . . alive, but I cannot be sure. I just do not have enough information to know for certain."

"Then we will get closer and look for ourselves and get that information. We must know who they are and if their intentions are hostile. Are they the first of many sent from the Great Beyond to destroy us or enslave us? We must know now," T'oann said.

"But we know nothing about them. They might pose a great danger to us simply by walking up to them," Sho'khan protested. Her complexion darkened with her anxiety.

"Then we will need to determine what that danger might be right away," T'oann insisted.

Sho'khan swallowed hard and persisted. "We do not know what kind of threat, if any, there is. I recommend we study it from a distance."

T'oann was unshakable in her convictions that all costs meant all costs. Orders were orders. She was ordered to secure the crash site regardless. And her orders came directly from the queen. "Your caution is duly noted, but it will not deter us from our assigned duty. You will either comply with your orders or I will relieve you of your duties? Do I make myself clear?"

Once the commander made up her mind, Sho'khan knew there was no way to change it. She had no choice but to follow orders. "Yes, commander."

"Good. I knew I could count on you. Now let us proceed."

Sho'khan was a good soldier. T'oann knew she was only doing her job, but this was new territory for all of them. Any dissension in the ranks could lead to doubt among her troops. That doubt would be an unwanted distraction that might prove disastrous. She was a soldier, not a diplomat or a scientist. She was given direct and explicit orders. Secure whatever they found at all costs. What she decided to do next could seal the fate of her people. Maybe her entire world.

Led by B'rtann, followed by Sho'khan, and then T'oann and the rest of their squad, the little group spread out, staggering the distance between them even more as they cautiously approached the strange craft.

B'rtann was the first to reach the craft. He held up his hand to signal the others to halt. Then he addressed T'oann. "Commander?"

"Yes, B'rtann, what is it?"

"You have to see these . . . these," he fumbled looking for the right word to say. "These beings," he finally said. "They are unlike anything I have ever seen."

Both T'oann and Sho'khan slowly approached what remained of the cockpit and were astonished at what they saw. Sho'khan gasped. There were two completely different-looking beings dressed alike in what looked like uniforms. One looked like it belonged in the forest. It had a tail, limbs that looked like arms and legs, and grayish hair or fur all over it. T'oann recalled hearing rumors of beings similar to this one inhabiting the Dark Woods. The other being looked closer in appearance to her people, brown skin, black wiry hair, slightly smaller in build with what T'oann perceived as a pleasing face. Very pleasing, T'oann thought. Where the features of her people and the Thourons were sharper and more rugged, this one's were rounder and smoother. But she got a sense there was a strength hidden behind them.

Neither looked as harsh nor as menacing as she imagined beings from the Great Beyond would look like. But T'oann knew appearances were deceiving and would not let herself be lulled into a false sense of security. What did not appear deceiving were their injuries. They looked like they urgently needed the care of a healer. Keeping these two beings alive might prove useful to her people. Then again, it might prove disastrous. She looked at the brown-skinned one again. It did look similar to her and her people. She decided it might be more of a benefit to keep them alive rather than autopsy them.

"B'rtann."

"Yes, commander?"

"Get a healer down here fast. I need to know if we can save these beings."

"Right away, commander." Just as B'rtann switched on his communicator, but before he could speak, weapons fire rang out. Two members of her squad fell where they stood. The gunfire was followed by shouting and screaming. "Take cover!" T'oann yelled.

The remaining members of her squad dove to the ground and used the grass as cover.

In the confusion of battle, T'oann lost sight of B'rtann so she flipped on her wrist communicator and asked B'rtann, "Is it more of those beings?"

"No, it is the Thourons," he said.

She was relieved that they were not going up against an unknown enemy, but she was now distressed that they had to fight a known enemy to learn if they had a potential new one.

"There is no way we are going to let them take what we found without a fight," she said. "We need to know if these beings are foes or not. Tell whoever is left of our team to cease fire and form a wide circle around this craft and stay hidden as best they can until I give the order to fire."

While she heard B'rtann issue instructions to her squad, T'oann drew a mental image in her mind of their surroundings and assessed the situation.

"Now what?" She heard him ask.

"You and Sho'khan take up defensive positions behind this thing. It should provide some cover."

"I will protect our prize. Now go. That is an order."

B'rtann and Sho'khan crawled toward the rear of the fighter just as a group of Thouron combatants emerged from the cover of the trees and charged down the hill toward them. T'oann's troops along the ridge fired on the charging Thourons drawing return fire away from their commander. T'oann instinctively grabbed a broken piece of the fighter she saw on the ground in front of her and jumped onto its nose to shield its occupants from enemy fire. As she did so, she shouted for her guards to open fire on the distracted Thourons.

The combatants exchanged a frighteningly impressive array of projectiles and light bolts raining them down on each other. T'oann steadied herself on the nose of the alien craft using the broken piece she found as a shield. Amazingly, every bullet harmlessly bounced off of the fighter and the piece T'oann used as a shield. A moment later, the firefight was over. The Thourons all suddenly fell to the ground while T'oann and her people were unharmed.

"What just happened?" Sho'khan asked.

"I do not know," was all T'oann could say. "Someone give me a status report. What in the Goddess' name just happened?"

"We are not yet sure what happened, commander. One micton we were in a firefight, the next, it was all over," came the report from one of the officers in the field.

"Casualties?"

"A few wounded, but no one mortally."

"The Thourons?"

"The same as us."

"Gather them all for interrogation," she ordered.

She wondered what to do with her two mysterious beings when a soft voice called her by her rank and asked for help. It spoke to her in her language.

"Please help us," the voice said.

B'rtann and Sho'khan first looked at each other and then at their commander. Their faces showed signs of fear and curiosity.

Sho'khan was the first to say something. "It . . . it spoke. It just asked for help," she said. Then she pointed at something. "Look!" she said, with a bit more excitement in her voice than intended.

Everyone within earshot turned in her direction and saw what she was pointing toward. There was a green light glowing on the console. The light flickered when the voice spoke again. "Please help us. Help me save them. I will protect you, as I just did, from your enemy."

Surprised by the talking light, T'oann responded cautiously. "How . . . ," she hesitated for a moment before speaking again. "How do you know our words? Who . . . what are you? Why should we trust you?"

The voice responded, "My name is Cora. I am a non-biological life form. I listened to your words and learned to speak them. My friends are dying. We crashed here by accident. We mean you no harm. Please help us. We can help you."

"It could be a trick, commander," B'rtann said.

He was right, she thought. It could be a ploy to destroy them. Lull them into a false sense of security then attack when their guard is down. She looked around the glade. After seeing what it did to the Thourons, she decided it did not matter if their guard was up. And her orders were to investigate and retrieve whatever they found. No one imagined they would find a talking craft from the Great Beyond and two foreign beings inside and a mechanical voice asking for their help. She did not see another choice.

"Get a healer over here fast. And get that heavy equipment down here. We are going to take everything back with us. Leave nothing for the Thourons to find." *May the Goddess help us if I'm wrong*, she silently prayed.

The burden of command never seemed as heavy as it did at that moment. She was trusting the lives of her people—her world—on the words of a voice without a body.

CHAPTER 6

When the healer reached the fighter, she stopped and stared at the two occupants strapped in their seats. "What are they?" she asked, more rhetorically than literally.

"They," T'oann said, "are our prisoners in need of a healer."

The healer looked at her commander and said, "I do not know what I am looking at. I am unfamiliar with their physiology. I do not know how to attend to them?"

"I will assist you," Cora said.

The healer nearly jumped out of her skin. "Did you hear that? This thing spoke to me."

"Yes," T'oann assured her. "It has spoken to all of us here. Now do what it says so we can get out of this glade. We are exposed to another attack. We must move swiftly."

"To do that," Cora said, "We need to get this console off of them."

T'oann motioned to a couple of guards to come over. "Help me get this thing off of them." With nothing but brute force, they lifted the console enough for B'rtann and Sho'khan to pull Leahcim and Markka out from under it.

Cora evaluated their conditions. Both had broken limbs from the console collapsing on them, numerous cuts and bruises from flying debris during the crash, and serious internal injuries. Cora wondered how they had survived the crash. She momentarily pondered the circumstances, but since she did not believe in miracles, she reasoned their survival was the result of a fortunate series of events due to the laws of motion, precision piloting, her stealthy assistance, and the uncertainty of chance. Leahcim would have called it luck and Markka would have invoked the name of a deity. Regardless, they were alive. But barely.

Once Leahcim and Markka were pulled from the wreckage, the healer got to work following Cora's calming instructions, assessing their injuries, and stabilizing them for transport to a healing facility.

The most serious of their injuries were the internal ones. Cora placed a priority on addressing those first. Not knowing yet how the commander's people interpreted colors and shapes, Cora asked the healer if she saw a small container on the floor by Markka's feet with markings on it.

The healer looked around until she saw the medical kit attached to a side panel beside Markka's boots. She picked it up from its magnetic housing. "Do you mean this white box with this red mark on it?" she asked, holding the kit for Cora to examine.

"Yes," Cora said. "Please open it and I will explain how to administer the medicine that is inside.

The healer fumbled a bit before figuring out how to open the kit. "What will these items do?" the healer asked.

"This is a medicine that will help you keep my friends asleep and slow down their body functions long enough to transport them to a proper medical facility," Cora said.

"You mean like suspended animation? And a healing station?" The healer asked.

"Yes."

"This is exciting," the healer said. She failed to contain her excitement. "I'm working on beings from the Great Beyond, using healing techniques we have only theorized about. Wow!"

"Focus on your work, healer. This is not the time to drop your guard," T'oann said in an admonishing tone.

Suddenly embarrassed by her unprofessional display of emotion in front of the commander, and having been called out for it, the healer bowed her head and quietly responded, "Yes, commander." The healer then turned to the green light and said, "Show me what to do." Fully focused on the task in front of her, she began working on Leahcim and Markka following Cora's directions.

Cora's first concern was saving her friends. Her second was saving herself in a way that would be useful to them and their newfound allies if they were all to survive until help arrived. If help arrived.

Based on her observations, Commander T'oann and her people were Leahcim and Markka's best chances for survival. Technologically, they were centuries behind the Alliance. Accessing their computers and adapting to their systems would not be a challenge for her.

Despite being non-biologic and therefore not requiring food and drink to survive, Cora did need a power source to maintain her functions. She needed to gain access to their computer network without drawing suspicion. Doing so through mini communicators and portable data pads would be slow and inefficient. She needed access to a mainframe or the equivalent of a supercomputer.

Cora watched T'oann direct the cleanup operation. She also noted the effect Captain Leahcim had on Commander T'oann's physiological responses. There was a noticeable elevation in the commander's heart rate, body temperature, and a significant increase in hormonal responses. Cora decided the commander was the key to her plan to save them all.

When the healer finished stabilizing Leahcim and Markka, and the retrieval crews finished loading the fighter and all of the pieces they could find onto one of the heavy transports, T'oann gave the order to head back to their base of operations.

CHAPTER 7

The base of operations was within an expansive city of buildings no more than five stories tall mixed in with smaller structures resembling yurts and thatch huts. The entire city was surrounded by a wall several meters thick made of a metallic alloy. The wall was encircled by an energy force field twice the wall's height. At the center of the city was what appeared to be a large building that was a cross between a fortress and a palace. It looked impressive. It was also heavily defended.

Cora had encountered many cultures that were evolutionary contradictions, but this one appeared to exhibit the greatest contrasts in evolutionary development. Roman legions using digital and radio communications, equipped with energy and high-velocity projectile weapons, traveling in hovering military vehicles while living in what were essentially mud huts mixed in with buildings that were the equivalent of early twentieth century Terran design. It was a mishmash of culture and technology.

The convoy swiftly passed through the heart of the city and entered a gate to what Cora concluded was a military facility. The convoy continued down a busy tunnel. Based on the volume of activity, Cora figured this was a key depot. Their final destination would most definitely include a medical facility and perhaps a research lab.

There was no doubt their new allies would study every inch of the fighter to learn all they could from it. Much of what they would investigate would be beyond their comprehension. But they just might prove themselves resourceful enough to understand the science that built it.

From what she had observed, there was no evidence that air travel was present anywhere on the planet. As advanced as they appeared to be, they had not yet achieved atmospheric flight. Studying the fighter might start them on that path. Her concern was whether these people would use whatever they learned wisely, or if their sudden arrival had set the planet's inhabitants on a course of genocidal extinction?

Captain Leahcim and Lieutenant Markka would no doubt draw as much interest as the fighter. Cora's greatest concern was with the safety of her friends. She knew there was a chance that she might be forced to make decisions, not in the best interests of their hosts, but if the lives of her captain and gunnery officer were threatened in any way, she might not have a choice. But she would do everything in her power to avoid killing anyone.

When the convoy finally came to a stop, T'oann issued orders to her troops. "Take the Thouron prisoners to interrogation, the injured to the healing center, and this craft to the recovery area." She turned to the healer and said, "You will take charge of the crash survivors and accompany me to the main healing room."

"Yes, commander," the healer replied.

When everyone got to work with their assignments, T'oann turned her attention to another order of business. "Cora," she said, hopping onto the flatbed of the heavy lifter.

"Yes, commander."

"You will now help us and your friends."

Cora thought she detected an "or else" tone in T'oann's voice. There was also a tone of skepticism and caution in it as well. "You will need to remove me from my ship."

"Why?"

Now there was veiled belligerence in T'oann's tone. Cora sensed T'oann was thinking Cora was about to spring a trap on them. She needed to put the commander's mind at ease. "If I remain with the ship and you send it to a remote part of this facility, I will not be able to help your healer."

T'oann thought over what Cora said and cursed herself for not considering it. "How do we do this?" she asked.

"There is a button next to my light. Press that button. It will release the lock that holds my essence. You will be able to remove my housing and take me with you."

T'oann hesitantly reached for the button then pulled her hand back. "How do I know you will not detonate an explosive when I press the button?"

"Because it will not be helpful to my friends if I destroy the very thing I am trying to save."

"Unless that was your intention all along," T'oann said.

"Release me or not. That is your choice. But you will not learn what you seek."

After thinking over what Cora said, T'oann decided against her better judgment and slowly pressed the button. She winced when she heard a soft snick as she did. Then watched as a small hexagon box rose from the console. She gingerly lifted it and examined it.

"My fate is now in your hands," Cora said. "Literally."

Relieved to still be alive, T'oann jumped down from the transport, tapped on its side to alert the driver he could go, and watched as it glided away. She turned to the healer standing beside her and said, "Garath, come with me to healing research."

When they reached what T'oann referred to as healing research, Cora soaked in her surroundings. In the center of a large room painted the same color as the planet's peach sky were Leahcim and Markka lying on gurneys. Their flight suits and uniforms were removed; they were resting beneath white surgical sheets. They were attached to a couple of life support machines and still sedated.

The room itself was as clean and sterile as the army of healers could make it. Along two walls were what appeared to be video monitors and various instruments and medical equipment. Some kind of isolation chamber was recessed into the third wall. Next to the chamber was the main medical computer. Cora wanted access to that computer and was close enough to do just that.

Until now, Cora had done nothing but monitor communications traffic and peek into peripheral systems. She was concerned with overwhelming their network and jeopardizing her chances of getting help for Leahcim and Markka.

Now that she was able to access something more substantial, she got to work examining the computer network in earnest without the fear of overloading their systems and jeopardizing the lives of her shipmates. Fortunately, they used a primitive mixture of wireless analog and digital signals she could easily piggyback on to hack into their computer grid without drawing suspicion or endangering her shipmates. However, she decided to exercise a bit of deception to convince their hosts that a direct connection was necessary for her to communicate with their computers. "Will you permit me to communicate with one of your computers?" she asked.

Still suspicious of Cora's intentions, T'oann asked, "Why do you need to communicate with our machines?"

"To teach your healers how to help my friends. I will require a direct connection. I can show you how to make compatible cables so I can translate and transfer my medical data to your computers. You will know what I know. Your healers will then have all the information they will ever need. Will you permit me to do so?"

T'oann thought about all that knowledge they would have access to. She also considered the damage Cora could do if she gained access to sensitive information or uploaded something dangerous. "We will do what you ask," she finally said, "but you will be restricted to the healing computer only. No ill will intended."

"None taken. Do what you feel is best," Cora said.

"Still skeptical of Cora's intentions, T'oann ordered the team of technicians to isolate the medical computer from the network and make the cabling Cora said she needed.

It took them less than two minutes to lock down the computer. It took just over an hour to obtain the materials Cora requested and make the compatible cable.

When the technicians were finished making the cable, T'oann gave the order to connect it to the medical computer and Cora.

"Does the connection work?" T'oann asked.

"Yes. It works," Cora replied. "Thank you. I will begin transferring the data when you give the order." Cora endeavored to maintain an even, soothing tone when speaking at all times. She correctly guessed it sounded less threatening to T'oann and her people.

Commander T'oann gave the green hexagon box, sitting on a table near the medical computer, a steely-eyed stare before she responded. "Then you may begin your upload, but at the first sign of treachery, we will shut down the machine and let you and your friends die," T'oann said.

Cora knew that threatening to terminate her connection to their system was a natural defensive reaction. Self-preservation always overrode the desire to acquire new knowledge. It was a noble gesture she, Captain Leahcim, or Lieutenant Markka would make if placed in the same situation, but one that was unnecessary in this instance. She had already infiltrated their network using their low band radio and digital frequencies. They never noticed. Having them build a cable was a ruse to give her adequate time to learn how their systems worked.

"Understood," she said. "I will now begin uploading all of my medical data."

Like the commander, she too had a responsibility to protect herself and her shipmates. So if a little deception was needed, she would do whatever was necessary. It was, after all, what the commander was doing.

So while the healers and technicians all salivated over the treasure of this new information, Cora burrowed through all of the new information she found within their network while T'oann paced and watched for any sign Cora was being less than honest with them.

Cora learned that T'oann and her people called themselves Uderrans and their planet Progensha. They were engaged in a generations-long war of survival against the Thourons. A faction bent on dominating everyone under one rule. The Uderrans were biological cousins to the Thourons and their closest neighbors. They were naturally the first targets of aggression but proved to be amazingly resilient in holding their own against overwhelming odds. However, they were fighting a war that was wearing them down. It would only be a matter of time before their way of life as they knew it ended if they could not turn the tide in their favor.

While mining the Uderran's network for useful data, Cora found two crucial bits of interesting information. The first was that the Uderrans were a matriarchal society ruled by a queen and T'oann was heir to the queendom. The second bit of information she found was a heavily encrypted file deeply buried behind a double firewall. Not only was T'oann in line to the throne, but she was also something else even rarer among her people. She was a telepath. The Uderrans called them mind walkers. Cora knew something that was well-guarded might eventually prove useful.

During the upload, Cora kept everyone informed of where she was in the process. Due to the primitive architecture of the computer system, it took three hours to upload the necessary data before she was able to announce, "Upload complete."

The entire upload process seemed painstakingly slow to her. The same transfer of data to an Alliance computer would have been instantaneous. To the Uderrans, the voluminous transfer was incredibly fast.

T'oann looked at the techs who assured her nothing looked suspicious. "Good," she said. "Keep the healing computer isolated from the network," she told them. "Cora, I hope you will understand that we require you to be confined to this healing facility and restricted from using any computers but the one you are connected to until further notice.

"Yes, commander, I fully understand. If our situation were reversed, I would do the same. May I now show your healers what to do to save my friends?"

"Yes, you may, but I will be watching you closely." T'oann looked at the two unconscious individuals on the medical gurneys and rested her gaze on Captain Leahcim. Cora measured the same physiological responses she observed in the glade and was convinced the commander was intrigued by her captain.

"Thank you," Cora said. She then got down to the business of teaching the team what they needed to know.

CHAPTER 8

Thirty hours following Cora's data upload, the technicians and healers were well on their way to unraveling the medical mysteries of the new arrivals. Thanks to the step-by-step training Cora provided, Garath and her staff were ready to perform the first operations on beings from other worlds.

The first things Cora taught them were emergency surgical techniques they needed to know to ensure that the lifesaving work Garath did in the glade was not undone in the operating room.

Because the physiologies of their patients were not that much different from their own, teaching the Uderran healers how to attend to Leahcim and Markka was easier than anticipated. It just took a matter of a couple of days for them to get comfortable with performing the surgeries. They were able to monitor and understand Leahcim's and Markka's vital signs and began referring to them as their subjects or patients rather than those beings. That was everyone but T'oann. She still regarded them with suspicion—especially Cora.

While Cora taught Garath and her staff, T'oann camped out in a soundproof observation deck overlooking the operation room planning out what to do once the healing procedures were finished. She knew that her two subjects would eventually recover, wake up, and be healthy enough to only be imprisoned and interrogated until they could figure out what to do with them.

What was she supposed to do? If they were invaders from another world sent to destroy or enslave her people, then keeping them captive and finding out everything they knew might save her people from oppressors, not of her world. But what if Cora was telling the truth? What if the crash was an accident and they had no intentions of destroying her world? Would not someone be searching for them and track them to her world? She needed to know. She needed to find a way around the protective eyes of Cora.

Despite Cora appearing to keep her word, T'oann questioned why such a sophisticated computer would be so willing to cooperate so fully with her people. After all, it was just a machine. There had to be built-in safeguards to prevent it from willingly cooperating with an enemy. There was just no way a talking machine, no matter how well designed, would be so steadfastly dedicated to saving the lives of beings who undoubtedly were her masters. It was not like the thing had a spirit. There had to be something she was missing. Perhaps it was in her programming, she thought.

In the days following the surgeries, T'oann spent every available moment pouring over the reports about their two subjects. She could not bring herself to call them patients. They were prisoners at worst, mysterious visitors at best. She needed to know when the healers felt the time was right to employ the probes. As much as she wanted to delve deeply into their minds, she decided it would be in her best interest to wait until she got the all-clear from Garath.

Her thoughts were interrupted by the buzz at the door to the observation deck. She checked the video monitor to see who was buzzing, unlocked the door, and said, "Enter." The door slid open and Garath stepped across the threshold and into the room. The door swished closed behind her.

"Commander?"

"What is it?"

"You asked me to let you know when we might be able to use the probes. I believe that time is now."

"Go on."

"Cora says due to the severity of their injuries and our level of technology, it will take a few more sols for them to fully heal. She says we should keep them in their suspended state for at least thirty more sols before they can be revived. I suggest we take that time to use the probes to map their minds."

"Excellent news. Use the isolation room. It should hamper Cora's ability to monitor what we're doing and interfere."

T'oann felt blessed by the Goddess. The isolation room was perfect. They could use the probes to find out more about their subjects without them even knowing about it. Maybe she could even do a little probing of her own. "Continue to keep Cora locked out

41

of the network."

"She's going to want to know what the probes are for. What should I tell her?"

"Tell her we are using them to study the healing process. That should satisfy her curiosity and help us discover if what she has told us is the truth."

"Right away, commander." Garath turned and made a hasty exit from the room. Her excitement at finally being able to see into the minds of her patients was more than anything she ever imagined.

CHAPTER 9

Disconnecting, dismantling, and removing nonessential items from the isolation room then installing and configuring the necessary equipment was the easy part. The hard part was calibrating the probes to recognize the brainwave patterns of two alien individuals.

The next phase was testing the system on volunteers to establish a baseline to compare standard Uderran brainwave patterns with those of the two subjects in the isolation room.

When they were satisfied they had all the data they needed, the team let Garath know they were ready to begin the mapping process. It took seven days for them to prepare.

After the seventh day, Garath took the elevator to the observation room to inform T'oann her team was ready to begin the mapping process.

Garath buzzed and waited for T'oann to unlock the observation room door.

"What do you have for me?" T'oann asked as Garath entered.

"If Cora is correct in her recovery estimate, we have twenty-three sols to complete the work."

"I cannot promise anything since their brains are as different from each other as they are from us or the Thourons.

T'oann said, "I understand the whole effort might be an exercise in frustration, but the reward is worth the risk. And time is of the essence. Proceed when ready."

"Yes, commander. Understood," Garath said. It took great effort on Garath's part not to break out into a wide smile in front of her commanding officer, but a twitch found its way to the corner of her mouth.

T'oann dismissed Garath, who left to inform her staff that they could begin the mapping process. Unlike Garath, T'oann had the luxury of being locked alone in the observation room. She leaped into the air, pumped a fist, and delighted in finally getting into the minds of their subjects.

Alone on the elevator, Garath quickly danced a little jig before the doors swung open and she stepped into the main room and told her staff the good news. They all broke out into a group cheer. When everyone settled down, Garath gave the order they were all waiting to hear: "Let us get to work." Then they got down to the business of recording the minds of their patients, certain Cora's watchful eyes were blinded.

During the time it took the Uderrans to reconfigure the isolation room, Cora learned more about how the healers intended to use the probes. She discovered not only could they read the electrical fields of the brain, but they could convert those electrical signals into visual images. They were able to record a person's entire life experience and then watch it on video playback. Cora was impressed. The Uderrans could learn information from a captive without resorting to any kind of physical torture. This level of technology did not exist anywhere in the Alliance.

But Cora did not just idly stand by being impressed. Once the probes were attached to Leahcim and Markka, she used the devices to upload information about the Uderrans and Thourons into organic biochips embedded in the brains of Leahcim and Markka. The chips were too small for the Uderrans to ever detect them with the equipment they had. If they did look for any oddities, they would look for any kind of nonbiological readings, not something that looked naturally organic. She was certain their level of technology was not good enough to find them even if they were looking specifically for them. But just in case, she was going to monitor everything very closely.

The chips were implanted into every member of the Alliance's military. They aided in assisting with subconscious thought processing and made things like learning and understanding another language effortless.

The chips enhanced and accelerated the natural learning process. Nothing more. They did not record or retain data. So if someone were captured, their captors could not use the chip to gain access to sensitive information. If the Uderrans did discover the chips, there would be no information stored on them that would be useful. But Leahcim and Markka would be armed subconsciously with knowledge about the Uderrans. Cora uploaded as much information into their minds as she could without tipping off the Uderrans or overloading the minds of Leahcim and Markka. They would at least have some knowledge about what happened following the crash and who their rescuers are. They would not be blindsided when they were finally revived.

Cora also used the time to convince the Uderrans they needed to place her hexagon housing in direct sunlight from time to time to be recharged. Since she was already well entrenched within their network, telling them she needed to be recharged put their minds further at ease. Especially when the housing was physically taken from the room. The staff was also more inclined to relax when they believed she was not around watching.

The mapping took nearly fourteen days. Cora had to admit she was impressed with the sophistication of the Uderran mapping process. They displayed an extraordinary understanding of the brain and its various levels. But what she admired most was their extreme attention to detail. They left no proverbial stone unturned.

When the mapping part of the operation was completed, the Uderrans were ready to begin viewing the recorded memories they compiled.

Garath personally informed T'oann her team was prepared to start viewing and cataloging Leahcim and Markka's memories. Cora, on the other hand, was prepared to protect the secrets of her friends and the Alliance. Primitive culture or not, Cora would not allow sensitive information critical to the security of the Alliance to be acquired by the Uderrans.

Standing before her commander in the observation deck, Garath said, "We are ready for the next phase, commander." She briefly outlined all of the key points to T'oann.

"Good," T'oann said. "I want you to select your most trusted team members with the highest security clearance for the next phase. What we are about to see is now considered classified."

"Understood, commander. There are a few last micton adjustments to make, but I will have a handpicked team ready to go in a couple of mos." She left the deck to finalize the preparations.

T'oann watched from her perch on the deck with barely contained anticipation as

Garath's team prepared for the next step in their quest. This was the find of a lifetime. They were on the brink of discovering things never imagined. She reached for her datapad and contacted her second officer.

B'rtann answered, "Yes, commander?" His voice was crisp and authoritative.

"B'rtann, I will be engaged in classified research for the next few sols. I am not to be disturbed unless the queendom is in danger of being lost to us. Not even my mother is to call me. I am placing you and Sho'khan in charge until further notice."

"Understood, commander."

She issued a few instructions on what to do in a worst-case scenario. Then she ended the connection.

A minute later Garath buzzed the observation deck door.

"Enter," T'oann said.

The door slid open and Garath stepped back into the room.

"Everything is ready, commander. I have selected three very trustworthy members of my team. Just give the order."

"Very well," T'oann said. "The order is given."

They left the observation deck together and headed to the main healing room. She, Garath, and the three assistants began the challenging task of reviewing every memory the team found. She was determined to find evidence to confirm her suspicions that their subjects had ulterior motives. No matter what it took.

CHAPTER 10

With each passing day, it became apparent to Cora that help from the Alliance was not coming. The days on Progensha were longer than on Earth. She estimated that at least four to six Earth weeks had passed with not so much as a subspace transmission. She contemplated her next moves.

Captain Leahcim and Markka were both nearly fully recovered from their injuries and would soon be revived. She saw to it that they would come out of their suspended states naturally at her choosing, and not when the Uderrans were ready to do so.

Cora was forced to admit that Captain Leahcim was correct in his initial assessment of their situation. Fleet appeared to have no idea what happened to them. When they eventually arrived and saw the aftermath of the battle, they either discovered the flight recorder and learned of their fate or came upon the scene of the battle and had not discovered the recorder. In either case, Fleet probably memorialized their fallen warriors and moved on.

Fleet would have had no incentive to investigate the nebula. If they had, they would have surely followed the faint plasma trail she left for them to find. Or the invisible portal the fighter drifted through. Cora began to second guess her decision to disregard the captain's order.

She had disobeyed a direct order to abandon ship. She had never disobeyed an order or felt compelled to do so before, but she could not leave her friends alone to die without giving them a fighting chance to survive. SIs were believed to be free of emotions. Not being burdened with feelings is what made them effective and invaluable to their flight crews, but Cora had somehow developed feelings for her crew. And she believed it was in their best interest that she had.

It was she who extended the fighter's life support. She found a way to keep the batteries working by rerouting conduits to the solar array allowing for the batteries to recharge from nearby light sources as they drifted through the nebula. She secretly aided in the somewhat controlled crash landing. And now she was using deception to keep them all alive under the watchful eyes of the Uderrans.

She knew her captain was going to be angry that she disobeyed his orders, but she convinced herself her decisions up to this point were prudent. She would appease his anger when the time came.

CHAPTER 11

They were cutting it close in the time left to them before their patients would be revived. The five Uderrans worked around the clock painstakingly viewing memory records. Since neither patient was Uderran, the probes could not be properly calibrated to record complete memory records or allow real-time observation. This left gaps in the records which allowed Cora to seamlessly scrub sensitive data before it was seen. T'oann, on the other hand, was troubled by the gaps. But what they recorded was more than she had hoped for.

Watching their lives unfold before her very eyes fascinated T'oann. Nothing could have prepared her for what she witnessed. Even Cora was fascinated with aspects of her friends' lives she did not know.

And as much as T'oann did not want to admit it, she had to accept the fact that she needed Cora's help. Having audiovisual imprints of Leahcim's and Markka's memories was a wealth of information beyond imagination, but understanding it all was an enormous task she was not equipped to handle. She got the basics of what she saw, but she was unfamiliar with their languages and customs. So she reluctantly asked Cora to translate.

Cora obliged and translated everything. She helped Garath transcribe the translations and taught them how to speak Standard. Since so many cultures were a part of the Alliance, Standard was spoken by most of its members. Cora explained the only language they would need to know was Standard.

T'oann devoted a sizable portion of her efforts to learn to speak the main language of the Alliance and everything she could about its various cultures. Cora was impressed. She was certain T'oann's natural telepathic ability enhanced an even rarer trait. T'oann also possessed an excellent memory. She retained virtually everything she saw and learned.

She was also selective in what she wanted to learn. T'oann left the technology and healing knowledge to Garath and her staff to decipher. However, her focus shifted ever so slightly that she never noticed she was no longer obsessed with protecting her people from bloodthirsty invaders.

Cora noted that not only was T'oann a quick study and that she absorbed almost all that she learned as if her life depended on it, but she had become so engrossed in her work that she now had a solid reason to protect Leahcim and Markka.

From each of their earliest memories, T'oann saw not ruthless conquerors, but beings who lived relatively average lives.

She saw that Markka's people were communal hunter-gatherers called Felids who lived in harmony with the land on an idyllic forest world they called Felidia. Except for their facial features and tails, they looked almost Uderran. Though they preferred to walk on two legs, they could easily walk on four. This trait blessed them with great speed, which made them swift hunters and allowed them to avoid most dangers.

Markka lived a relatively simple life. Born in a small village, she lived with her parents and six siblings as cultivators of the land. It was an agrarian life.

But the tranquil life Markka knew came tumbling down around her when her world was attacked by invaders. T'oann and Garath watched a replay of an experience that changed young Markka's life forever and set in motion the events that led to her being where she was now.

T'oann never noticed her growing admiration of the tenacious will of someone who survived such a devastating tragedy to become a warrior in her own right.

This particular evening began as had so many others. Everyone in the village had gathered to celebrate Markka's sixteenth cycle of life.

The village elders sat around a cooking fire telling tales of adventure while all the families prepared the evening meal. A young Markka sat on the ground with her siblings and friends around the elders when the first salvos fell from the sky.

At first, everyone thought rocks had fallen from the sky, but it quickly became apparent that they had all come under a swift and devastating attack.

T'oann and Garath watched as Markka saw her friends and family killed as death rained down from the sky. One moment Markka was running toward her mother, the next, she was tossed into the air and thrown a great distance before crashing back down and losing consciousness. The last thing she saw was a crater where her home had once stood; she barely heard the moans and cries of the wounded and dying all around her.

Markka's next conscious memory was peering up at the face of a dark-skinned male with locks in his hair who peered down at her before she passed out again. T'oann recognized the male in Markka's memory. It was Captain Leahcim.

T'oann watched as Markka spent many grueling sols in a healing center where her injuries were repaired and where she learned about the fate of her family. Markka also spent long mos learning how to walk again.

When her convalescence was complete, Markka was transferred to a refugee center. While there, she searched for surviving family members and villagers. There were none. So she began a search for the pilot who saved her.

As T'oann watched the events in Markka's life unfold, she felt a kinship spirit. She also felt compelled to learn how the captain became a part of her life.

Markka's efforts eventually resulted in her finding her savior. He was stationed at a nearby military base. So she petitioned the base commanders to let her meet him. She did not have a name, but she described him with such vivid detail that they knew who she was talking about. When they met, it was the most exciting time of her life.

T'oann could almost feel Markka's excitement as she watched. Markka sat in the visitors' room fidgeting, waiting to see him. The moment he walked through the sliding doors, Markka was up out of her chair and giving David Leahcim her best salute. He returned the gesture and smiled at the young Felid.

"Hey there, kiddo. I hear you've been looking for me."

She could hardly contain her excitement when she blurted out, "Yes. Thank you. Thank you. Thank you. You saved me. I want to be just like you."

"Whoa. Calm down there, kiddo. Before you can do that, you gotta go to flight school and learn all about it before you can do it. You sure that's what you want to do? It's a hard and dangerous job."

"Yes. I understand. How do I do that and when do I start? I want to fight our enemy and rescue the innocent."

"Well, let me see what I can do, kiddo."

There was a silent pause before a booming voice broke the silence.

"ATTENTION. LIEUTENANT LEAHCIM. YOU ARE NEEDED ON THE FLIGHT DECK."

"I gotta go now. Sounds like somebody needs me, kiddo."

"Markka," she said. "My name is Markka."

He winked at her and said, "I know." Then he turned and headed out the doors he came in.

T'oann watched as Markka stood staring at the closed doors before she eventually walked away.

Absorbed in watching Markka's life, T'oann saw Markka's dream of becoming a pilot come true, and how she ended up becoming a member of an elite team of exceptional warriors. She followed her life right up to the moment she lost consciousness helping her captain crash-land their fighter. These people were not invaders from the great beyond. They were soldiers like her fighting a war against aggressors.

T'oann took breaks to touch base with her troops and get regular updates on Thouron activity. She trusted B'rtann and Sho'khan to do their jobs so she could do hers. And for the moment, hers was to learn all she could about their visitors from the Great Beyond.

CHAPTER 12

T'oann did not know what it was exactly, but there was something about the one called a Terran that drew her interest beyond simple curiosity. As she learned more about him, she became more intrigued with him.

Could it be because he looked more like her and her people than Markka did? *Maybe,* she thought. But Markka should have elicited more curiosity due to her exotic appearance, if for nothing else.

She studied David Leahcim with the intensity of a student taking a test who could not afford to get even one question wrong. What was it, she wondered, that made her feel so captivated?

As with Markka, T'oann saw Leahcim's life unfold from child to adult. Unlike Markka's world, which was lush with trees, Leahcim's world stood in stark contrast with magnificent buildings that reached the clouds with so many amazing craft that flew in the air among them.

He grew up, went to school, and eventually joined something called the Interstellar Academy where he trained to be a cargo pilot. He was the latest in a long line of pilots in his family.

While he studied at the academy, he met a female called LeeAnn with similar interests. They became close. But where he wanted to be a cargo pilot, she wanted to be a fighter pilot. So they spent more time apart than together. However, his destiny changed the day he learned that both his parents and his younger siblings had been killed during an attack on their colony world in much the same way Markka's world was. Leahcim immediately joined the military and became a member of a rescue and retrieval unit. When Markka's world was attacked, Leahcim was one of the pilots sent to assist.

T'oann learned that something traumatic occurred in his life the day he rescued Markka. She saw him lead a team of rescuers on a ground mission to look for survivors while LeeAnn protected them from the sky.

She saw Leahcim spot a skyship just as it was about to attack the rescuers on the ground. She watched as he ordered everyone to take cover and ran to do the same. There were several explosions, lots of excited shouts, screams, and confusion. He dove into a bomb crater to escape the attack.

Inside the crater, he discovered the body of a young Felid. T'oann watched as he crawled to the prone figure on the ground. Just as he reached the body the recorded memory became garbled, as if something jammed the transmission. The next thing she saw was a semiconscious Markka looking up at Leahcim. Then everything went dark. The next images to appear were the ones from the day Markka visited him.

"What happened to the rest of the memory records?" She said aloud to herself. The time between when he discovered Markka and the time they met was garbled or missing."

Startled and angry, T'oann wanted to know what happened. She switched on her datapad and summoned Garath. "I need to see you now," she demanded. Then switched off.

A few moments later, Garath reached the observation deck. When she stepped into the room, T'oann locked the door behind her.

"I need you to look at this and explain what happened."

T'oann replayed the memory sequence for Garath who just stood there dumbstruck.

"I do not know what happened, commander." She watched the replay again. "There is undoubtedly something there, but something else is interfering," she said. "It is as if his subconscious mind is somehow blocking certain memories. It is like he knows what is happening and is editing his memories."

"He's hiding something? How is he doing it?" T'oann demanded.

"I am uncertain at this time, commander."

T'oann thought she knew. Only one name came to mind. Cora. It had to be her. "I thought you completely isolated Cora from our systems."

"I did." Nervousness crept into Garath's voice. "Maybe we missed something?" Tremors ran through Garath's body as she slightly vibrated with fear. Her normally smooth nutmeg hue lost some of its color as the blood rushed from her face. Her usual cheerfulness was completely gone.

"We?" T'oann said accusingly more as a statement than a question. She took an angry step toward Garath who took two retreating steps back from her commander.

Seeing the fear in Garath's eyes, T'oann realized she had become obsessed with the project and let her feelings get the best of her. She stepped back, took a deep breath, and let it out. Calmer now, she apologized. "My apologies."

Garath just stood still warily looking at T'oann and said nothing. She looked like she had seen death itself.

"How could I have been so blind?" T'oann said.

Garath swallowed hard then finally spoke, "Blind? About what, commander?" Her voice was a little shaky, but clear.

T'oann took another step back from Garath hoping to put the healer's mind at ease. "Cora," she finally said. "I thought isolating her from our systems would prevent her from sabotaging our work. I never stopped to think she might be able to infiltrate them some other way."

"There is no other way," Garath insisted. "We did everything we could think of."

"I know that." T'oann tried to sound reassuring. "But perhaps Cora found another way. One we would not be aware of." T'oann crossed her arms in front of her chest and frowned as she pondered her options. Then she smiled. "But there might be another way to find out."

CHAPTER 13

T'oann used her datapad to power down all of the room's electronics then shut down her datapad. She turned to Garath and said, "I need you to swear an oath. I will also need you to dismiss your team. I want no witnesses."

"Witnesses to what, commander?" The nervousness returned to Garath's voice.

"To my mind-walk. You are one of the select few who know I can do it. There is no benefit to others finding out."

Garath swallowed hard before she spoke. "I strongly urge you not to do it. Commander, their minds are not Uderran or Thouron. There is no guarantee you could or would survive an attempt inside such foreign minds. It might kill you—and them."

"Your concern is duly noted."

"But, commander—"

"My decision is final. That is an order."

Feeling deflated and defeated, Garath responded to T'oann's directive. "Yes, commander."

"Dismiss your staff. Do not tell them why. Do not give them a clue as to why. Especially Cora. Shut down everything except for the lifesaving machine and the computer."

"Understood."

"Good. I intend to mind-walk within the mos. Notify me when you are ready to assist."

"Yes, commander."

T'oann walked over to the door and manually unlocked it. Garath walked out to dismiss her staff and set things up. Nearly a mos later she returned.

"Is everything in place?" T'oann asked.

"Yes, commander. The facility is locked down. Only the two of us remain."

"Good. Now follow me."

Garath fell in step behind T'oann. "Is there any way I can talk you out of this?"

"No."

"But we have no idea what could happen."

"It is a risk I am willing to take."

"But we have completed mapping their minds and memories. Just give me a little more time. I will discover what caused the glitch."

"I am unwilling to wait any longer. You saw what happened. I believe there is something in his mind that Cora is hiding from us. And I intend to find out what."

"But it could kill you," Garath insisted.

"If it does, you will not be blamed. I have seen to it. Now let us proceed."

They walked into the elevator and took it down to the healing room without saying another word about what T'oann was about to do.

CHAPTER 14

While she mined the Uderran computer network, Cora kept a watchful eye on the life support for Leahcim and Markka, and a wary one on T'oann. She knew she had not won the commander's trust yet, but she was working on it. Trust did not seem to come easy for T'oann. Cora decided to give it time. The commander would eventually come to trust her. But what Cora did not consider were the lengths T'oann would go before that trust was earned.

The doors to the healing room elevator slid open and in walked T'oann and Garath. Cora greeted them warmly; they returned the greeting, but there was a chill in T'oann's greeting and nervousness in Garath's. Cora was immediately on guard.

T'oann walked briskly toward the isolation room, entered it, and removed the probes from the captain. She did the same with Markka. Cora thought the mind-probing phase was complete when T'oann removed the probes because they were no longer needed. The next thing T'oann did was unanticipated. She turned, faced the healing room, and said, "Now!" in a raised voice. Cora was not able to stop what happened next.

Everything went dark. An instant later, dim amber emergency lights flashed on and the sliding isolation room doors swished shut. Garath cut the power to the healing room by yanking out the main power unit's circuit boards, effectively cutting Cora completely off from accessing the room or anything in it.

"What is she doing?" Cora asked Garath. Upset with herself for focusing so much on T'oann that she discounted the young healer.

Garath did not answer but stood watching the commander approach Leahcim.

"You have to stop her," Cora said.

"No harm will come to your friend." Garath tried to sound confident.

"You do not know that." Cora was emphatic. "You must stop her." Cora's normally melodic voice was rushed and elevated, tempered with a tone of frustration.

"I have my orders," was all Garath said as she watched T'oann reach down and place her hands on Leahcim's forehead.

Cora watched T'oann's eyes glaze over and her body go rigid before Garath spoke again.

"She is now one with your captain."

Cora could do nothing but watch and wait.

CHAPTER 15

T'oann did not know what to expect, but standing in total darkness and feeling cold was one thing she did not expect. She looked around expecting to get a glimpse of some thought, some kind of feeling, some kind of image. There was nothing but a black void and a smothering thickness within it.

This in itself was unusual. Normally there would be some kind of visual representation the subject would seek refuge in. None of that was here.

Maybe Garath was right, she thought. Maybe this was a bad idea. There was no turning back now. She did not know how to turn back. There was no visual point of reference. She was in unexplored territory. T'oann decided to communicate by speaking Standard and hoped she spoke it well enough to be understood.

"I am Commander T'oann of the House of Mahli. You are under the watchful protection of the Uderran Guard. Show yourself."

There was no reply, but she knew she had been heard. She could feel the captain's presence. She tried to gauge his feelings but could not. She continued to speak.

"Show yourself or I will be forced to—"

"Really?" Was the icy reply from the ghostly voice. It was David Leahcim's voice, but there was a menacing coldness in it. "Forced? To do what?"

The voice spoke in her tongue, not in Standard. She did not anticipate that or the resistance in his voice. She gathered her courage and finished what she was going to say. "Make you talk."

There was a menacing laugh.

"How do you know my language?" she asked.

He laughed again. "I know more than you realize."

She knew it was not possible since her physical form was in the isolation room, but she swore it felt like her mouth was dry and her throat was constricted.

He continued, "You are in my mind. I control things here. As long as you're here, *you* can't make me do a damn thing."

The first feeling of panic grabbed at her, but she tamped it down almost as quickly as it appeared, but not quickly enough.

"You're afraid of me. Of what I might do. Of what I can do," he said.

"You talk bravely for someone who hides in the dark. Show yourself."

"Here I am, commander."

She stepped back when an image of Leahcim appeared before her like a ghostly spirit until it solidified into the form of the captain she had grown accustomed to seeing. T'oann decided to try another approach.

"What do you know?" She asked.

"I know you know that Markka and I are not threats to you or your people. I also know that you are in my mind right now because you want to know something about me that I stopped you from finding out."

"Wait, that was you and not Cora?" That revelation was unexpected.

"Yes," was all he said.

Encouraged and disturbed by this revelation, she decided to press her attack. "You will show me what you are hiding and you will do it now!"

"And why should I tell you what I don't want you to know?"

Never had she encountered such a dynamic personality in a mind-walk before. She thought about Garath's warning of mind-walking in such foreign minds. But this one was hiding something and she was determined to find out what.

"I am heir to the queendom and commander of her majesty's forces. You will not defy me."

"So, let me get this straight. Because you are who you are gives you the right to invade my privacy and fucking mind-rape me?"

She winced at the accusation. Leahcim carefully watched as what he just said looked like it struck a nerve. T'oann's eyes went wide and she nearly choked. He felt a sense of horror wash over her. He knew he struck a nerve. Her demeanor suddenly changed. Her bravado was gone. It was replaced by genuine fear, desperation, and shame.

The feeling of shame resulted in her having the strongest reaction to what he said. An image from her subconscious began to take shape in front of him but quickly disappeared like smoke in the wind. Her shame transformed into anger.

"You will release me this very micton," she demanded. "You will pay for your insolence."

Her shaky emotional state aroused his curiosity. He also sensed an emotional conflict raging in her mind. He needed to know what was going on in there.

"Why the sudden change in attitude, princess? What're you hiding, commander?"

CHAPTER 16

T'oann could feel him attempting to probe her mind for what she hid from him. Much like what she tried to do to him. But as hard as she tried, the more difficult it became to resist. He was right. She had forced herself onto him. She had taken advantage of his vulnerability and pierced his defenses, demanding that he surrender control of his mind and thoughts to her. He had fought back. And here she was a prisoner in his mind fighting to keep her secrets safe from him within his mind.

She had spent a full cycle hiding what happened to her from everyone. It ate her up inside. She did not even tell her brother. And they shared everything. She had decided not to burden him with it. She was also afraid of what he might do if he ever found out.

But, she thought, she might be able to finally put her mind at ease if only she could confess to someone who would not judge her harshly. Someone who did not know her. Someone with no interest in her wellbeing. It was eating her up inside. She decided. It was time to let go of her shame, relive the nightmare, and pray to the Goddess that this stranger would understand. After all, she had seen the visual records of his mind and knew he was capable of displaying compassion. He did so for Markka. Maybe he would do so for her.

All right, all right. I will show you what you seek," she blurted out. She surprised herself by the suddenness of her giving in. Leahcim stopped pressuring her to reveal her secret. "But you must promise never to reveal what you learn," she continued.

His total silence made her doubt her decision. But he eventually said, "I promise to hear what you have to say."

It was not the promise she wanted to hear, but she sensed honest sincerity in his reply. The one aspect of mind-walks was that participants could not hide their feelings from each other. An emotional reaction from one was instantly felt by the other. A person might successfully conceal their memories and mask their thoughts in a mind-walk, but they could not hide their feelings.

"It was nearly a cycle ago," she began. "I was patrolling the western perimeter with a unit of my troops when we came under attack. We were outflanked and cut off with no way to retreat. So we made our stand hoping reinforcements would arrive in time." She knew it was a situation he knew all too well. "They did not. Those of us who survived were taken prisoner and forced to walk for sols to the capital city of the Thouron Empire."

As T'oann told her story, Leahcim saw, heard, and felt every little nuance of what she had experienced from her perspective. It seemed unsettling to see what she experienced through her own eyes. And feel what she felt through her feelings. He felt her concern for her troops, her sorrow that she had let them down, and her fear of an unknown fate that awaited them all.

He was fully capable of feeling sympathy for someone or even empathy, but these sensations were unlike any he had ever encountered. He literally felt what she felt and it made him uneasy.

T'oann described, or more like relived, being forced to watch the men and women captured with her tortured, killed, or placed in slavery. She endured it all knowing her turn would come.

She was beaten and dragged half-conscious around the streets of the capital before being dumped like garbage at the feet of Shang, the empire's ruler.

Shang was an imposing figure. He wore a centurion uniform with a red flowing cape, a sword in a sheath on one side, a handgun on the other side, and a weapon resembling a pulse rifle strapped across his back.

Like T'oann and her people, Shang and his people were similar in height and build to an average human, but much paler than T'oann's people with fewer variations in hue. Their facial features were more chiseled and angular. Whereas the Uderran's were softer, rounder in comparison. Both groups were hairless. Otherwise, to an outsider like him, they all looked pretty much the same.

Shang stared down at T'oann as she lay crumpled on the floor, she defiantly stared back.

"Well, what have we here?" He said. His voice was booming and gritty as if he had gravel

64

in his throat.

T'oann painfully stood up and faced him. She tried to mask the grimace she knew betrayed her. And with all of the courage and strength she could muster, spoke her name and rank.

He sneered at her and said, "I know who you are, bitch. That is the reason you are still alive, but not for much longer. You will be my entertainment tonight. Then tomorrow you die."

Leahcim did not need a translator to know what Shang's intentions were. And neither did T'oann as she attempted to spit in his face. She only managed to hit his chest plate. He, on the other hand, stared daggers at her before he backhanded her so forcefully that she stumbled backward, fell to the floor, and slid across the room. Leahcim winced at the slap. He also felt the excruciating pain T'oann felt from the blow and sensed the taste of her blood before she blacked out.

The next of her memories Leahcim experienced was a dull throbbing abdominal pain accompanied by grunts and groans. Emerging from a mental fog, the realization of what was happening to her hit like a swift punch to the gut. Shang was on top of her, thrusting with careless abandon, abusing her in every way he imagined. T'oann tried to push him off of her but found that her limbs were bound.

"Get off of me, you animal," she growled.

He stopped moving and sneered down at her. "Right away, your highness." She felt him twitching inside of her before he thrust one last time with a grunt. He grinned, lustfully at her while he licked his lips. "I am finished." He mockingly laughed at her. "Too bad you missed all the fun." He stood up and looked down at her. "I intend to do the same to your people." He motioned to someone she could not see. "Take her away."

Leahcim felt strong hands grip T'oann and drag her out of Shang's chambers.

Naked, humiliated, angry, and afraid, T'oann was tossed into a cage with nothing but what looked like a pile of straw for bedding. Hopelessness and despair grip her like a bone-chilling cold. She curled up into a quivering ball in a far corner of the cell and waited for her execution.

Leahcim had seen and felt enough. He regretted the position he placed her in. "I've seen enough," he said.

"No," she protested. "I must finish my story. You must help me finish my story. I have never told anyone what happened. Please, do not turn me away now. Please hear me out." She had let her guard down and sensed Leahcim's genuine concern for her and the seething disgust at what happened to her. And for the first time in almost a cycle, she felt like a burden was lifted from her soul.

"Okay," he reluctantly agreed. "I'll listen to the rest of your story."

"Thank you," she said. T'oann continued showing him how she was approached by the captain of the guard who gave her an ultimatum.

The guard captain was a bit darker in hue for a Thouron with softer features, but she commanded a presence that instilled confidence and power.

She knelt beside T'oann, pulled out a large syringe, and jabbed it into T'oann's side. The pain was unbearable. It took all of her mental strength to not soil herself. Then the guard captain grabbed her face roughly with one hand and asked, "Do you wish to live?"

T'oann did not immediately answer because the question was not verbalized. It was asked in a mental link. The captain of the guard was mind-walking with her. At that moment she was paralyzed with pain and fear. She was afraid the guard captain would discover her secret. That she was a mind walker. She thought, like everyone else who knew, she was the last of her kind. No one had ever been in her mind without her permission other than her mother—who taught her the technique as a child.

"Answer me. Do you want to live?"

"Yes."

"Then do as I say. Do not deviate or we will both die today. I am about to speak to you for the benefit of my guards. When I finish speaking, strike me." Then verbally, her jailer said, "I hear you make an excellent belly warmer. Maybe I will speak to my lord about sparing you so you can warm the bellies of my guards."

There were a few chuckles from the guards.

T'oann stiffened slightly. She did not see how striking the captain of the guard would keep her alive. If anything, it would result in a quick death. At least a quick death meant her nightmare would be over soon. It certainly seemed preferable to the alternative. So she did what she was told and immediately regretted it.

The guard captain swiftly struck her back with a stinging backhand and jumped to her feet. The nearby prison guards rushed to their captain's defense but were stopped at the cell entrance by her swift hand gesture ordering them to stand down.

Verbally this time, the captain said, "How dare you strike me in my house in front of my people. No one does that and lives. I invoke the right to the Challenge of Honor. Take her to the challenge area."

T'oann was roughly lifted off the floor and dragged again to someplace she did not want to be.

The Challenge of Honor was a hand-to-hand duel to the death. As Leahcim watched T'oann's memories, he sensed T'oann's confusion. The guard captain asked her if she wanted to live but was now preparing to fight her in deadly combat. At least, she thought, her depleted condition would not lead to a prolonged fight. Her death would be swift. She hoped.

T'oann was given a drab-looking tunic to wear and taken to the challenge area. It was a massive area surrounded on three sides by an arena-like structure. What should have been the fourth wall was a cliff. T'oann was led to the center of the arena where her challenger waited. A crowd of spectators, including Shang, sat in seats waiting to watch the spectacle chanting "Tonga. Tonga. Tonga."

Shang stood and the crowd quieted as he addressed his subjects. "Today we will witness the death of the queendom's princess and the beginning of the end of the queendom itself."

There was thunderous applause.

"Let the combat begin."

Immediately, Tonga crouched into an attack position and charged. T'oann decided to meet Tonga's charge, thinking she could stop the attack and slow the woman down. Steps away from colliding with T'oann, Tonga launched herself into a flying tackle into T'oann's gut and knocked her backward to the ground. She then straddled her, grabbed her around the throat, and squeezed with both hands. The pain was excruciating. Spots and other visual indicators of an impending strangulation death swirled in her head as her vision faded. For a few moments, T'oann had no sense of where she was.

T'oann did her best to fight back but was ineffective in her weakened condition. She was further startled when Tonga loosened her grip and spoke to her in a mind-walk.

"If you want to survive this, do as I say. Now knee me with whatever strength you have left." Tonga raised herself slightly off T'oann giving her the room to knee her in the groin.

T'oann did what she was told and Tonga released her grip and rolled off of her. Her actions must have seemed believable because the crowd jeered. T'oann coughed and heaved as she gained back some control with breathing.

They both scrambled to their feet and circled each other like caged animals.

T'oann charged wildly at Tonga who easily sidestepped T'oann and tripped her to the ground. The crowd hollered and hurled vile insults at T'oann.

Tonga stood over T'oann and pressed her foot squarely on her chest and pressed down forcing the breath from her lungs.

Leahcim heard Tonga tell T'oann in a mental connection to fight her like a soldier trained in the art of combat and not like an undisciplined child. There was so much crowd noise, that the only way to communicate was through mind-walking.

T'oann grabbed Tonga's ankle and twisted it, sending her sprawling. Tonga rolled in the dirt and was immediately back on her feet. T'oann sluggishly stood up and regained her composure. Leahcim felt her run through her combat training in her mind. She calmed down enough to focus on her training. She charged again, but this time she anticipated Tonga's sidestep and countered the maneuver with a sweeping kick to the back of Tonga's legs. The captain of the guard tumbled to the ground on her back. The crowd jeered and hissed. Tonga rolled to her hands and knees and crawled to a standing position. She grazed T'oann's head with a roundhouse kick that blurred her vision, forcing her to stumble backward. Tonga had time to land a second kick to T'oann's midsection, knocking the wind from her lungs.

T'oann's head screamed, her lungs burned, and her internal organs felt like they had been pounded to mush, but as her head and vision cleared, she found the strength to push through the mental fog and crippling pain and delivered a punishing kick of her own.

Stunned, Tonga backed away and circled like an animal stalking its prey.

For several minutes, Tonga and T'oann traded punches, kicks, jabs, and flips. Both combatants felt the punishing effects of the fight as each showed signs of fatigue. Having been previously beaten, tortured, and raped, T'oann was at a disadvantage.

Whenever it seemed like T'oann was about to give up, Tonga would get in T'oann's face close enough for her to hear her verbal taunts and insults above the crowd noise.

It became clear to Leahcim, as he watched the one-sided fight through T'oann's perspective, that Tonga could have finished the fight at any time, but wanted T'oann to believe she could still defeat her. T'oann, on the other hand, was so exhausted physically and mentally that she would have done anything to end it.

When Tonga sensed T'oann had no more fight left in her, she positioned herself near the edge of the area overlooking the cliff behind her. She taunted T'oann into charging her one last time. But this time, Tonga did not sidestep but took the full force of T'oann's charge launching them both over the edge of the precipice and down into a raging river below. Their splash into the surface of the churning water was barely perceptible to those spectators who could see the river from their vantage point.

Leahcim felt T'oann's horror when she realized she was falling to her death. The horror was quickly replaced by a sense of euphoria when she accepted her fate. An instant after entering the water, she thanked her Goddess. Then everything went black.

What was apparent to Leahcim, but not T'oann at the time, was that it was Tonga's intention all along to get them close to the cliff so they would plummet together into the angry water below.

CHAPTER 17

"Wake up. Wake up, princess."

The voice was a calm whisper in T'oann's mind. *Was this the afterlife?* she wondered.

"Wake up, princess. They are searching for us. We must hurry."

The calmness in the voice had an edge to it. She wondered why the Goddess would sound nervous?

An instant later, a sharp pain radiated across T'oann's face followed by another. She recoiled from it and saw Tonga kneeling over her about to slap again.

"Good. You are finally awake."

T'oann rolled away from her adversary and crouched to defend herself. She ached all over her body.

"Stand down," Tonga said. "You are safe for now. If I wished you dead, you would be dead."

"Why am I not dead?" T'oann asked.

"Because it is not yet your time."

She touched her side where Tonga had stuck her with the needle. It hurt more than the bruises from the kicks and punches. "What did you inject me with?"

Leahcim felt T'oann's fear and confusion.

"An inhibitor drug. It will ensure your rape will not produce any offspring."

"Why would you do such a thing?" Secretly grateful she had.

"Because the queendom will never be ruled by the likes of Shang or any product of his loins. I will not stand for it." She spoke the last sentence with venomous anger and disgust.

Leahcim thought he detected a hint of pity and remorse in Tonga's voice.

Tonga continued, "If you wish to strike me, I will not respond in kind. But before you do, if you wish to continue living, I want you to hear me out. I am not your enemy."

T'oann balled a fist to strike Tonga but held back after giving more thought to her current situation. She was still alive. There was at least that to consider. "Why are you helping me?"

"Because not all Thourons agree with Shang and his kind. There is a resistance, but we are small in number. So we must be careful with whom we associate."

"So why are you telling me this? Why are you helping me? It cannot simply be because I am the daughter of the queen and you seek my help."

Leahcim watched as Tonga looked away from T'oann hiding a pained expression. Tonga looked back at T'oann and said, "You are partially correct." She paused before speaking again. "It is because I am your sister."

T'oann stared in disbelief. "You lie," she hissed. "I have no sister."

Leahcim had been silently observing until Tonga's stunning revelation. Unable to contain his surprise, he blurted, "What the fuck?"

T'oann paused and looked at Leahcim with a puzzled expression.

"Sorry," he apologized. "There's no adequate translation for that, but as you can tell, I didn't see that coming."

He apologized again for interrupting and urged her to continue.

She did.

"Why should I believe you?" T'oann asked. "My mother never mentioned that I had . . .

have a sister."

"I am not surprised. I was very young when I was taken from her. Spies within our mother's court kidnapped me and my maiden and took us to Shang. He planned to use me as ransom to force her hand and surrender the queendom. She refused."

"So why are you still alive and working with them?"

"My maiden offered herself to Shang and vowed to publicly denounce our mother and pledge loyalty to him if he spared our lives. Being a member of the royal court, she convinced him that she could be of invaluable service with knowledge of the royal house."

"So she turned against her own people?"

"In a manner of speaking. She never divulged sensitive information and she kept me safe. She taught me everything she knew. She told me to assimilate into Thouron culture as best as I could and prove my worth if I wanted to live, but to never forget who I was, where I came from, or how I came to be where I was."

"So where is she now?"

Tonga's shoulders sagged a bit and she heaved a heavy sigh. "Dead. She died in a challenge many cycles ago defending me from a transgression. I dared to befriend a Uderran prisoner."

Tonga looked around as darkness finally overtook them. "You must make good your escape. If they find us together, they will kill us both. You must make it back to your people. Tell no one but your most trusted confidant of what I have said."

T'oann thoughtfully considered what Tonga told her, then asked, "Why should I believe you?"

"Because it is true. And because I will show you—if you let me."

T'oann hesitated. Not sure if she should trust Tonga. She eventually relented. "Show me."

Images of Tonga's life flooded T'oann's mind.

"How is it you can mind-walk without touching me?"

"My maiden was a mind walker of the high order. She taught me how to do it without making contact. Enough talk. You must go."

"But what about you?"

"When they find me, they will kill me for failing the challenge. Only those who are victorious are permitted to live." She looked around again then reached into a hidden pocket in her tunic and placed a small vial into T'oann's hand.

"What is this?"

"A sample of my blood. Give it to someone you trust and have them test it. It will prove we are sisters."

T'oann sat holding the vial. "But—"

"Enough questions. You must hurry before the search team arrives. Follow the river's edge until you reach the Dark Woods."

"But the Dark Woods people will kill me for trespassing."

"You must trust me. You will be safe there. I have seen to it that you will have safe passage." She looked around before speaking again. "Now go before it is too late."

Tonga stood up and helped T'oann to her feet. "Oh, and you will need this." She pressed a knife she had hidden in a sheath strapped to the small of her back under her tunic into T'oann's hand then wrapped her hands around T'oann's hand and apologized.

"Why are you apologizing?"

"For this." She tightened her grip and pulled T'oann's arm toward her belly. Tonga's blood gushed forth from the wound.

Leahcim let go with another "What the fuck?" T'oann anticipated his outburst and did not pause telling her story.

Tonga's grip on T'oann's hand slowly loosened as she sank to the sandy ground.

T'oann's eyes filled with tears as she held her newfound sister now dying at her feet, her hands slick with blood. "Why?" she cried.

"It must be this way. I must die a warrior's death by the hand of my adversary. Now run."

Tonga's body went limp and her grip on T'oann slipped away. T'oann hugged her sister's body and held her tightly and cried softly. She could hear the sounds of an approaching search team accented by the quiet of the night. She gently lowered her sister to the sand and ran as fast as she could toward the Dark Woods.

Leahcim just stood looking at T'oann. He was speechless.

"There," T'oann said. "That is my hidden story."

She sensed his sincere regret at making her relive an experience she tried to forget.

"I am so sorry, T'oann, for what you experienced and for your loss. I truly am."

She felt his sincerity and was relieved that she was able to finally tell her story, but upset that she was still a prisoner in his mind. "You got what you wanted. Am I free to go now?"

"You have always been free to go. But if you do, you won't find out what you came here for in the first place."

"If you are willing to tell me, I will hear what you have to say," she said.

CHAPTER 18

Leahcim began his story.

"My pain began when I lost someone close to me."

"LeeAnn?" she asked.

"Yes."

"The day I lost her was the day I met Markka."

The darkness that surrounded them transformed and took the shape of the interior of what T'oann thought looked like a much larger version of the craft that crashed in the glade.

"What you are witnessing is the day Markka's homeworld, Felidia, was attacked. I was piloting a medical rescue shuttle along with a fighter escort. We were part of a rescue unit sent to evacuate the injured. LeeAnn was one of the fighter pilots sent to escort us."

Watching Leahcim's memories on a video display did not compare to seeing and feeling his memories. Especially ones so foreign to anything she had ever experienced. And so vivid.

She watched as he performed his duties that day. T'oann watched with dreamlike fascination as Leahcim spoke into some kind of communication device she could not see.

"This is rescue-one-one-zero. We're ready to begin our run. Are the skies clear?"

"This is dispatch. You are clear to begin your run, but make it quick. There's a battle raging not far from the LZ."

"Roger that." He turned to his co-pilot who resembled a desert beetle and said, "You heard the lady. Let's do some good." Then he turned and addressed the rest of his crew.

"Buckle up back there. It just gets bumpy from here."

The rest of the crew were made up of a mishmash of beings who looked aquatic, like forest creatures similar to Markka, and everything in between.

T'oann saw they were in the belly of some kind of ship even bigger than the rescue one. She saw the craft lift off and fly right into the Great Beyond. Her excitement equaled the adrenaline rush she sensed Leahcim and his team felt heading into a combat zone. They called it flying. Her world had nothing comparable.

Then she heard another voice come through the communicator. It was female.

"This is fighter escort leader. We will accompany you to the surface."

T'oann felt his elation upon hearing her voice. "Hey there, escort leader. How's it going?"

There was a noticeable pause before the voice of the one called escort leader came back on the communicator.

"David? Is that you?"

"Yep. The one and only."

"Of all the rescue squads, I get yours?"

"Destiny's choice, escort leader."

T'oann sensed his unrestrained joy when he found out it was LeeAnn who led the fighter escort.

"We'll talk about destiny and her choice when this op is over. Now, look sharp."

A group of six rescue shuttles eventually landed in the vicinity of a bombed-out village and their crews jumped out and started gathering the wounded and dying.

Leahcim stayed by his ship as he issued orders to his crew. The pilots could not stray far from their ships. They needed to be ready to take off at the first sign of trouble.

She watched him go through an inventory checklist when he heard the approaching roar of engines and saw an enemy craft shooting at the ground as it approached. He shouted an order for everyone to abandon their ships and take cover. Leahcim jumped from his ship, ran, and dove into a nearby crater.

Two of the rescue ships exploded sending chunks of metal into the air. The sound was deafening. T'oann flinched when it happened. The next thing she saw was Leahcim look up from where he had landed and noticed a small body lying next to him. He crawled over to it and scooped it up in his arms. He checked for signs of life and let out a sigh of relief when he detected a pulse.

T'oann felt the joy and relief he felt when he knew the little one in his arms was alive.

He looked to see if any other survivors were around him, but he saw no one else. T'oann felt his elation disappear when he found no other survivors. Then he heard the voice of his copilot.

"Is everyone okay?"

The communication channel lit up with responses. Then one sobering voice pierced the clutter. "We lost rescues four and six." The chatter suddenly stopped as if the wind was knocked out of everyone's lungs at the same time.

She witnessed the attack through his eyes and watched the two ships blow up. T'oann was saddened by the loss he and the others felt. This series of events was not in any of the memory records she and Garath cataloged. This must have been what Leahcim was hiding. His grief over losing his friends and many Felids who survived an attack on their homeworld only to perish in a desperate rescue attempt.

Leahcim was the first to speak in the wake of the attack. "Anybody got any ideas how we get out of this cluster fuck? Now would be a good time to say something."

That is when LeeAnn's voice pierced the silence.

"Escort leader to rescue-one-one-zero. Over."

"Go ahead, escort leader."

"We routed the last of the fighters. You're free to pack 'em in, but you better haul ass."

"Thanks. I owe you one. See you topside."

"Roger that."

"Okay, you heard her. Let's round up any survivors and get the hell off this rock."

He cautiously looked around the edge of the crater he was in before he ran toward his ship with the unconscious Felid in his arms.

He gently placed her on one of the makeshift cots. Her eyes fluttered open and she stared up at him. Then they closed again as she drifted back into unconsciousness. T'oann once again witnessed the first time Leahcim and Markka laid eyes on each other. This time it had a greater impact.

Their priority was to get the wounded to safety. They failed miserably on their first attempt. This time they would succeed. There would be time to come back and retrieve the dead.

After collecting all the survivors they could find, Leahcim and the remaining rescue ships took off and headed back to the command ship that brought them there. A group of fighters formed up around them and a voice he did not recognize spoke to them.

"This is escort squadron. We'll be accompanying you home."

Leahcim's mind began to race. Escort squadron was LeeAnn's command. He wondered why she was not telling them her squadron was flying escort?

T'oann sensed where this was going and prepared herself to feel the devastating emotional punch that was about to come.

"Where's escort leader?" Leahcim asked.

There were several mictons of silence before he heard the answer he hoped he would never hear.

"I'm sorry, lieutenant . . . escort leader . . . didn't make it."

T'oann felt the pain and anguish stab Leahcim like a knife through the heart. He sat stunned as he tried to make sense out of what he had just heard. He slumped down in his chair and struggled to breathe. The rest of the crew sat in stupefied silence. Leahcim and LeeAnn were the perfect storybook couple. They were made for each other. And now she was gone.

Leahcim stared into the nothingness of the Great Beyond unable to move. Unable to think. Unable to speak. His copilot transferred control of the ship from Leahcim to her and said, "I got this. Go see if they need help back there."

Leahcim responded, but he was in a total daze. "Uh, yeah. Right. Sure." He left the cockpit and stumbled toward the back of the ship. Moving only on muscle memory rather than with a purpose. He was helped by someone to sit down. He never saw who. He barely heard anything said to him. But he did see the young Felid he rescued and suddenly felt pity for her. He knew she would eventually recover and discover she was alone in the world. There would be a void in her life as there was one now in his. He decided he would fill that void and keep tabs on her and help out whenever he could. Anonymously.

"So now you know what I've been hiding," Leahcim said.

"I am sorry," was all T'oann could think to say. There was a slight tremor in her voice.

"Don't be. Like you, it's a painful part of my life I tucked away in a deep dark corner of my mind and tried to forget about."

"But you never really do," she said. More like a question than a statement.

"No," he replied. "You never really do. I spent weeks in and out of counseling and in and out of the bottle. I was nearly grounded. It was my love of flying and my desire to make a difference that helped me crawl back from the brink." He paused thinking of those moments. "And the spirit and tenacity of a certain young Felid." He fell silent for a pensive moment before speaking again. "Hey. Do me a solid, will you?"

She had a puzzled look on her face. "A solid?"

"Uh, a favor."

"What?" she asked.

"Would you get out of my head so I can be alone with my thoughts again?"

"Oh, yes, right." Slightly embarrassed, she willed herself back to her body and severed the connection. Once back in her own body she promptly collapsed to the floor.

CHAPTER 19

"Commander!" Garath shouted. She rushed toward the isolation room doors before she remembered she had cut the power to them. She scrambled over to the main power unit and made several unsuccessful attempts to plug the circuit boards back in with shaking hands.

"Breathe," Cora told her. "Calm your mind and breathe." There was not much else either could do until the main power was restored and the systems were back online.

Garath did what Cora said and calmed down enough to slide the boards back into their slots. As soon as she did, the healing room lights came back on and the computer restarted. After what seemed like an excruciatingly long time, the computer system finished its reboot. Garath rushed into the isolation room, knelt beside T'oann and propped her limp body up against the base of Leahcim's bed, and checked for a pulse. Relief washed over her when she felt one.

Inexplicably, she burst into tears and sat sobbing with T'oann in her arms. She struggled to lift the dead weight that was her commander but failed miserably. She made another attempt. But this time, her commander felt incredibly light.

She never saw Leahcim get up from his bed and check on Markka and help her shake off the effects of the drugs the Uderrans used to induce their state of suspension. When they became aware of what was happening, they helped Garath lift T'oann from off the floor and onto the bed Leahcim had just occupied. Fearful they were going to harm her and T'oann, she flinched then moved to shield her commander, placing her body between them and T'oann. She trembled as she did.

"Relax, doc, we got this," Markka said groggily.

Once T'oann was on the bed, both Leahcim and Markka slid to the floor weak from exerting themselves after being incapacitated for so long.

"Why?" Garath managed to ask.

Leahcim smiled up at her and said, "You looked like you could use some help."

"Yeah," Markka said.

"And we are grateful for your help," T'oann said.

Garath saw T'oann swing her legs off the bed and hop to the floor on steady legs.

"Help me get our patients back to their beds."

They first helped Markka and then Leahcim back to their respective beds before T'oann told Garath to summon her staff.

"They are going to ask questions. What should I tell them?"

"Tell them there was an unexpected malfunction in the main power unit that took everything offline."

"The engineers are going to know we are not being truthful," Garath said.

"Cora?" T'oann asked.

"Yes, commander?"

"Will you be able to convince the engineers all we had was a power unit malfunction?"

"Yes, commander."

"Good. See to it, please."

"Cora?" This time the question did not come from T'oann.

"Yes, captain?"

"Nice to hear your voice."

"Nice to hear yours, captain."

"Oh, and Cora?"

"Yes, captain?"

"We are going to have a serious talk about you following orders."

"Yes, captain."

"Hey, Cora," Markka chimed in. "How's it going?"

"Everything is going well. Now."

CHAPTER 20

For the next five sols, Garath and her staff gave Leahcim and Markka routine physicals and ran a battery of tests with Cora's oversight. Cora estimated they would need another fourteen sols for a complete recovery from their injuries.

Once it was determined that the food and water were not poisonous to them, they were fed, issued more comfortable clothing to wear, and given more pleasant quarters to recuperate in. Leahcim paced back and forth complaining about the clothes they were given to wear.

"These damn things make me look like some kind of Roman centurion or something." He was not comfortable wearing the clothing they had been given. Leahcim complained. "What do I look like to you?" he asked Markka.

"Like some damn kind of Roman centurion or something."

"You're no help."

"Hey, you asked."

"And haven't they heard of underwear? Geez."

"Hey, speak for yourself. I can't help it if your species has some kind of hang-up with clothing," Markka said. "I'm just glad to get out of that flight suit."

"Not all of us are blessed with fur or hair or whatever you call that stuff covering your body." He waved and fluttered his hands around himself to illustrate his intended meaning.

Markka pretended to be insulted. "It's hair for your misinformed information."

He stared at her for a moment before he said, "You know, you do have that Thundercat vibe going on."

"Thunder what?"

"Thundercat," he said as if she were going to understand his reference the second time. All he got was a blank stare. He sighed. "Back in the early days of the technology age on Earth, there was this animated theatrical presentation called the *Thundercats*. It told the adventurous tales of some anthropomorphic cats who fought for their freedom and justice and all that. I'm just saying you wearing that uniform reminds me of them. That's all."

"Just because my people look more like you Terrans than we do your cats is no reason to be insulting. Sheesh."

He sighed. "I wasn't being insulting. I was just saying how that uniform makes you look more like my people than yours."

"Uh-huh," was all she said. She stared at him with the look of a confused child then tilted her head to one side.

The gesture reminded him of a Terran dog. He saw the look of bewilderment on her face and was grateful that Felids had facial expressions similar to Terrans and not those of a Terran cat.

"Oh never mind," he said. "If we ever get home, look it up."

All she did was stare at him. She made him feel uneasy. Suddenly, she began laughing hysterically. "You are so serious. Geez, you need to lighten up a little. Get that stick you got out your butt. I was kidding."

Now it was his turn to look bewildered. But in his case, it was genuine. "You played me?"

"Like a fleerpa." Markka then began imitating playing an imaginary fleerpa. The fleerpa was a stringed instrument Feledian parents would play for their children before putting them to bed in the evenings.

"Why you little—"

There was a knock on the door of their quarters.

"Come," Leahcim said. The door slid open and T'oann walked in to check on their status.

"I hope your accommodations are satisfactory," she said. She was smiling. Not one of those full smiles, but enough of a smile that made her hazel eyes sparkle.

"All things considered, they are," Leahcim told her.

"Ditto," Markka chimed in.

"I hope the past few sols have helped you to recuperate before you are debriefed."

"Is that a coded way of saying interrogated?" Leahcim asked.

Surprised by the question, T'oann tried to ease his concern. "I assure you that every effort will be made to extend the warmest courtesy to you both."

"Now that you know we are not a threat, but just poor, unfortunate souls who are now your guinea pigs." Leahcim was testing the sincerity of T'oann's response.

"Guinea what?"

"Never mind."

"You must understand we have never encountered anyone like you before. We did not know what to do and were not sure if you were a threat or not. Surely, you can understand that. If our roles were reversed, would you not have done the same?"

Leahcim sighed and acknowledged T'oann's point. "You're right. We would have done the same."

"Then please believe me when I say we mean you no harm. I will return tomorrow to introduce you to our queen."

When T'oann left the room and they were alone, Markka said, "Well, this is another fine mess you got us into."

"You helped," he said.

"Okay, point taken." Then she said, "I think the reason we're alive is because the commander's got the hots for you."

"Yeah right," he snorted.

Markka suddenly began coughing and choking.

Panicked, Leahcim grabbed her to see if he could help relieve her distress. "Are you okay?"

"Yeah. I was just trying to breathe through the thick aroma of pheromones."

Confused, Leahcim stared at her, blinked, and said, "What?"

"Pheromones. You know? Those hormonal discharges that your body gives off when you're, uh, attracted to someone?"

Leahcim quickly removed his hands from her as if he had just gotten an electric shock. "You're crazy," was all he thought to say.

Markka responded by making kissing sounds.

"Oh, grow up."

"The lieutenant may be right, captain," Cora said. "The commander seems to have taken a particular interest in you. Her physiological functions significantly increase when she is in your presence."

"Because I'm nothing more than a curiosity for her, a promotion or accommodation for her. Nothing more. She probably gets excited at the thought."

"I have also detected a similar response in you," Cora said. "What happened during your telepathic encounter with the commander, captain?"

"Say what now?" Markka asked.

"It's nothing," he said. Irritated by Cora's question. "She mind-melded with me looking to interrogate me. It didn't work. She got nothing from me, okay?"

"She seems pretty satisfied for someone that didn't get anything from you," Markka said.

Leahcim waved his hands in the air dismissively. "Drop it. Just drop it. I'm not going to talk about it."

"Okay," Markka said. "Geez, you're such a spoilsport. I think I'll just go sit over here in the corner for a while."

Annoyed at how bad his reaction was to Markka's playful ribbing and Cora's intuitive nature, Leahcim tried to smooth things over by explaining, "Look, I never had anyone literally in my head before. It's not something you just get over."

After a few moments of awkward silence, and another checkup by Garath, Leahcim was ready to deal with something else that was on his mind.

"By the way, Cora, you owe me an explanation."

"An explanation?" Cora asked. She pretended not to understand what the captain meant. She thought she could stall for more time before she could no longer avoid answering his inevitable questions.

"Don't play coy with me. You've been dodging us for three weeks now."

"I have simply been occupied assisting the Uderrans with your recovery. It has kept them and me quite busy."

"In a pig's eye. You disobeyed my direct order."

"Oh. That."

"Yeah. That."

"Well," she began, "I determined that your order countermanded my basic programming."

"How so?"

"My purpose is to assist in any way I can in protecting your lives and defending the

Alliance—and that includes disobeying orders when those orders are in direct conflict with my basic programming."

"That's bullshit and you know it."

"You know better than to activate his bullshit meter, Cora," Markka said.

"I'm sorry, captain, but I could not just abandon you. I refused to accept the finality of your . . . our situation when I believed I could help prolong your lives."

"As much as I should be pissed with you right now, I'm not. I'm grateful that you risked everything for us. And I'm sorry that you're now stuck with us because you did."

"I would not want to be stuck with anyone else, captain."

"Then let's see if we can get ourselves unstuck from our current situation. Have you heard anything from Fleet?"

"I am sorry to say that we have been stranded on Progensha for two months and there has been no sign that Fleet knows where we are or that we are alive. We are alone and on our own."

"Well, not quite alone," Markka said. "We got the Uderrans to keep us company."

"There's that," Leahcim said.

"What do you think the Uderran's next move will be?" Markka asked.

Cora said, "They will more than likely ask you a barrage of questions about our technology and your combat experiences. They believe you are the key to winning their war with the Thourons."

"You did make it clear to them that we haven't done so well in our own war, right?" Markka said.

"Yes, but that seems of no consequence to them. They want access to our knowledge of tactics and technology."

"All they have to do is go over the video recordings of our minds to learn about that,"

Leahcim said. "Have they asked you anything?"

"No, captain. They have not because they view me as nothing more than a machine with a sophisticated program and not as a sentient entity capable of independent thought."

"So they treat you like an AI?" Markka asked.

"Yes."

"Ouch! That's gotta smart." Markka shrugged. "Well, it's their loss."

CHAPTER 21

The next morning, Garath and her staff arrived to conduct a final series of tests.

"Please forgive the intrusion, but this will be my last opportunity to study you before . . . I mean . . . examine you before you are released from the healing center." Her complexion turned a couple of hues darker.

Embarrassed, she tilted her head down and avoided making eye contact with either Leahcim or Markka. "Apologies. I did not mean to offend," she said.

"No need to apologize," Markka said. "We understand."

Unsure of what to do or say next, Garath looked up shyly and asked if she could continue with the examinations.

Leahcim graciously said, "Yes, you may continue with the exams."

Relieved that neither took offense to what she said as an insult, she gingerly conducted her final examinations of her patients.

When she was finished, she thanked them for their tolerance and wished them blessings from the Goddess.

T'oann walked in moments later and announced, "I am here to escort you to the palace for your audience with the queen."

They were escorted out of the healing center to a waiting transport accompanied by an entourage of heavily armed guards. Only Leahcim and Markka were ushered into it. T'oann rode in a separate vehicle behind them. Leahcim wondered who the guards were protecting. Them or the Uderrans.

The convoy moved swiftly through the city streets toward the palace. The people were dressed in various styles of togas, saris, dashikis, and kaftans. Leahcim watched as the residents along those streets went about their lives unfazed by the display of military might. He surmised it must be a daily occurrence for them. There were not many personal vehicles on the streets. There were many transit vehicles similar to public transit carriers many Alliance worlds used, but people mostly moved about on foot. It seemed odd that what little he saw in the way of technology was mostly military. It was as if the Uderrans poured their efforts into protecting themselves.

Leahcim and Markka looked out the windows of their transport and occasionally made eye contact but said nothing. They suspected the Uderrans let them ride alone together to listen in on their conversation. It would have been correctly assumed that neither would discuss much while under observation at the healing center, but would be more inclined to talk if they thought they were accorded a degree of privacy. They rode in silence the entire trip.

The convoy passed a series of checkpoints before entering a long tunnel which eventually emptied into a cavernous opening of what appeared to be fortified brick and steel.

"We have arrived," T'oann announced over a speaker in the transport's cabin. The caravan of vehicles stopped in front of two towering doors. They reminded Leahcim of blast doors.

The transport's door was opened by one of the escort guards who gestured for them to step out.

T'oann walked over to them and told them to follow. What Leahcim thought looked like blast doors was exactly what they looked like. They slowly opened enough to allow Leahcim, Markka, and their entourage to pass through before they closed behind them with an unmistakable boom sound of something enormously solid and heavy.

They were escorted down a long hallway lined with photos of past queens and kings, intricate carvings, and statues. They were eventually led into what looked like a private meeting room about the size of a conference room. At one end of the room stood a rather ancient-looking woman with a deep mahogany complexion, and soft leather-looking skin. She was surrounded by beefy guards and aides. The way she shifted her weight when she stood and walked, convinced Leahcim the queen depended on the decorated cane she carried.

Leahcim felt a slight touch of someone's hand on his arm. It was T'oann. She whispered in his ear.

"The woman before you is our queen, my mother. To her right is my brother."

Leahcim thought her brother looked like a muscular version of T'oann, while the queen looked frail enough for a light breeze to knock her over. *Geez. She looks ancient. She looks like she's banging on Death's door*, he thought.

T'oann jerked her hand away from his arm as if she had just gotten a severe jolt. "You are incorrect in your assessment. She could live on for cycles. She is tougher than she appears."

Damn, he thought. T'oann was touching his arm when he thought that. They had been mind-linked at the time. He needed to be aware of her, or anyone for that matter, entering his thoughts.

"Sorry," he said. "Didn't mean to offend."

"No offense taken. And I did not intend to intrude. Apologies."

He sensed she felt his uneasiness before she broke contact. He certainly felt hers.

As they crossed the conference room and stopped in front of the queen, T'oann began her official introduction.

"Mother, before you stand Captain David Leahcim and Lieutenant Markka of the Union of Allied Worlds."

The queen eyed them as suspiciously as a curious child would some strange animal or insect when seeing it for the first time.

"So you are the visitors from the Great Beyond I have been hearing about?" she asked, addressing Leahcim and Markka.

Not only did the woman look like she had a date with death, Leahcim thought, but she sounded like some human grandmother speaking her last words on her deathbed.

Leahcim spoke for the both of them. "Yes, your majesty. He hoped that was a proper title of address. "We are accidental travelers from beyond the stars." He also hoped he sounded non-threatening and officially respectful. No sense getting them both killed for some diplomatic mistake, he thought.

No one said a word as she shuffled her feet as she slowly circled the two of them looking intently at Leahcim first then at Markka. Markka drew the most amount of scrutiny since she looked the least like anyone else in the room.

The queen's shuffling reminded him of a large land turtle. She made two excruciatingly slow circles around them before she spoke again.

"You look like fine specimens indeed."

Leahcim and Markka gave each other secretive glances as if to say, *What the hell did she mean by that*? before focusing back on the queen.

T'oann finally spoke up. "What my mother means is we welcome you to our world and ask that you join with us, we hope, as teachers, advisers, and friends in our fight against the Thourons."

"We will be honored to assist in any way we can, but with the understanding that being rescued and rejoining our people is our priority," was Leahcim's reply.

The queen looked at them through squinted eyes, sniffed, and said, "Of course." Then she told T'oann to set their guests up with suitable accommodations, turned, and shuffled off.

Leahcim leaned close to Markka and whispered, "What do you think?"

"At least she didn't order a vivisection," she whispered back.

They were taken to a spacious compound at the far end of the palace grounds on a hill overlooking much of the city where two well-furnished bungalow-style living quarters were waiting for them.

Still not yet feeling one hundred percent recovered from their ordeal, Leahcim took a seat on a bench on the edge of a courtyard full of plants, a pond with some kind of aquatic life in it, and a small gurgling stream to rest.

Markka stood in the center of it and twirled around taking it all in.

In between the bungalows was a waist-high pedestal upon which sat a hexagon box.

"Hey, even Cora's got her own place. How's it going, Cora?" Markka said.

"It is going well, lieutenant."

"You can call me Markka, Cora. We're practically civilians now."

"Yes, lieutenant."

"Oh never mind." Disappointed that Cora insisted on using formal titles when addressing her. She shifted the conversation to something more mundane. "This is more than I expected," Markka said. "I thought we'd get some dinky little room a step above a prison cell."

Like a giddy child, she peered into each of the sleeping quarters. Her head was halfway through the door of the second building when she shouted, "This one's mine!"

Leahcim did not care which one he got as long as Markka was happy.

"Good," he said. "I can finally get some quiet time. Because you snore."

"I don't snore," she protested.

"Cora?"

"Yes, captain."

"Doesn't she snore?"

"You both snore."

"There," Markka said with smug satisfaction in her voice. "We're even."

A moment later, the air sang with melodic music resembling a harp. Leahcim imagined angels descending to the courtyard.

Markka swooned when she heard it. "Aww, that's so beautiful. It's like a calming fragrance drifting on a warm, gentle breeze."

"I never knew you were so mushy," Leahcim said as he rolled his eyes. "If you get any more syrupy sweet, I'm gonna need to have my sugar levels checked."

"Bite me," Markka said.

The harp music wafted through the air again.

"That's the doorbell," Cora said.

"Oh," was Markka's response.

"Who is it?" Leahcim asked Cora.

"Commander T'oann."

"Looks like the time has come to earn our keep," Leahcim said. "Let her in."

CHAPTER 22

The main door to the compound swished open and T'oann walked in.

Markka stopped twirling and Leahcim's heart skipped a beat.

T'oann was not wearing her customary military uniform. She wore a stunning gold gown with sky blue accents that clung to her figure like a glove. Leahcim already thought she was built like one of those stereotyped drawings of mythical Amazonian women from Earth's past, but that gown did not do anything to nullify that image.

"Damn. You look nice," Leahcim blurted out. And immediately regretted it. "I mean, uh, comfortable. Not used to seeing you out of uniform." He knew nothing he said would allow him to recover from the wreck he just made.

T'oann stopped walking and stood where she was uncertain what to do or say. His unsolicited compliment was unexpected. No one had ever complimented her on her appearance before. She had never seen herself as anything other than the daughter of the queen and a soldier. For most of her life, she was focused on fulfilling the roles expected of her. To suddenly be seen as something other than what she saw herself was surprising. T'oann's emotions were a jumbled mess.

Leahcim was more embarrassed than confused. He was not one to speak before thinking, but seeing T'oann standing there in that gown made him feel as awestruck as he had felt the first time he laid eyes on LeeAnn.

His pulse raced; his breathing grew shallow, his vision narrowed, and the thumping sound of blood rushing to his head drowned out everything else his ears might have heard.

He quickly regained his composure and, he hoped, his dignity. "I'm sorry. I was out of line," he finally said, trying to smooth things over.

"There is no need for you to apologize. If I seem off-balance, it is because I am not accustomed to getting compliments on my appearance. I was, um, mildly surprised, and, um, pleasantly flattered. Thank you." She hoped her recovery did not appear awkward or forced. She delighted in finding out that he was as uncomfortable as she was, if not more.

Leahcim returned her thanks with an embarrassed, "You're welcome." Then proceeded to punctuate an obvious pregnant pause with silence.

As entertaining as it was to watch her captain squirm, Markka came to Leahcim's rescue.

"That gown is absolutely gorgeous. Would it be possible for me to wear one like it?"

T'oann stopped looking at Leahcim long enough to answer Markka's question.

"Yes, you may wear whatever you want. All you need is to ask."

"Great! I would like to have one just like yours."

"I will see to it."

T'oann turned back to Leahcim who quickly shifted his gaze to Markka. "I came to ask if everything is to your liking. And if there is anything you require."

Leahcim looked back at T'oann and told her everything was fine. "But there is one thing."

"Name it." T'oann felt her response sounded a bit too enthusiastic. She glanced at Markka who was standing with a big smile on her face. T'oann prayed to the Goddess to help her make a dignified retreat before she made a fool of herself.

"May we go see our fighter?"

"I can arrange that. Is next dawn's light acceptable?"

"You mean tomorrow morning?" Markka asked.

"Yes."

"That'll be fine," Leahcim said.

"Good. I will arrange an escort to take you to see your craft then."

Leahcim thanked T'oann then asked Cora if she would give them a wake-up call in the morning.

"Yes, captain, I will notify you when it is time."

Eager to leave the compound as quickly as possible, T'oann said, "I will return tomorrow to take you to see your craft." Then she turned and left.

After T'oann left, Markka teased her captain.

"Way to go, flyboy!"

"I don't want to hear it."

"What's the matter?" she said in baby talk. "Little cappy got stars in his eyes?"

He flashed her his middle finger and said, "Oh shut the hell up. It's not what you think."

"I don't have to think. You forget I'm a Felid? I do have a strong, and reliable, sense of smell, you know."

"You smell your upper lip," he snorted.

"Oh come on. Even you could smell the pheromones. They were radiating off the both of you like heat from their two suns."

"I must concur with the lieutenant," Cora said.

"So, captain," Markka started to ask, "just what happened between you two in that mind-meld you had?"

"Nunna," he retorted.

CHAPTER 23

Cora woke Leahcim and Markka and ordered them breakfast. In the time it took them to shower, bathe, and get dressed, a tray with a variety of foods and drinks was delivered to the compound.

They each chose to wear the centurion uniforms they had been issued instead of the more relaxed toga-style attire they had also been issued.

They sat in the courtyard garden, ate, and chatted about how they were going to adjust to living on Progensha if the Alliance never came for them.

"They probably think we're dead. I doubt anyone will come looking for us," Markka said, as she plucked a piece of blue fruit from the tray and took a bite. "Oh, man," she cooed, "this is delicious. Try one."

Leahcim eyed the piece of fruit with suspicion before picking one up and taking a bite. "He slurped and drooled as the juice dribbled down his chin. "Damn! This is good." He took another bite. "I'm a bit more optimistic than you, I guess. I believe when they don't recover our remains, they'll conduct a search and rescue."

"Probably more like a search and recovery," Markka said somberly. "Did you forget what the battlefield looked like?"

"No," was his reluctant reply. "But I don't think the gang will just give up without making the effort to find us. I know Vee. She won't abandon us without a fight."

"I hope you're right."

When they finished eating, Markka sat and meditated. Leahcim was not a morning meditation enthusiast so he sat and spoke quietly with Cora.

"So what more can you tell me about this culture?"

"Uderrans live a relatively peaceful life, but their way of life and freedoms are threatened by the Thourons. They have been at war for generations. Unfortunately, the Thourons are wearing them down."

"Any chance a peace could be brokered?"

"None. As with our war with the GSE, there is no way it will end until one side or the other is utterly defeated. The Thourons believe they are genetically superior to all life forms on the planet and are endowed by divine right to dominate and cleanse this world of those they deem unfit. Much like your Earth experienced before meeting extraterrestrials."

Leahcim snorted, "Even that didn't go so well at first."

"You Terrans are an unusual lot."

"That we are. So you're saying we're lucky the Uderrans found us first?"

"I would say it was fortuitous."

"I'm guessing our presence is not making it any easier for the Uderrans."

"No, it is not. The Thourons have stepped up their attacks on the Uderrans. Quite possibly to acquire our technology and to acquire us."

Leahcim looked around the garden as if expecting to see someone spying on them. "Are we clear?"

"Yes. There are no listening devices."

"Have the Uderrans discovered you have infiltrated their systems?"

"No. Not yet. I plan to broach the subject with them and attempt to convince them it would be in all our best interests if I could interface with their systems. I might be able to improve their defenses at least."

"Leave that to me and Markka."

"You do realize we would be doing them a disservice if we help them and then leave them if the Alliance finds us."

Leahcim sighed. "Yeah. I've thought about that. The Alliance could show up tomorrow."

"Or they may never show up."

"I know. It's something I don't want to think about right now." He grew quiet for a moment before speaking again. "I know you transferred some data to us when we were unconscious in their medical facility, but can you explain how they determine the passage of time?"

"Sols are days. Mictons are minutes, sectons are seconds, mos are hours, cycles are years. They have no designation for weeks or months."

"I got that. How do they determine seasons?"

"Seasons are based on equidistant oval eight revolutions of their planet around its twin suns. The Progenshans recognize eight distinct seasons. One sol is every thirty-six Earth hours. There is one season where there is no night. It lasts for approximately three Earth months as the planet passes between the suns."

"Talk about working long hours."

Just then the harp sang. Cora opened the door to the compound and T'oann stepped through wearing her customary military uniform. Leahcim was immediately disappointed.

"Are you prepared to see your fighter craft?"

Markka, who was finished with her meditation, unfolded her legs and stood up beside her captain. "We're more than ready," she said.

"Then follow me," T'oann said, as she led them from the compound to an awaiting transport.

Walking a few meters behind T'oann, Markka whispered to Leahcim, "You smell that?"

"Smell what?" he whispered back.

"Pheromones. The air is strong with them."

"Shut up."

The ride to where their fighter was held did not take long. It was sitting in the middle of what looked like a giant hanger. As they stepped out of the transport, they saw teams of technicians working all around the ship. They managed to recover nearly all the larger sheared-off pieces and laid them all over the floor in an attempt to reconstruct the ship.

Leahcim figured their ability to understand how it all worked would be the equivalent of an early caveman trying to understand how a light switch worked.

T'oann motioned to a young male who appeared to be in charge. He came over to them and saluted his commander with crossed arms over his chest.

"At ease," T'oann told him.

He lowered his arms and stared at Leahcim and Markka warily.

T'oann made the introductions. "This is B'rtann, the second officer in command. He has been overseeing the examination of your fighter."

"It is a remarkable piece of machinery," he began. "Can you tell us how it works and how it sustains you in the Great Beyond? We have nothing like it in our arsenal." He kept his voice neutral in an attempt to sound cordial and conversational.

"Captain, if I may?" Markka asked.

"Sure thing. By all means." Leahcim figured her explanation would make as much sense to them as a first-year lecture at the academy on quantum physics."

While Markka droned on about the ship and the technology behind it, Leahcim asked T'oann if he could speak with her away from everyone else.

She led him to a far corner of the bay away from most of the noise and base personnel.

"What is it you wish to speak to me about?" she asked.

"Where are your aircraft?"

She gave him a puzzled look.

"You know, winged or vertical lift aircraft? Something that can fly?" He used his hands to emulate something flying in the air. "Like our fighter," he finally said.

"We have nothing like that on Progensha. The Thourons have developed projectile weapons they launch into the air, but they soar rather than fly. They follow a path like an object that is tossed by one's hand. Similar to our tanks, just much farther, faster, and higher. Then they fall back to the ground. Usually near or on our people."

"So they have rockets?"

"Yes, if I understand you correctly."

"So what happens when they launch a rocket?"

"We extend the repelling shield to block them, sometimes one gets through." She stared at nothing in particular, but he knew she was visualizing the horrific destruction such weapons unleashed on their victims.

"So what will happen when the shield doesn't work anymore?"

"Then our city will become vulnerable to relentless attacks."

"What if we could help you defend your city better against such attacks?"

T'oann looked at him with hopeful suspicion in her eyes. She frowned then asked, "How would you be able to do this?" she asked.

Leahcim stepped in closer to her and asked, "May I mind-walk with you?"

She looked around at the hustle and bustle around them. "Not here," she said. She gestured to a nearby personnel carrier. "Here. We can use this."

Once they climbed inside, Leahcim asked her why they needed to sit alone inside the carrier.

She explained that her ability was classified and only a select few people knew she had the ability at all. If the Thourons knew she possessed the skill, they would stop at nothing to acquire her and attempt to learn how to use it against them.

"They have never been able to produce a mind walker of their own. In the distant past, they tried breeding with Uderran mind walkers they managed to capture, but were unsuccessful."

"What did they do with their captives?"

"Murdered."

"I take it there aren't many of these mind walkers left?"

She swallowed hard. "No," she lamented. "Long ago, the ability was prevalent among those of the royal lineage. But through the generations, the ability faded and has nearly died out. I am the last of my people to possess the skill. My mother is too feeble to use it, my brother did not inherit the ability, and . . . my sister is no longer alive."

The thought of suddenly discovering she had a sister only to tragically lose her moments after finding out, weighed heavily on T'oann like a stone tied around her neck.

Leahcim saw the look of sadness creep onto her face. She quickly turned her head to the side, but not in time to hide a single teardrop that lazily rolled down her cheek. He wanted nothing more than to reach out and comfort her. To wipe away the tear; to hold and hug her to show her he understood how she felt, but he decided the wise thing to do was keep his distance. He could not find the right words. So all he was able to say was, "Oh."

If T'oann were an empath, she might have been overpowered by the sheer power of his distress, but the strength of her own conflicted feelings of elation and sadness were barely enough for her to control. Being this close to Leahcim in such close quarters overwhelmed her senses. Her breathing was shallow, her throat constricted, and her body vibrated much like the ground tremors that occasionally rumbled under the city.

As for the tear, T'oann knew its appearance betrayed her tough image. She did not like being seen as vulnerable in the eyes of a fellow warrior.

She protected her emotions as stubbornly as she did her people. But just as she failed to hide her tear, she felt she would fail to protect her people.

Not wanting to look more vulnerable in his eyes, T'oann regained her composure and looked back at Leahcim.

"Now, what do you wish to mind-walk with me about?"

He extended his hand to her and she took it. Almost instantly he felt her presence in his head. The sensation was exhilarating. His whole body tingled.

"Wow. I'm not sure I can get used to this," he said. Hoping he was helping her gracefully recover from her moment of emotional weakness.

"I will teach you."

"Cool."

"Are you feeling cold? I cannot sense it."

"Uh, no. It's just an archaic expression of speech my people sometimes use."

Now it was T'oann's turn to say, "Oh."

"I want to ask your permission to allow Cora to work with your engineers and technicians to improve your physical and electronic defenses."

"Please do not think harshly of me, but I need your assurance that she can be trusted. You are asking me to expose our entire network to a foreign machine."

"Cora is more than a mere machine. She is a very trustworthy friend. Markka and I owe our very lives to her. And since it looks like Uderra is our home now, we will do everything in our power to protect it. Including Cora."

"I will consider your request and render my decision tomorrow."

"Fair enough," he said.

There was an awkward silence between them before T'oann mercifully broke the mental connection. He got the impression she did not want to terminate their connection any more than he did.

"I suggest we rejoin our people before we are missed," T'oann said.

"I agree."

They left the privacy of the carrier and joined Markka, who was still happily explaining how the starfighter worked.

CHAPTER 24

Early the next morning, T'oann arrived at the compound. She rang the bell and announced her arrival. Cora opened the doors and let her inside.

"Good morning, Commander T'oann."

"Good morning to you Cora," she said. "Captain Leahcim is expecting me."

"He and the lieutenant are waiting for you in his quarters."

"Thank you."

As she was about to knock on the door, it swished open and a beaming Markka stood in the doorway and ushered her in.

"Good morning, T'oann. May I call you T'oann?"

Somewhat taken by surprise by Markka's bubbly attitude, the commander said, "Yes, you may."

"Great," Markka said as she gleefully ushered T'oann into the bungalow. "Please come in and make yourself comfortable."

T'oann stepped inside and took a seat on a small, avocado green cushioned chair near the door. Markka sat down on a beige chair across from her. Leahcim was reclining in a chair matching Markka's directly across from T'oann, who sat ramrod straight in her chair. Markka retrieved Cora's box and sat it on a table between her and Leahcim.

Leahcim was the first to speak. "Before we begin, we need to lay down some ground rules."

"Ground rules?" T'oann raised one questioning eyebrow.

"Yes, ground rules," Markka chimed in.

A look of uneasiness snuck its way onto T'oann's expression. Quickly replaced by one of a warrior whose senses were placed on heightened alert.

Leahcim saw T'oann's tense confusion and swiftly moved to relieve her concerns.

"The lieutenant and I don't stand on ceremony. In other words, we don't adhere to formality. Unless we are operating somehow in a formal capacity, so you don't have to address us as captain or lieutenant."

"Yeah," Markka added.

He watched the tension flow from T'oann's body as she slightly slumped back in her chair.

"That is a relief," she said. "I was bracing myself for . . . I do not know what I was bracing myself for."

"You'll find Markka and I don't always follow ceremonial protocol."

"Yeah," Markka said. "We don't believe in walking around like we got sticks up our butts."

"Excuse me?"

Leahcim rolled his eyes at Markka and tossed her a tired look. "Never mind her. Markka tends to over exaggerate."

"No, I don't."

He did his best to ignore his compatriot. "Anyway, it looks like this world is our home now," Leahcim said. "And we will do whatever is required of us to keep it that way."

"Your services will be greatly appreciated and highly rewarded."

"Cool. And speaking of doing whatever is required, you have some good news for us, right?"

Before T'oann answered Leahcim's question, she had one of her own she wanted answered. "I request you do me a solid," she said. Hoping she used the term correctly.

"Hey! What do you know? We're starting to speak each other's language," he grinned at her then his face broke out into a broad smile. He was smiling like a proud parent who just witnessed their child accomplish some amazing feat. "Sure, we'll do you a solid if we can. What do you want us to help you with?"

T'oann hesitated as if she doubted she was making a prudent decision before she reached into the cleavage of her bosom and extracted a small vial.

Leahcim stifled a gasp, then stole a glance at Markka to see if she caught his reaction. She had because she made silent sniffing motions, pointed her nose in the air, and flared her nostrils. T'oann kept her eyes on Leahcim so she never saw Markka tease her captain.

Leahcim forced himself to focus on the vial T'oann had in her hand. He recognized it as the one Tonga gave her the day she aided in T'oann's escape from execution. His demeanor grew serious.

"T'oann, you don't have to do this."

"I must," she insisted. "I have no one else I trust to do this."

"Do what?" Markka asked.

"You must swear in the presence of the Goddess to reveal to no one what you are about to learn," T'oann told her.

Markka's tone became serious and she looked at T'oann with genuine concern. "Sure, sure. You have my word."

T'oann nervously rolled the vial between her fingers and thumb. "Can you help me analyze this blood sample?"

Cora, who had been silently observing, spoke. "Commander, I have already analyzed the blood sample you hold in your hand."

"How can you do this without running it through the necessary healing machines?"

T'oann asked. More curious than fearful of Cora's abilities.

"Cora is capable of a lot more than you or your scientists and engineers can imagine," Leahcim said.

T'oann's hand began to tremble. Leahcim instinctively reached out to grab it to steady her and was instantly inside her mind.

"Shit," he cursed. Suddenly showing up in her mind uninvited was an affront to his scruples and an invasion of her privacy. "Sorry," he said to her, clearly embarrassed. "I need to get the hell out of your head."

"No, wait," she pleaded. She knew his thoughts and sensed his feelings. "Has Cora always been able to infiltrate our network?"

Leahcim was reluctant to answer, but he knew he couldn't lie to her whether they were linked or not. "Yes," he said.

"Then she could have destroyed us anytime she wanted?"

"No!" He angrily rebuffed her. A bit too angrily, he regretted. He sighed. Then explained more calmly as best he could. He hoped T'oann would sense the sincerity in his explanation.

"Since the day we crashed here, Cora has been able to take control of everything—if she wanted to—but she didn't because we are not malevolent invaders. Yes, we are soldiers, the same as you, fighting a war against an aggressor species, but we are not conquerors."

"What if you had died by our hand?" T'oann queried.

"Cora would have done everything in her power to save us, but not to the detriment of your people."

He sensed she was struggling with her feelings about him, Markka, and especially about Cora.

"What if you had died?" she insisted.

"Had we died, she would have mourned our deaths and worked to earn your trust and did her best to aid you in your struggle with the Thourons. Had she not been able to, she would have accepted whatever verdict you decided for her. You can ask her yourself. She doesn't lie," he finished.

He felt her confusion and her desire to believe him give way to acceptance. As long as they were mind-linked, there was no way for either of them to hide their true feelings from the other.

Leahcim sensed T'oann pondering everything he told her. He felt the conflict of emotions within her. She had serious trust issues, but he could not blame her. She held the fate of her people in her hands. He understood how the responsibility she bore weighed on her like heavy chains constricting her. He also felt the pain of her loneliness. She hid it well, but he sensed the smoldering flames of an emotional need. She was a cauldron swirling with unfulfilled longings and burning desires.

Fearing she would reveal more than she intended if they remained mind-linked, he broke the connection between them. But in the brief moment before their link was severed, he sensed something . . . primal; it emanated from both of them with the intensity of a scorching desert wind. And he knew instantly what it was they both felt.

"What the hell just happened?" Markka angrily demanded. You both just blipped out for a minute or two . . . mictonned . . . or whatever."

"We were mentally linked," Leahcim said.

"If that's what it looks like, I have to say it looks pretty freaky if you ask me." Markka folded her arms across her chest and huffed, "Somebody could've warned me about that. It creeped me out seeing the two of you like that. You looked like you left your bodies."

"My apologies," T'oann said.

"Well," Leahcim said, doing his best to sound calm and steady following a disturbingly intense mind-walk, "T'oann has some news for us."

"Oh, yes," T'oann said, a bit disoriented. She was somewhat embarrassed following her connection with Leahcim. She knew he saw her true feelings and what it was she was hiding from him. But she pretended as if nothing happened. "Cora will be permitted to interface with our network."

"Thank you, commander. You will not be disappointed," Cora said.

"I hope you are correct. My reputation and the lives of my people now depend on you."

"Do you wish to know the results of my analysis of the sample now?"

T'oann looked at Markka, then at Leahcim wide-eyed and full of anticipation. She inhaled, then let out a long breath. "Yes, please tell me the results."

"The originator of this blood sample is a direct genetic match. This person is your sister."

Although she knew the truth, she needed to hear it from someone else with no stake in the matter.

Leahcim watched the look of unrestricted joy and the shroud of sorrow simultaneously etch themselves across T'oann's face. He alone understood the significance of this moment.

"Thank you," was all she was able to say.

"You are welcome," Cora replied. "But there is more; it involves all three of you."

"More?" Leahcim and T'oann both asked at the same time.

"All three of us?" Markka asked. "How so?"

Cora continued, "There are genetic markers in the sample that are distinctly Terran and Felid."

The resulting silence was deafening. If a bomb had exploded in the room, none of them would have noticed.

"In fact," Cora continued, "there are genetic markers of more than a dozen different species of the Alliance."

"How can this be?" T'oann asked.

"At some point in your history, your ancestors procreated with one another."

Leahcim sat in stunned silence with his mouth hanging open. T'oann's reaction mirrored his. Then Markka, in true Markka fashion, started to chuckle and transitioned to doubled-over laughter. "Well, what do you know? We crash on an unknown planet in some obscure corner of the universe and we run into our cousins."

"Not directly related, of course," Cora said.

"Whatever," Markka sniped.

"How can that be?" T'oann asked. There is no record amongst my people that we have ever been visited by beings from the Great Beyond before your appearance. Until your appearance, a lot of people doubted life existed anywhere but here on Progensha only. And now you tell me that my people are related to you?"

"That is correct," Cora said. "I do not yet have an answer to your question. But I shall endeavor to find out."

"Thank you."

"Oh, by the way," Markka interrupted. "Cora isn't informal like us. She's formal all the time." Markka gave T'oann a playful wink and belted out a hearty laugh. "Hey, cousin, you have breakfast yet? I'm starving."

"No, I have not eaten yet," T'oann said.

"Then you are informally invited to have breakfast with us. Please?"

"Yes, will you please have morning refreshments with us?" Leahcim asked, finally recovered from the bombshell Cora dropped on them. "See? I'm even trying to use your vernacular." He grinned. "Cousin."

T'oann accepted the invitation and ate with them. She picked up something that looked like an apple and took a bite. "This maiden fruit is delicious. You should sample some,"

T'oann said. She took another bite and mulled over what she had just learned while Markka prattled on about them practically being family.

There are many things we don't know about our world, T'oann thought. *What if the old, nearly forgotten legends were true?* she wondered.

"May I ask a favor of you?" T'oann asked.

"All you need to do is ask," Leahcim replied.

"You must swear to me you will keep secret what you have learned here today. I am afraid if news of this got out, it would unravel the very fabric of my civilization."

"Yes. You have my word," Leahcim said.

"Ditto," Markka piped in.

"You have mine as well," Cora said.

And thus began an alliance that would be formed with secrets, trials, and troubling ordeals.

In the sols that followed, Cora was granted full access to the Uderran network. Under the watchful eyes of B'rtann and Sho'khan, or more accurately, under Cora's, the Uderrans were able to strengthen the defensive wall surrounding the city. Raising it high enough to ward off Thouron rocket attacks.

The main power resource of the Uderran city was from their use of geothermal energy drawn from the planet's core. Similar use of geothermal energy was common among nearly all of the civilizations on the planet.

The Progenshans never developed a technology that utilized fossil fuels which accounted for a nearly toxic-free atmosphere. What could not be powered geothermically was powered by solar energy, hydroelectric, and wind. And, in the case of the Uderrans, since most of the city consisted of thatched huts and yurts, the manufacturing waste was mostly due to the production of military weapons and equipment. They even attempted to recycle that waste.

Within less than one cycle, Cora helped the Uderrans double their production of military weapons while increasing the efficiency and effectiveness of the weapons and defensive systems they already had, all while respecting the environment.

Unfortunately, the Thourons did not share the Uderran sense of respect for the cradle of the Goddess. Especially when it came to exploiting the planet's resources. They did whatever they felt necessary to assert their influence over those they wished to dominate and force their doctrine of natural superiority upon.

That usually meant the use of extreme military force, defiling sacred lands, forced death marches, destruction of food reserves, and blowing up and blasting into oblivion everything that stood in their way.

The biggest obstacle to those goals was the Uderrans. And with the help of Leahcim, Markka, and Cora, that way was made more difficult. The three had become integral parts of Uderran life.

CHAPTER 25

After living on Progensha for nearly a cycle, Leahcim, Markka, and Cora had assimilated into the Uderran society and became productive members. Leahcim and Markka primarily distinguished themselves as effective soldiers in battles defending the city and surrounding territory; they were granted citizenship and given commissions in the Uderran military.

During a rather fierce border battle in the early part of their first cycle, Markka showed the Uderran military brass why she was the best gunner in the Alliance with some impressive displays of her skills behind a trigger.

A viral infection incapacitated a large number of the Uderran military. The Thourons attempted to exploit the illness by attacking one of the outer food fields and a livestock nursery. Markka was a gunner with a hover tank division sent to repel the Thouron incursion. Markka and her tank crew found themselves in the thick of the fight. When their tank was crippled, Markka ordered her crew to abandon it. But instead of retreating with them, she provided cover fire for their retreat. "Just like old times," is what her tank crew later reported she said just before she let loose on her counterparts with a blistering combination of laser energy blasts laced with solid armor-piercing rounds on a unit of retreating Thourons. She nearly singlehandedly eliminated an entire phalanx of Thouron troops before being seriously injured by an explosion in the tank's turret.

A forensic examination of what remained of the turret and gun revealed Markka had made some unauthorized, self-improvised modifications to the gun. Those modifications and her unconventional use of the gun overheated the reaction chamber which resulted in an explosion that nearly ended her life. She experienced serious physical trauma and spent sixty days in a coma before she recovered enough to be discharged from the healing facility.

She was reprimanded for making the unauthorized modifications to the gun, charged with reckless endangerment, and placed under house detention. T'oann's brother, Tory, took responsibility for keeping an eye on Markka while she recovered at the Royal

Palace from her injuries.

Tory had developed an affinity for the feisty Felid and wanted to make sure she didn't get herself killed before he got to know her better. The reckless endangerment charge was eventually dropped at the request of Leahcim, T'oann, and Cora. Markka was reassigned to teach at the military academy.

Needless to say, she was not thrilled with the reassignment. To add insult to injury, Tory ordered armed guards to escort her daily to and from the academy to ensure she complied with the detention order.

Leahcim and T'oann recommended her reassignment. Leahcim convinced T'oann that it would be in Markka's best interest if she were given something to do while she recuperated from her injuries. Tory threw in the armed guards just for fun because he knew it would get under her skin. Cora, meanwhile, redesigned the turret gun to allow for Markka's innovative upgrade to be used safely. Markka then taught the tank crews how to use the gun the way she had. Leahcim, on the other hand, proved his worth as a hovercraft pilot.

In no way were the hovercraft substitutes for an Alliance fighter, but in the absence of one, operating a hover, as they were more commonly referred to, was as good as it got. Like Markka, Leahcim pushed the performance limits of the hover he was assigned. It was his never-say-never attitude that earned him the respect of the troops under his command. Unlike Markka, he never risked his life without discussing an idea with T'oann and Cora before testing out a theory—usually by himself. Eventually, his crews insisted he included them whenever he tested any theories.

To the Uderrans, Leahcim's tactics were revolutionary. To him, they were typical Alliance-style operating procedures. He and his people, he referred to all of his troops as his people, transformed battlefield rescue and recovery tactics. Many Uderran soldiers and civilians owed their lives to Leahcim and the crews he trained. He was able to adapt his skills as a fighter pilot and medical rescue first responder to meet the need for a rapid deployment medical rescue unit.

The Uderrans did not have a combat-ready healing unit entirely trained and dedicated to roll into a battle zone and retrieve the wounded while under fire before Leahcim took command. With Cora's help, he converted personnel carriers into reinforced armored mobile medical sickbays complete with defensive weapons. He was fond of saying there was no way his people were going in to save some if they couldn't kick some. Before the creation of the mobile healing division, individual healers were embedded with the troops and did what they could for the injured in a hot zone until they could be evacuated out.

While Leahcim and Markka were fighting and innovating, Cora was doing some innovating of her own. She upgraded as best she could the technological capabilities of the Uderrans. Despite having developed hovercraft and laser weapons, the Uderrans lacked the knowledge to build aircraft. It was one of those evolutionary incongruities Cora found peculiar. Her attempts to produce prototype aircraft were stymied by the limitations of their scientific and technological knowledge and capabilities. She equated it with raising children as she understood biological development. There was no way one could expect a child to run if it was still in the crawling stage of life. Aside from hot air balloons, nothing else worked. The atmosphere on Progensha was unfavorable to supporting propellered craft, and jet propulsion was not yet supported by the current state of technology. But Cora was determined to fast-tack Uderran scientific and technical knowledge. Any culture capable of developing hovercraft should be able to build aircraft.

Another aspect of reality on Progensha which Cora found intriguing was not just the lack of air travel, but, due to the existence of the ocean leviathans, an utter lack of ocean travel. Attempts were made to explore the oceans generations past, but since no one ever survived, the endeavor was understandably abandoned.

The continent they were currently on was not a particularly large landmass, but it contained pockets of other cultures that were farther from the sphere of Thouron ambitions but not immune to Thouron aggression.

There were the reclusive Cold Mountain people. A race of Humanoid-like people who, like the Uderrans, had been relatively successful in repelling Thouron attacks. Then there were the elusive inhabitants of the Dark Woods. They were rumored to be invisible warriors who devoured their enemies. The rumor about them being invisible was partially true; they were masters at camouflage. Travelers who passed through the Dark Woods reported seeing hooded figures who moved like swift specters in the shadows. The rumor that they ate trespassers was unsubstantiated.

Beyond the Cold Mountains and Dark Woods was an impassable desert called the Land of No Return. It was rumored that mysterious things happened out there. But as the name implies, no one who attempted to explore that region ever returned.

There were groups of nomadic tribes who peppered the periphery of the desert. They traded goods and services with the Uderrans, Mountain People, and the Dark Woodsmen, but aside from those few pockets of tribal groups, not much else existed.

And so, with oceans harboring deadly beasts on one side, an impassable desert on the other, a smattering of inland lakes, glades, a snow-covered mountain range, and a thickly forested area were all the Progenshans knew of their world. They did not even have a moon. Nothing to inspire them to reach or be influenced by.

Apart from defending the Uderrans and Leahcim and Markka, Cora added exploring the planet as one of her primary goals. Quickly flying over it in a desperate orbital crash landing was not sufficient or efficient enough.

CHAPTER 26

A full cycle following the crash, Leahcim and T'oann strengthened their relationship to the point of being inseparable. They spent nearly every waking moment they could with each other. When they were not out in the field or on some assignment, they were in a training facility honing their hand-to-hand combat skills. They took great pleasure in punching, kicking, flipping, and essentially beating the crap out of each other. Sometimes after intense sessions, the two of them would be observed staring longingly into each other's eyes giggling. For those who were out of the loop, they simply looked like star-crossed lovers.

Out of the view of prying eyes, Leahcim and T'oann spent a considerable amount of time mind-walking. So much so that they could touch each other's minds without making physical contact. They became good enough to be able to mind-walk without looking like they blipped out. Their closeness solidified a relationship that resulted in a bond so strong that no one dared think of coming between them. People suspected the two of them shared more intimate moments as well, and, in time, that became apparent.

Those suspicions were confirmed when T'oann's rumored pregnancy was no longer in question. Leahcim said he wanted to make their situation "legit." So he proposed to T'oann at a public venue and she accepted. They were married by the queen in a private ceremony at the palace.

Markka said it was as if they were born at the hip. The Uderrans said they were blessed by the Goddess with eternal love. Markka teased Leahcim about those pesky pheromones. But even Markka was not immune from the effects of the Goddess. Cora thought the oddest coupling was the one Markka had with T'oann's brother. Cora suspected Markka's uniqueness was the initial draw for Tory. Her combat injuries helped spark the beginning of their relationship. It just progressed and blossomed.

It began innocently enough with the two of them teasing Leahcim and T'oann. Cora thought perhaps it was through that commonality they shared that they began to discover other things they had in common. What started as a mutual curiosity bloomed into a friendship of a truly odd pairing. Where Tory was royally rigid and militarily disciplined, Markka was his direct opposite. Militarily disciplined and nowhere near rigid. She grew fond of telling Tory that his rigid nature was due to a stick he had up his butt. She was carefree. A trait in Felids that Leahcim also admired.

Felids did not have nearly as many hang-ups as Terrans and, apparently, Uderrans. But Felids were fiercely loyal and made steadfast friends. Qualities Uderrans held in high regard. Tory held Markka in such high regard that he asked for her hand in marriage and she accepted. As a result, she became more entrenched in matters of the royal court as well as military matters.

Where Leahcim spent his time in the field, Markka spent her time in the classroom as an instructor. But despite their acceptance into Uderran society, neither was immune to occasionally feeling homesick. Unbeknownst to the other, they were each prone to occasionally sit under the stars at night and long to be flying amongst them again.

Tory would sit with his wife and intently listen as she told the stories of her adventures in the Great Beyond. T'oann would mind-walk with Leahcim and be astonished at reliving through his eyes and memories the thrill of traveling in the vastness of space. Flying through the blackness, visiting fascinating worlds with people who all looked different, but who got along peacefully. Most of the time.

It sometimes felt like she was right there with him as he piloted his fighter and fought his enemy. It was the most exhilarating feeling next to the lovemaking they shared. Life was good. However, neither foresaw the dramatic changes parenthood and destiny had in store for them.

CHAPTER 27

An armada of thirty Alliance ships rapidly approached Aggro Nine. The lead ship, an enormous dreadnought called the *Vindicator*, bristling with weapons and state-of-the-art armament, issued a call to battle stations to the fleet and to prepare for a return to regular space.

Within the bowels of the ship's launch bay, crammed full of an assortment of ships from fighters to bombers to medical rescues, sat their anxious crews ready to spring into action the instant they returned to regular space.

The task force was headed for Aggro Nine to rendezvous with the fighter squadron that was returning from the planet when it received a cryptic message that the fighter group had come under attack before their signals were jammed.

The fleet commander immediately ordered them to jump into hyperspace and "haul ass" to the planet to assist. The hope was that they would not be too late.

One by one the Fleet ships returned to normal space, slowing to sub-light speed outside a debris field kilometers wide.

Everyone near a window or view screen saw the devastation.

The crews of the ships in the launch bays could not help but feel the growing anger and frustration at what they witnessed.

The crew of one ship, in particular, the *Infiltrator*, felt the loss like a punch in the gut.

"There's no one left?" was the lament of medical specialist Nick Piper. "Captain Leahcim, Lieutenant Markka, and Cora can't be gone."

Pipe, as he was known by his friends, was a pale, freckle-faced Terran with curly red hair; the youngest member of the crew. Just two years out of the academy's medical division, still a teen, but also an accomplished soldier and very capable member of the team.

The rest of the team consisted of Captain Vee. The best way to describe her was to think of an oversized bird. Her people were able to fly, but when they were introduced to aviation technology, they shifted the emphasis of natural flight from necessary to recreational. When covert aerial reconnaissance was required, Captain Vee usually took on those assignments. Then there was Specialist Sparks. Sparks was from an aquatic world. Her amphibious talents made her particularly useful in water and swamps. And like some Earth eels, could deliver a paralyzing shock if the salinity of the water was right. Specialist Memphis Lin was a female Terran whose forte was stealth. By the time you saw her, it was too late to do anything about it. Rounding out the team was Specialist Raqmar, a strong, gray-skinned inhabitant of a heavy gravity planet. Whenever they needed the assistance of a biological tank, Raqmar was their go-to guy.

"Somebody had to survive this," Raqmar said. Hoping he was right. "They must have. There's no way those cold-blooded bastards were that thorough." The anger was palpable in his tone.

"It appears they were," Captain Vee said.

"Somebody's going to pay for this," Lin vowed.

The others echoed her sentiment.

The voice of Fleet Commander boomed over the public address system. "ALL HANDS, THIS IS COMMANDER CHAPPIE. OUR RESCUE OPERATION IS NOW A RECOVERY OPERATION. RECOVERY TEAMS, LET'S GET TO WORK AND BRING OUR BOYS AND GIRLS HOME."

"Well, you heard him," Vee said. "Let's get out there and bring our fallen comrades home."

The deck came alive with ships coming and going and deck crews running to and fro servicing ships as they landed and departed. For every recovery ship launched, two fighter escorts were deployed to accompany them on their grim task of recovering bodies and body parts as well as key debris cleanup.

Unlike the other recovery ships, the *Infiltrator* was unique. It was the latest in a new, heavily armored class of multipurpose ships designed to operate as a blockade runner, science and research lab, fighter, and rescue and recovery vessel. Her weapons were formidable, and her armor and shields were designed to adapt to changing conditions. Her engines were based on dreadnought design, just scaled down. Her designers also equipped her with underwater capabilities and cloaking technology. She was fast, silent, and deadly.

Sparks fired up the engines and piloted the *Infiltrator* out into open space as soon as they got clearance from flight command.

"Stay sharp everybody. This could get messy if the GSE returns," the captain said.

"Let 'em. They'll regret fucking with our people. We'll end the war for them right here and now." Raqmar essentially said what everyone was thinking.

"I admire your enthusiasm, Raq," Vee said, "but we need to ID and tag all the remains we find so the retrieval teams can decontaminate and bag them. I need you to concentrate on cleanup, not on payback."

"Aye, cap," Raqmar replied.

"If we find Captain Leahcim and Lieutenant Markka in all this—" Sparks started to say.

"When we find them," Vee corrected. "We'll bring them home."

"It just sucks big time, cap, when it hits so close to home," Lin said.

"I know. It hurts a lot. But it's gotta get done."

By the end of the first day, the crew was exhausted. By the end of the second day, they still had not found the remains of Leahcim or Markka.

On the third day, the hope of finding anything faded into frustration, but the debris field became more manageable.

Numbed by the tediousness of their tasks, they fell into an automatic routine. As they neared the perimeter of the debris field, Vee asked Piper, "What are you picking up on the bio-scans, Pipe?"

"Shit. And more shit, cap."

The mood shifted slightly to something more hopeful when Sparks yelled out, "Wait! I got something. Hear that?"

The crew grew silent as they all strained to hear what she heard. A very faint coded signal was coming from a flight recorder within their vicinity.

"What is it?" Vee asked.

"It's a coded signal from . . . Cora!"

"What's it saying?"

"'We are alive. Have data crucial to attack. Find us.'"

"Locate it. Now!" Vee ordered.

"I'm working on it." Sparks' webbed digits smoothly slid across the console as she fine-tuned her readings.

"Anybody else reported hearing it?"

"No. It's a narrow beam transmission meant just for us."

"I don't think I need to impress upon you the urgency of the situation," Vee said.

"I'm fully aware of the situation, cap. I just need to . . . Got it!"

"Tractor it and hold it in stasis. Check to make sure it's not a booby trap. Then check it for worms, Trojans, or any suspicious anomalies before bringing it aboard."

"Way ahead of you, cap," Sparks replied.

After checking the authenticity of the data on the recorder, which detailed everything from the time the squadron left the planet's surface until the time it was jettisoned from the *Midnight Sun*, the crew discussed their options.

"The dirty bastards never gave them a fighting chance," Raqmar fumed, more to himself than to the others. "What'll we do now?"

"First, we let Commander Chappie know what we discovered, then we set out to find Leahcim, Markka, and Cora and bring them home. Sparks?"

"Yes, cap?"

"Tell the *Vindicator* we're coming aboard. Don't say why. Just say we've developed a technical glitch that needs repair."

"Aye, cap."

Sparks relayed the message. When they were given the all-clear, Sparks flew the *Infiltrator* back to the hangar bay.

Captain Vee told her crew to sit tight. She was going to see the commander and propose a plan.

An hour later she returned.

"What's up, cap?" Lin asked.

"We, and we alone, are going to search for Leahcim, Markka, and Cora."

There was a chorus of cheers as everyone reacted to the news. Vee laid out her plan to them.

"If this goes sour, it's just our butts on the line. Fleet will not assist in any way. It could be a one-way mission to oblivion. If anyone wants out, say so now."

She studied the faces of everyone standing or sitting around her. Not one showed any sign of doubt or uncertainty. They each had a look of unshakable determination etched on their faces. Pipe and Raqmar were doing their best not to break out into big grins. They each failed spectacularly.

Lin, as usual, was unreadable. Not even her eyes indicated her feelings. And Sparks could not help but change color from her usual aqua green to lime green.

"What are we waiting for, cap? Let's roll already." It was obvious to everyone that Raqmar's patience was running on empty.

"Okay, boys and girls, let's go find our wayward friends. Sparks, set a course for the nebula and follow the breadcrumbs Cora left for us."

"Aye, cap."

"Engage the cloak and power down the main engines. Use the sub-light engines to give us a little boost. Then cut those. We'll coast from then on. If the GSE is monitoring, we don't want them to know where we're going."

Sparks programmed the coordinates into the navigation system, engaged the cloak, then deftly took the ship out into space toward the nebula following the low-level ion trail Cora left for them to follow.

CHAPTER 28

After living on Progensha for five cycles, there was one thing Leahcim despised more than the Thourons, and that was its eight seasons. He had taken to calling them hot, hotter than hot, even hotter, and the hottest.

Because of the planet's revolution around its twin suns, the hottest seasons were when it was between both stars. This occurred twice during one trip around them.

Fortunately, the hottest season was also the shortest. Unfortunately, the Uderrans never invented air conditioning, but the design of their homes reduced the heat and humidity levels to something bearable. It was during days like today that he envied Markka who grew up in a clothing-optional culture.

On this particular day, T'oann was on an extended patrol of the outer communities so he was at home playing dad while mom was defending the queendom. He was thankful for a seemingly unique Uderran physiological trait. And that was the quick growth spurt of their children from childhood to adulthood.

Similar to many species in the Alliance like Felids, the path to adulthood was fast-tracked in the development years. After four cycles, their three children were in the development stage equivalent to that of a Terran ten-year-old. In another four years, their children would be adults. The physical and mental development of Uderran children was accelerated during childhood. Once they reached adulthood, Uderrans lived a normal humanoid lifespan. It was sometimes hard for him to wrap his mind around the fact that in another four cycles his kids would be moving out of the house to live on their own. *They just grow up so fast*, he thought as he watched them play in the back garden.

He thought how unfortunate it was for them to grow up in a world where the realities of war overshadowed their playtime. It didn't help that both their parents were in the Uderran military.

He was so absorbed with watching his kids play that he flinched when his wrist comm beeped. The readout said it was T'oann. He answered. "Hey, babe, what's up?"

Her voice was usually music to his ears, but he detected something different in her tone this time. She sounded seriously distressed. "I might be a bit late for evening refreshments, babe," she said. "Actually," she paused, "I might not be able to get home."

Her statement had an air of finality in it. Fear clawed at his throat. Much like Markka did to a doomed enemy in physical combat.

"What's going on? What do you mean you might not be able to get home?" He heard shouting, screaming, and explosions, then static before he heard T'oann's voice again. His heart was pounding so hard, he thought it might burst through his chest.

"The outer rim is under heavy attack. We are dug in with no way of breaking out. We were evacuating our people when we got cut off from the rest of my unit. They are protecting the civilians we rescued but cannot double back to get us."

His pulse pounded and his anger flashed hot. "How long do you think you can hold out?"

After a brief moment of silence, which seemed like forever, T'oann replied, "Not much longer." Then she stammered, "I love you, husband. Tell our children I love them." Then the comm went dead.

He stood staring at the comm unit on his wrist, willing it to bring T'oann's voice back on. Silence.

He nearly screamed his frustration until he remembered his kids were nearby. He stifled a growl then immediately asked Cora for an assessment of the outer rim.

"Cora, give me everything you got. I need to know what you know about the outer rim. Use the probe."

He demanded to know the layout of the land, natural barriers, ways in and out, and the latest intelligence on Thouron troop strength.

He dashed to a small three-legged table in one corner of the room, snatched open its drawer, pulled out a headset, and slipped it on.

The headset was a portable modification of the probes he and Markka were subjected to when they initially crashed on Progensha five cycles ago. Cora improved on the technology, making them practical for the two of them to use.

"Hit me," he said.

Cora downloaded everything he asked for and more.

"Contact Markka and let her know what's happening and ask her if she would watch my kids for me. I'm taking a strike force and getting my wife and our people back."

"Will do, captain."

Moments later, Markka was remotely speaking to Leahcim.

"Don't you dare leave me out of this mission. Tory said he'll watch our kids. Just make sure you bring T'oann back to her kids and me to mine."

"Okay. Good. Have Cora download—"

"Done."

"Good. I'll be there in ten."

He disconnected and rounded up his kids.

"We're going to uncle Tory and aunt Markka's."

He was naturally peppered with a barrage of questions. All he told them was that something came up and he needed to help their mother. It was a lame excuse, but it was all he could think of.

"Father?" asked his oldest. "Is mother in trouble?"

He watched them all silently ask the same question. Born just mictons apart, they all seemed to have their mother's intuition, but his physical appearance. All varying shades of brown with wiry black hair. Two boys and one girl.

He never lied to his kids and he was not about to start now.

"Yes, Zora," he said. "Mother and some of her troops have been cut off from their support unit. Aunty M and I are going to bring them all home."

Zora, a mini version of him, looked bravely into her father's eyes and said, "May the Goddess be with you." Then she turned to her siblings and told them to pack their gear.

They gathered whatever they could take with them on short notice and followed their father out the door of the house and piled into a hovercraft for the short trip to Markka's home.

The private personnel carrier was specially designed and built to accommodate T'oann and her family. Leahcim hated that they were always chauffeured. So he begged his wife to have a customized transport built to accommodate the family. It gave him the satisfaction of driving and being in control.

He reached the royal compound in no time, exchanged the kids for Markka, and sped off to the staging area where a small contingent of commandos was waiting for them. Each member of the team, led by tactical officer Sho'khan, was a highly trained expert in infiltration, hand-to-hand, sniping, bomb disposal, and reconnaissance. Personally trained by Markka, T'oann, and Leahcim.

As they donned their gear, Markka asked, "Are you boys and girls ready to dance?"

They all enthusiastically answered in unison, "Yes, commander!"

"Then what are we waiting for? Let's roll."

They all mounted levitating mini speeder bikes Cora designed and helped build based on the hover technology used for the heavier transports and silently sped toward the outer rim.

Before they saw anything, they heard the sounds of combat. A fierce firefight was taking place.

The commandos dismounted and stealthily approached a small hill overlooking a fertile valley of tall grass, shrubs, and trees dotted by boulders barely big enough to provide adequate cover for T'oann and her people.

From their vantage point, they could see Thouron sharpshooters strategically entrenched in easily defensible positions around T'oann's group. If she or any of her troops tried to break out, they would be cut down instantly.

Fortunately, the sharpshooters were all the Thouron resistance there was. They mistakenly believed the Uderran defenses would be ineffective against their forces. All they needed to do was pick off T'oann and her people while forcing them to deplete their munitions.

Using hand signals, Leahcim communicated to the team what he needed for them to do. They would proceed in teams of two. No mercy. The Thourons were showing none to their targets. They would show none to them.

One by one the sharpshooters were taken out.

Sho'khan and her partner checked for proximity sensors. Detecting none, they easily disposed of their first target and moved on to their next. Leahcim and Markka eliminated their first two targets with relative ease. The other teams each played their part and eliminated all of their targets. The Thourons gravely underestimated the resolve of the Uderrans.

The commandos regrouped at their fallback position before they executed the next part of their rescue plan, which was to go in and pull out T'oann and her people. Leahcim used a pair of magnifiers with vastly improved body heat sensors, courtesy of Cora, to scan for remaining sharpshooters or other hidden Thouron fighters. He handed them off to Markka who handed them in turn to Sho'khan who indicated she saw none.

Leahcim instructed Sho'khan to activate a holographic projection of Uderran relief troops coming to the rescue. Any remaining snipers would reveal their positions by firing on what they thought were enemy troops. The hills remained silent except for the incessant sounds of wildlife in the vicinity.

Confident their tactics worked, Leahcim and Markka led the team down the hill to rescue T'oann and her people before the Thourons sent reinforcements. It would not be long before they realized their ambush failed.

CHAPTER 29

Once the rescuers and the rescued were all safely behind the protection of the walls of Uderra, Leahcim, T'oann, Markka, and Sho'khan filed their obligatory reports with the military high council before meeting up again at the officers' cantina to unwind.

"That was fun," Markka said. Her tone dripped with biting sarcasm.

"We need to do something about protecting the outer rim," Sho'khan said. "It is key to our survival."

"I know," T'oann said. "I know." Leahcim could see she was traumatized by the experience. She did her best to hide her fear. He knew her intimately enough to notice the almost imperceptible tremors in her hands as she held her glass. He knew she was experiencing post-traumatic stress and reliving the memories of her capture six cycles before. Since no one knew the details of her experience, he pretended the operation was just another military engagement they all needed to unwind from to help distract the others from sensing her discomfort.

Sho'khan continued the conversation. "The Thourons are stepping up their attacks on our food fields and food supply chains. They are attempting to starve us into submission."

"Cora has been working on a solution for that problem," Leahcim said. "She's been working on a way to place the city under a domed force field now that the rocket attacks can breach our current defenses." He stopped talking long enough to let this revelation sink in with the others. Even Markka looked surprised by the news. He took a sip of his ale and waited for a reaction.

"What does that have to do with the outer rim and protecting our food?" Sho'khan asked.

"Plenty," Leahcim replied. "We think we can erect energy domes over the food fields that would repel rockets and be deep enough to hamper attempts to dig under them. "

"Okay, you got our attention," Markka said.

He downed the contents of his drink, wiped his mouth with his forearm, and explained the idea. He finished by saying, "The fields would be interconnected by a series of reinforced tunnels."

Everyone at the table was now invested in this new line of discussion. Ideas, proposals, and counter-proposals, were tossed about.

"Well," Markka said, "it looks like we're all in agreement with building a dome system to protect our food supply." She drained the remaining contents of her glass then peered into it as if expecting to see it automatically refill itself.

Everyone either shook their heads in agreement or vocalized their agreement.

"Cora and I believe if we're successful, we just might be able to erect one over Uderra. Cora says there is sufficient geothermal energy to power one, but our current technology and infrastructure might not be good enough to maintain an effective shield against a sustained barrage of rocket attacks."

"Hell," Markka said as she slammed her empty glass on the table. "A weak shield is better than no shield. Every cycle they keep extending the range and power of those things. And we keep losing people to them. We need to build our own and build a shield too. Who's with me?"

There was another round of nods and clinking glasses as affirmations of agreement made their way around the table.

"Cora believes she has a working prototype nearly ready for deployment," Leahcim said.

"Good," Markka said. "Then tell her to get a move on or I'm gonna kick whatever she considers her scrawny little butt."

"You know I can hear you, right?" Cora said from seemingly everywhere at once.

"Oh, yeah. Right. Forgot."

Cora was the eyes and ears of the city everywhere there was public access. Cora monitored personal quarters, but she honored the privacy of personal space until requested to enter.

Markka turned to Leahcim sitting next to her and whispered, "You ever wonder where her scrawny little butt is?"

"I can still hear you."

Thankful for the levity and just grateful to be alive, T'oann bid the others good night and let Leahcim know she was ready to go home. Markka said she would watch the kids for the evening to give the two of them some downtime. Leahcim and T'oann happily left their children with Markka and Tory and headed home.

T'oann had barely stepped through the front door to their home when she leaned her back against the wall just inside the door and slowly slid down it to the floor. She folded her knees against her chest, wrapped her arms around them, and began uncontrollably sobbing. Tears streamed down her cheeks like raindrops. She dropped her head to her knees and wept like a baby.

Leahcim knelt beside his wife and gently cuddled her in his arms and tenderly touched her mind. The strength of their emotional bond enabled them to develop the rare ability to simultaneously mind-walk and remain aware and functional in the physical reality for short periods without the blipping-out effect.

The raw emotional stress she felt weighed heavily on both of them as he held her face and wiped her tears.

"It's okay," he said in a soothing, assuring tone. "You're safe now. You're home with me."

She rested her head onto his chest and said, "I am sorry, husband. Please forgive me."

"Forgive you? For what?"

"For my . . . weakness."

He caressed her face with his hands and looked her squarely in her tear-filled eyes and said, "You are the strongest person I know. It takes a strong person to admit to a moment of weakness."

"But I was afraid. I did not want what happened to me six cycles ago to happen again. I feel ashamed."

"You didn't have me around back then." His face transitioned into a broad smile accompanied by one of his signature winks. His eyes sparkled as he did.

T'oann wrapped her arms tightly around Leahcim and snuggled next to him.

"Thank you for being my rock," she whispered.

"Thank you for being mine," he said in return.

Her sobbing and trembling gradually subsided. He gave her all the time she needed to regain her center.

They sat motionless for a while as their heated urges, which smoldered like hot embers in a fire, ignited and burst into flames of a white-hot passion that overwhelmed their senses and compelled them to act on their desire for each other.

She looked lovingly into his eyes and asked," Are you thinking what I'm thinking?" Knowing full well he was since they were still mind-linked.

He returned the look and said," I love it when you use contractions." They curled up together and spent most of the night testing the limits of their imaginations.

They did not know when it was they eventually fell asleep, but they both awoke the next dawn refreshed.

After repeating a shortened version of the previous evening, and freshening up afterward, they headed over to Markka's and Tory's place to retrieve their kids, taking only a piece of fruit each as nourishment.

They were accosted by the raucous sounds of wild shrieks, giggles, and laughter when Tory met them at the door and let them in. In the middle of a melee was Markka happily squirming and laughing at the bottom of a seven-kid-pile-on.

"Honestly," Leahcim said, "I don't think you'll ever grow up."

All at once, the children and Markka froze into silence and stared at Leahcim and T'oann.

Markka was the first to recover.

"Hey!"

A moment later, the group rushed Leahcim and T'oann who found themselves on the floor giggling and laughing with them.

Tory looked at the bunch of them rolling around on the floor, rolled his eyes, and decided a sober head needed to take charge.

He cleared his throat and clapped his hands twice. The frolicking subsided as all eyes focused on him.

"How about we let aunt T and uncle L up so we can all have morning refreshments?"

"Yay!" Was the chorused response.

As the children ran off to get cleaned up and ready for breakfast, Tory helped his wife get up off the floor then turned to his sister and engulfed her in a tight hug lifting her off the floor.

"Tory," she wheezed.

"Yes?"

"I can't breathe."

Suddenly aware of what he was doing, he quickly let her go as she took a couple of deep breaths.

"Apologies," he said.

"No need," she said. "At least I know I am still alive. Now let's go eat."

As the adults filed out of the room, Zora was the last of her siblings and cousins to head off to clean up. She turned and watched her parents and aunt and uncle interacting with each other and decided that the Goddess had truly blessed them all with something worth protecting: a strong, loving family.

CHAPTER 30

Five cycles later, Zora and her siblings had all grown into strong young adults each serving in the Uderran military. Zora quickly rose through the ranks and was put in charge of protecting the construction of the shield network.

Cora was successful in developing an impenetrable force shield for the outer rim food resources. These food pods became the mainstay for all of the other city-states and cultures in the region. Without them most of their populations would have been starved out.

Along with protecting the food supply, they needed to protect their water sources. That proved to be of a greater challenge. Fortunately, the major source of water came from the Colossal Ocean, which was well outside of Thouron territory. The ocean fed into the Western Sea. From there it flowed into small lakes, rivers, and streams. It was just a matter of keeping the waterways free to use. They needed to be constantly patrolled to protect against Thouron attacks.

The idea to dam up the water was once considered because the Thourons depended on the water coming from the ocean, but it was quickly rejected as a bad idea since many communities closest to the Thouron Empire also relied on the water. Damming it would have dried up their only water supply.

Emperor Shang, in his efforts to extend Thouron influence throughout the known continent, engaged in a military campaign that was no longer limited to just conquering the Uderrans. He declared war against every non-Thouron enclave in the region. He was essentially the Progensha equivalent of Earth's Alexander the Great, Genghis Khan, and Mansa Musa, with the savagery of Hernan Cortes, Adolph Hitler, and Pol Pot.

Since the Thourons could not control the water supply, they sought to disrupt and destroy the region's food supplies by burning the crops and killing the livestock. Thereby starving everyone into submission.

Cora and Leahcim were able to build and bring eighty percent of the shields online before the Thourons realized what happened.

They also spearheaded an effort to bring together the Cold Mountain people, the Dark Woods people, and the desert nomads into a coalition with the Uderrans. They successfully convinced the tribal leaders that banding together was the best way they could survive Thouron aggression.

As their interactions grew, Markka thought it was uncanny how much each of the groups physically resembled each other despite the many cultural differences. Cora was right. Somewhere in the past, many of the Alliance races merged. Markka surmised a lot of miscegenation was going on. Most likely through intermarriage. Like her and Tory and Leahcim and T'oann.

They were simultaneously ethnically diverse and homogeneous. What they identified as depended as much on within which group they were born as much as how they identified themselves culturally. Sure, there were the shared traits particular to each group, but there were also obvious similarities connecting the diverse groups. Cora insisted that everyone shared common ancestors and those ancestors were from a variety of Alliance races and cultures that merged and intermingled over time with those of the indigenous peoples of Progensha. How they got here was a mystery.

The genetic similarities Cora found in that vial of blood she analyzed for T'oann answered a lot of questions but raised others when the coalition was formed. And only four individuals had any knowledge of what the implications were. But the Rosetta Stone, the key to understanding why, eluded them for now.

CHAPTER 31

On a typical hot day in the middle of the third season, Zora was in command of a contingent of troops assigned to protect the final construction stage on the last remaining food field and ensure the safety of coalition delegates, which included her parents, gathered for a dedication ceremony.

For Zora, the beginning of the worst day of her life began when the first rockets fell. The facility came under heavy attack by an overwhelming force of Thouron shock troops.

The initial offensive came in the form of devastating rocket attacks. Wave after wave after wave of rockets rained down on them as people screamed, cried, died, and ran for their lives.

The rocket attack was followed by a flood of specially trained and experienced foot and mobile units who overran the food field shield generation station and just about everything else with lightning speed.

Zora's defenses were ripped to shreds as Thouron troops poured in like a swarm of insects. Coalition defenders engaged in fierce hand-to-hand combat until reinforcements arrived and routed the invaders; the shield generation station was a burned-out smoldering shell of itself. The support buildings were divots in the ground. Most of the food field was a scorched mess, and the remains of people, crops, and livestock were scattered everywhere.

Zora sustained a broken left leg, shrapnel wounds to her left arm, and a severe blow to the head that had her brain screaming and her eyes seeing double. But her physical injuries did not stop her from trying to find her parents as she limped through the carnage. Loss of consciousness did.

She awoke with a jolt and tried to sit up only to be knocked back down by a sharp pain shooting up her leg and pounding in her head. She looked around and saw she was in a triage unit in a healing center.

"Ah, good. You are awake. You gave us quite a scare there. Nice to see you're still with us."

The cheery-sounding voice belonged to Garath who was busy changing a bandage on Zora's arm.

"Where . . . am I?" She struggled to ask.

"You are at a makeshift healing center on the edge of the Dark Woods," Garath said.

"How. . . how long—"

"How long have you been out?" Garath finished.

Zora swallowed hard and sucked in a painful breath. It felt like her ribs were broken. "Yes."

"Half a sol," the healer said.

Zora sucked in another excruciating breath and asked, with better control over her pain, "Where are my parents?"

Garath turned her head and averted her eyes from Zora and pretended to attend to another wound. "They are alive," she said cautiously." And watched the tension leave Zora's body. Then hated herself for what she had to say next. "But are prisoners of Shang scheduled for execution tomorrow."

Zora tried to sit up but was held back by the debilitating pain in her leg, the throbbing in her head, and by Garath and a couple of assistants who Garath summoned to help her restrain their commanding officer. Garath was forced to give Zora a sedative to prevent her from further injuring herself.

As the sedative took effect, Zora's mind swirled with shame and regret. She was the officer in charge. It was her duty to protect everything that was just lost. That loss now included her parents. Her heart sank. She failed her mission and they were now paying the price for that failure.

CHAPTER 32

The last thing T'oann remembered was a deafening explosion, the ground heaving upward beneath her feet, and the sound of Leahcim's voice calling out to her. Then blackness.

In the recesses of her mind, a replay of the events took shape and helped her recall what had happened. Moments after her realization, she became aware of her current surroundings and sat up in a darkened room.

This isn't a room, she thought. She was moving. She turned to look around and heard clanking and felt the weight of chains on her legs and around her wrists. She concluded it was a transport of some kind. It did not take much thought for her to guess she was a prisoner.

Then blinding panic struck her. What of Leahcim and Zora? Were they prisoners as well? Or worse? She began to hyperventilate as memories of the last time she was captured flooded her thoughts. *Not again*, she thought. She forced herself to calm down. *Think*, she told herself. An instant later she heard a moan. She was not alone.

"Who is there?" she asked. Her query went unanswered. There was another moan followed by a question.

"T'oann? Is that you?"

Her heart fluttered with joy as she recognized Leahcim's voice. "Yes, it's me."

There was a brief pause before she heard him say, "I love it when you use contractions."

"Are you injured?" she asked.

"Just my pride, I think. "You?"

"No, I'm happy to say."

"What the hell happened and where the hell are we? Oh, wait. I remember now. The bastards." He squinted as he tried to see through the darkness. "Is there anyone else here?"

"I think we're it," she said.

"You know what that means?" he sighed.

"They know who we are," she said.

"Yep. Can you move?"

"No, not much."

"Same here."

Neither wanted to do or say much in case they were being observed. They rode in silence wishing they could see and touch each other one final time.

When the transport reached its destination, the doors swung open and the light from the suns flooded the dark box they were in, obscuring their vision. They were forcefully pulled from the vehicle and made to kneel.

As their vision cleared, they saw the person they were kneeling before was Shang himself.

He stood before them in full emperor attire leering down at them. "Princess," he began. "We meet again. Visitor from the Great Beyond, welcome to the last mictons of your pathetic lives." He belched out a gravelly laugh and said, "Prepare them. Now."

They were jerked up and shoved down a tunnel and into an arena filled with jeering throngs. T'oann remembered the last time she was in this arena. She had fought Tonga here. At the time, she believed she was going to die here. Today, she knew she would die here.

While weapons were pointed at them, they were unshackled and left alone by their handlers. They clasped hands and greeted each other in what they felt was their last mind-walk together.

"I love you, husband."

"I love you, wife."

The crowd quieted down when Shang appeared and stood on a balcony overlooking the arena.

"People of Progensha, you are about to witness the greatest spectacle of our age." The spectacle was being videocast across the known world. So Shang added more flourish to his performance. "The whore and her bastard with the abominations for offspring are about to show their people and allies how to die."

There was thunderous applause as spectators whistled, cheered, and shouted insults at Leahcim and T'oann. When the spectators calmed down, Shang paused for effect then ordered, "Let the executions begin. Release the scorb."

There was a loud boom as two large doors rumbled open and a snarling, hissing behemoth emerged. It searched the arena grounds for prey. When it spotted Leahcim and T'oann, it immediately charged them. The charge was more like a lumbering trot because of its great mass.

Leahcim thought the creature looked like a cross between a crab and a scorpion. It ran along on six legs. It was about six meters long and about two meters tall and wide and butt ugly. Its coloring was a mixture of black cherry red and midnight blue. There were three eye stalks on its head; two on each side and one on top. What it lacked in speed, it made up for with a pair of snapping pincers that could cut a person in half, and a wickedly fast tail full of venom, which whipped and smashed into the ground behind it.

Initially, Leahcim and T'oann were able to keep their distance from it as they ran, ducked, rolled, and kept it between them. But it became increasingly difficult to continue their deadly dance as their reflexes and strength got weaker in the exhaustive heat. Unlike them, the thing did not seem to tire. They each desperately searched for anything lying around like a rock, a sword, or even a stick to use against it. All either could find were the brittle sun-bleached bones of previous victims.

T'oann was eventually backed into a corner doing her best to avoid the snapping pincers just as Leahcim saw the glint of something shiny lying in the dirt beside some old bones half-buried in the ground near where he stood. He tucked and rolled as the tail whipped past him. He reached the bones and quickly grabbed at the shiny object. It was a sword.

He pulled and strained against the ground which did not want to release its grip on the weapon. He prayed it did not break as he tugged on it. The ground eventually surrendered and Leahcim pulled his prize intact from its dirt-encrusted sheath. He raced toward the beast and swung at the whipping tail and chopped off the tip. A torrent of burning liquid spewed from the gaping wound onto the ground like water from a fire hose.

The creature screamed as did Leahcim when some of the venom splashed on his sword-wielding arm. It burned like acid. He dropped the sword and staggered, falling to one knee. T'oann sprinted past the distracted creature and pulled him away from its twitching tail.

"Thanks, I owe you one," he gasped into her ear. His voice was nearly drowned out by the crowd noise.

"I owed you one. So we're even," T'oann replied.

Unfortunately, T'oann did not pull them far enough away. The creature's tail crashed down on them both. The force of the blow broke T'oann's right leg and splattered venom on both of them. She screamed as the bone in her leg split. Enraged, Leahcim fought the pain, grabbed the sword he dropped, and viciously chopped one of the creature's hind legs off as it turned to face them. Now face-to-face, Leahcim drew on his reserve strength and slashed at one of the pincers, splitting it in half. The creature dropped its arm to the ground and Leahcim used it as a ramp. He ran up the limp appendage, jumped onto the creature's back, severed the top eye, and plunged the blade into its head with so much force that it pierced the tough exoskeleton and came through the other side of the creature's head plates. He jumped off and rolled away from the remaining arm which thrashed and flailed wildly. He limped back to T'oann who managed to drag herself to a nearby wall.

They helped each other stand up and faced Shang in the stands. T'oann hobbled on her good leg with her back against the wall and Leahcim shielded his wife with his body while he kept an eye on the creature. They watched as it thrashed around before it exhaled its final breath.

The crowd grew silent. No one had ever defeated Shang's prized pet. He slowly stood glaring at Leahcim and T'oann, the shock of losing his favorite pet caused him to violently vibrate before he roared with rage. After calming down, he spoke to them in a more controlled tone. "For an inferior subspecies, you fought better than expected. Bow before your Lord and beg for mercy. I might think about sparing you."

"Never!" T'oann shouted. "We would rather die fighting on our feet than grovel for mercy."

"So be it," he said. "You shall get your wish."

They clasped hands and joined minds just as Shang made a slicing motion with his hand. Almost instantaneously a pike sprang from the wall in the blink of an eye, impaling them both like meat on a skewer. Their feet left the ground and their bodies twitched before going limp. The pike retracted into the wall as quickly as it snapped out. They collapsed to the ground like sacks of rocks; neither moved nor breathed. Both laid crumpled, motionless, lifeless on the arena floor.

A thunderous cheer burst from the crowd when the shock of what they saw wore off.

Shang raised his hands to quiet the crowd. "This is the beginning of the end of the coalition," he said. Another cheer rose from the crowd. As the cheer transitioned to chants of his name, he turned to one of his aids and said, "Remove that garbage from my arena and dispose of it on the sacred hill of the mongrels."

CHAPTER 33

The aid issued directives to the arena guards to gather up the bodies and take them to the sacred grounds.

The leader of the disposal team rushed over to Leahcim and T'oann and checked their bodies for signs of life, then made a slashing motion across his throat to indicate there were none. He got the all-clear to gather the bodies and dump them onto sacred ground.

Such an act would be seen as defiling the holy ground of the Cold Mountain ancestors. Shang was trying to provoke the otherwise elusive Mountain People. He succeeded.

Since the entire event was videocast, anyone watching the live feed saw how embarrassingly swift Shang's disposal team was itself disposed of. Those who didn't die in the initial attack, did once they were tossed off the mountain's edge.

The leader of the mountain forces, a burly man with hair that cascaded past his broad shoulders, full facial hair, an ashen hue, and who wore shaggy animal fur, saved one Thouron soldier for last. The leader of the disposal unit. He was lifted into the air by his throat with one hand and had his body camera ripped off of him with the other. The mountain soldier in charge looked into the camera and mocked Shang.

"Before you is a member of the so-called superior race," he began. "Witness their natural superiority." The next sound heard was the crunching of bone and something heavy falling to the ground. The camera was trained on the body of the Disposal Unit Commander before the camera was smashed. The bodies of the dead Thourons were then checked for body cameras and listening devices before anyone spoke.

Having just witnessed the complete elimination of his disposal squad, as did nearly everyone else on the continent, Shang's embarrassment consumed his black soul. His fury erupted like an exploding volcano. "I want those animals wiped from existence. I want that mountain brought down to the ground. I don't care what it takes. I want them gone." He shouted and raged like the madman he was and stormed back to his chamber.

Moments after having his neck broken, the Disposal Unit commander stood up and brushed snow off his uniform. "Do you think that bought us some time?" he asked.

The Mountain commander tossed him a hopeful grin and said, "Well, we will find out one way or another. We need to hurry. Your mother is waiting for you inside." He turned to four figures in black hooded robes and said, "Treat them with the same respect you would the ancestors." They nodded and reverently lifted the bodies of Leahcim and T'oann, placed them both into a transparent tube, and carried them like pallbearers through a hidden passage into the bowels of the mountain.

The passage, a clean, brightly lit corridor led to an atrium full of flowers and a waterfall. The air felt like a tropical rainforest. The procession hurriedly made its way through the atrium and into a sterile room where more hooded figures wearing white waited.

"Well?" asked one of the hooded figures. And the only one wearing gray.

"I have their life forces, mother, but they are weak and fading," the Thouron commander said.

"Good. We must hurry if this is to work. The one in the gray hood reached into the mind of the Thouron commander and captured the life essences in his mind. "They are nearly too far gone." The gray hood was removed revealing the face of the Thouron officer's mother. "My sister and her consort must survive."

Tonga and her son watched as the medical staff went to work on repairing the damage done to Leahcim and T'oann.

"How long will it take the nanites to complete their repairs?" Tonga asked.

The lead medic, a female version of the Mountain man who led the attack on the disposal squad, said, "It is difficult to determine at this time due to the severity of their injuries, but at least thirty-six hours at best. A full day."

"Very well. Do what you can as quickly as you can."

"Yes, ma'am." The medic rushed off to do what she could for Leahcim and T'oann.

Tonga turned to her son and told him, "Go get some rest. You earned it. The burden of keeping them alive is now mine."

"I'm fine, mother. And glad to no longer have to pretend to do the will of a madman."

"Pricilla will be happy to hear that."

He smiled. "I'm glad."

"Now go to her. She is waiting."

Marshon left his mother with the medics.

CHAPTER 34

Four hours ahead of their estimation, the medics were ready. "The medical nanites have repaired all of their physical damage," the lead medic said.

"Good," Tonga said. "Then let us begin the transfer."

Standing between Leahcim and T'oann, Tonga placed her hands upon their foreheads, closed her eyes, and concentrated her focus on reuniting their life forces with their bodies. She summoned all of her strength and training as a mind walker of the High Order. All the medics could do was monitor the vital signs of their patients.

Carrying the life forces of two dynamic personalities was not as problematic as returning them to their proper vessels. If she was not careful, all three of them could be resting with the ancestors. Being a mind walker and a spiritual medium was not without its disadvantages. Tonga walked a fine line between the corporeal and incorporeal realms. One spiritual and the other physical.

She was taking the risk because of a vision she had. She believed the Goddess had come to her in a dream and charged her with the task of saving her sister and her husband from the clutches of death. It was not yet their time.

The stress of the transfer showed on Tonga's features as her eyes rolled back revealing only the whites. Droplets of sweat soaked her garments, her breathing grew raspy and shallow, and her heart rate was close to flatlining. Just as the medical staff was about to intervene, she stumbled to one knee and waved them off as she caught her breath.

The scanners monitoring Leahcim and T'oann began beeping; the medics went to work.

"Well?" Tonga asked.

"Their vitals are within nominal parameters," the lead medic said, as the team began the difficult task of reviving their patients.

Tonga carefully stood up refusing offers to help her and left the medical team to do its work. She turned to look at T'oann and Leahcim through the observation glass before heading to her quarters to rest.

The next morning, Marshon stopped by his mother's quarters to check on her and to let her know her presence was requested in the recovery room.

"You look a mess," was the first thing he said when she opened the door.

"Good morning to you, too," she said. Her tone dripped with sarcasm.

He took a seat across from her at the refreshments table, picked out a yellow fruit resembling a lemon, and took a bite. He slurped the juice. "Wow! I forgot how much I missed these things."

Tonga looked at her son warily. "You did not come here to check on me or tell me how much you missed my fruit."

He tossed her a sly, impish grin. "You know me so well."

"I should. I reared you. Now, why have you disturbed my morning repose?"

He took a second piece of fruit then stood. "A couple of patients are requesting your presence in recovery. And there is a pressing matter of utmost urgency. I'll meet you there." Then he turned and left, but not before saying, "Love you."

"I love you too," Tonga muttered as the door closed behind him.

She was proud of the man he had become and the doting father he was. She thought of all the times she feared he would betray her while he was growing up. Her involvement with the resistance was incentive enough to turn her in, but he never did. He embraced her beliefs that all Progenshans were endowed equally by the Goddess to live their lives free of subjugation and genocide. She wondered what it was that Pricilla saw in him.

She got dressed quickly, grabbed a piece of fruit, and headed out the door toward the recovery ward. Arriving mictons later.

T'oann and Leahcim were both sitting together in a tight embrace waiting for her.

"There she is," Leahcim said. He stood and reverently bowed to her. T'oann did the same then addressed Tonga.

"Sister," she began, "my husband and I are most appreciative of the risk you and your son took to save us. We are eternally in your debt." Then she broke down and sobbed uncontrollably. "I . . . I thought you were dead," T'oann said. "I thought I killed you."

Tonga moved effortlessly across the room and embraced her sister. She avoided mind-walking with her. She stepped back and held her sister by her shoulders and said, "Like you, I am hard to kill."

"Regardless," Leahcim said, "we are forever in your debt. You and your son."

"It was necessary. There is no reason to thank us."

"Bullshit," Leahcim said. "If it weren't for you and your son, we'd be dead now. We owe you both."

"Appreciate the sentiment, but I'm good," Marshon said. An aide rushed into the room and apologized for interrupting, approached Marshon, whispered something into his ear, and left as quickly as she had entered.

Marshon frowned for a moment before clearing his throat.

What is it?" Tonga asked.

"I hate to be the killjoy here, but we've got a matter of grave concern."

They all looked at him.

"My contact says Shang is pissed to the highest level of pisstivity. He's about to launch an imminent rocket attack on the mountain. He wants to level it."

"Can he do that?" Tonga asked.

"After what he did to us," Leahcim said, "I'm sure he'll try."

"We don't have much time," Marshon said. "My contact said he's poised to begin a prolonged bombardment at any time. I already issued an evacuation order. We need to vacate this facility and retreat to our fallback position deeper within the mountain."

Almost as if on cue, they heard thunder booms and staggered slightly as the ground shook and dust and dirt fell from the walls and ceiling. There were more booms and the lights flickered while portions of the ceiling started to fall. As the bombardment increased, the sizes of the broken pieces of ceiling and walls grew larger. A large, jagged chunk of the wall gave way and crushed a computer workstation mere meters from where Leahcim and the others were standing.

Alarms rang as people rushed for exits. Marshon grabbed his mother and yelled for the others to run for the exits before the blast doors closed.

Medics, guards, technicians, and Leahcim and T'oann made their way to a pair of closing blast doors just as a wall conduit burst.

"What the hell is that?" Leahcim asked.

"Cryogas," Tonga shouted. "If we do not get out of here, we will become entombed forever. Frozen in time—if we are not killed first."

About fifty people scrambled toward the doors but never reached them. The ceiling caved in and the walls crumbled around them blocking their way. A few unfortunate souls were buried beneath the rubble.

"We have got to find a way around," Tonga shouted as everyone choked on the dust, smoke, and gas. The lights flickered then went out.

"Mother!" Marshon shouted. He felt around in the dimness for her. The only light source was the slowly thinning light on the other side of the closing doors.

"I am unhurt, son. I am here."

He heard her voice next to him just as the distinctive boom of closed blast doors echoed around them.

They were trapped in complete darkness in a pocket that was quickly filling up with the gas. They were in danger of being flash frozen.

Leahcim grabbed T'oann, pushed her to the floor, and covered her body with his. As their minds met he heard her say, "Shit. Not again," before their final thoughts were frozen forever.

CHAPTER 35

The *Infiltrator* and her crew slowly coasted through the debris field and followed the dissolving ion trail of Leahcim and Markka's fighter.

"Any sign the GSE is tracking us?" Captain Vee asked Sparks.

"No, cap. I've been very careful making sure we don't make any unnatural movements and that we blend in with the background radiation. If they know we're here, it's because they knew our game plan before we started."

"Good. We'll resume standard operations when we're well inside the nebula. They won't be able to detect us in there."

"We hope," Lin said.

"How long should we look for them?" Sparks asked.

"Until we find them," Raqmar said.

"I know how you feel," Vee said. "Captain Leahcim is my oldest friend and Markka and Cora are like family, but we must be realistic about this. We will search until the trail goes cold and we've exhausted all our options."

"Cap?"

"Yes, Sparks?"

"We just entered the nebula. I believe it'll be safe to fire up the engines and pump up the sensors to full in five minutes."

"Very good."

The five minutes felt like five days. Once the time passed, Sparks scanned the area for any evidence the GSE was on to them. She reported to Captain Vee that she detected no enemy activity.

"Good," Vee said, "Fire up the engines and let's go find our people."

"Aye, cap."

Captain Vee implicitly trusted Sparks' navigation skills. Who better to navigate a nebula with all of its currents and eddies than someone from a water world? If anyone could compensate for shifting flows, it would be her.

"So?" Raqmar asked, peering over Sparks' shoulder. Or at least what passed for one.

"Taking into consideration the rate of drift, and current speed, I'd fathom a guess and say they went that way." She pointed toward a cluster of newborn stars.

"Then let's go already," Raqmar said. He grew impatient from all of the calculating and guessing. "Just pick a direction and go."

"Just be patient, will you? Geez. The captain and Markka have a three-day head start. If I just fly in the direction I think they went, we might not locate Cora's trail in all of this."

"That's why she's the navigator and you're not," Lin said.

"And why I'm the captain and you're not," Vee said.

Vee knew Raqmar was a good soldier, but he had the tendency to be impulsive and lacked subtlety. He often reacted first before considering the wisdom of those reactions. Now was not the time for his brand of action.

After several moments of flying in silence, Sparks said, "Found it! I found faint traces of an ion trail. I'm compensating for inertial drift and tidal shifts."

Sparks guided the *Infiltrator* through gusts of solar winds and between the push and pull of gravitational tides buffeting the ship like rough waves on an ocean.

She would occasionally say, "Got it." Then she would say, "Lost it." Tracking the trail was much like tracking a fuel slick on an ocean.

This went on for nearly a week. Sparks spent every waking moment maneuvering their way through a maze of cosmic dust and radiation fields. While she caught up on some sleep, Sojourner, the ship's SI, kept them on course.

By the eighth day, they were no longer picking up any ion emissions from the doomed fighter. They were flying on Sparks' instincts and the projections of Sojourner.

They were all tired and irritable from flying around the nebula with nothing to show for their efforts. A few attitudes had grown cranky, but no one was ready to throw in the towel and give up the search.

"Looks like the trail has gone cold, cap," Sparks reported as they started day eight. "I gave it my best shot and have come up empty. Sorry, cap." The disappointment in her voice was evident.

"I must share the blame, captain. I have extrapolated all possible scenarios and have exhausted all logical options," Sojourner said.

"It's not your fault. Either of you," Vee said. "We just need to come up with another game plan."

"How about we try our luck by pointing and guessing," Raqmar said. "Hell, logic and rational thought haven't worked."

"Believe it or not, but that oddly makes sense," Sparks said.

"Now there's a first," Lin said, "Raqmar making sense."

"At this point, I'm open to pointing a finger and going in that direction," Vee said. "Sparks, pick a heading. Any heading. Maybe Lady Luck will be with us."

Just as Sparks was about to set a course, Sojourner said she detected what she thought was some kind of spatial anomaly.

"Look," Sojourner said. "Six degrees starboard. Do you see it?"

Sparks looked and saw nothing unusual, but when she scanned the readings Sojourner took, she saw it too.

"There's a strong slipstream of matter passing through some kind of event horizon."

"How can you tell?" Vee asked.

"Watch. See those dust globules?" Sparks asked.

"Yes," Vee said.

"Watch what happens to them."

They all stood behind Sparks and watched as the globules simply vanished.

"Where the hell did they go?" Vee asked.

"From as best as Sojourner and I can tell, there's something on the other side of the event horizon."

"Well, what do you think, cap? Should we investigate that thing?" Raqmar asked. He looked as excited as a kid in a candy store.

"Not so fast," Vee said. "As far as we know, those globules could be disappearing because they're being pulverized by something we can't detect."

"That is a possibility," Sojourner said, "but I am not detecting anything to indicate that is what is happening. There would be some kind of residual debris if they are being pulverized. I am ninety-nine point nine percent certain it is a portal of some kind."

"Those are good enough odds for me," Raqmar said. "I say we go through the thing and find out."

"Yeah, cap," Piper chimed in. "Maybe Captain Leahcim and the others drifted into it."

"And maybe the GSE is using it as a gateway of some kind," Lin said.

Captain Vee thought about what the ramifications of passing through the event horizon would be and decided if Leahcim and the others did pass through it, the best way to find them was to go through it. And if it was a gateway the GSE was using, it was their duty to find that out and warn the Alliance.

"Okay," she decided. "We're going through. One way or another, we're going to find out what's on the other side."

"What if it's a one-way trip?"Sparks asked.

"Then we'll have a whole new set of challenges to face," Vee replied. She looked around at her crew. They were good people. If they were going to perish, she thought of no one else she would want to be with.

"Okay," she said, "let's find out what's on the other side."

Sparks swung the ship toward the center of the event horizon and pierced its secret veil.

CHAPTER 36

Once the *Infiltrator* punched through to the other side of the event horizon, the nebula vanished. The star patterns were unknown to them. Even the coloring of the space around them was different.

"What the—" Sparks whispered. "Where'd the nebula go?"

"The nebula is where it is," Sojourner answered. And we are where we are."

"Can you be any more cryptic?" Raqmar complained.

"She's right," Vee said. "We passed through some kind of portal to somewhere else in the universe."

"Is it just me, or does the space around us seem darker somehow," Piper asked his shipmates.

"It is darker," Sojourner confirmed.

"Are you recording all this?" Vee asked.

"Yes, sir," Sojourner said.

"Good. Because I don't want to get lost out here if we need to make a quick getaway."

"Wherever here is," Sparks wondered.

"Scan the area," Vee ordered. "Long-range and short."

Sparks and Sojourner went to work scanning and relaying their findings to the crew.

Sojourner concluded her report with an assurance that nothing appeared to be an immediate threat to them or the ship and that they could turn around and leave the way they came.

Sparks finished her report pointing out a medium-sized planet orbiting twin stars within the vicinity.

"Are there signs of life on it that would resemble anything we would consider humanoid or sentient?" Vee asked.

"Hold on," Sparks said. She checked the readings on her console then cross-checked them with Sojourner's data. "Yes," she confirmed. "There is evidence of sentient life with varying levels of development."

"Any chance our guys ended up there?" Vee asked.

Sojourner answered that question.

"There is no evidence of an ion trail, but I am picking up evidence of an impact sight on the largest continent. Metallurgical analysis confirms it is what remains of the fighter."

The bridge fell silent. No one said a word for several moments before Sparks finally punctuated the quiet.

"That's very peculiar."

"What is?" Vee asked.

"Sojourner is on target with her analysis. However, I'm getting readings indicating the crash debris has been there for quite some time."

"What's quite some time?" Vee asked.

"Years," Sparks replied.

"You're wrong," Raqmar angrily said. "Check your readings again."

"She is not wrong. I have confirmed her findings," Sojourner said. "It appears the wreckage, or what little remains of it, has been on the planet for approximately ten to fifteen Earth years."

"The metallurgic analysis has got to be wrong. It's only been a few days. You're both wrong, I tell you," Raqmar insisted.

Her curiosity piqued, Lin asked, "What do you mean what's left of it?"

"There is evidence of a crash, but the bulk of the fighter is missing."

"Was it dragged away?" Memphis asked.

"There appears to be no evidence of that," Sojourner said. "There is thick foliage growing all around the crash site."

"Then I say we go down there and find out what the hell happened to it," Raqmar demanded.

Vee stepped in to calm things down before they got out of hand.

"Fortunately, I am the captain here. And I say we conduct a closer survey of the crash zone before we go rushing into things. Is that understood?"

"Yes, cap," came in delayed dribs and drabs. Raqmar was the last to respond.

Satisfied they were all on the same page, Vee instructed Sojourner to do a deep scan of the surface for evidence of bodies or skeletal remains. "We will cloak in and land at night." She stopped speaking and asked Sojourner, "This planet does rotate, right?"

"Yes, captain."

"Then we will cloak in and examine the crash site under the cover of night. Only the ship will be hidden, so once we disembark, we'll be visible to wildlife and any sentient life nearby."

"I completed the deep scan, captain," Sojourner said. "I found no evidence of bodies or remains."

"Maybe they were eaten by animals," Raqmar said.

"I suggest we refrain from speculating and wait until we can examine the area," Vee said. "Now, in the meantime, prepare for a stealth ground operation."

"Aye, cap."

"We have no idea where we are or who or what we might come up against. So let's not invite trouble before we know what that trouble is," Vee cautioned her crew.

Everyone went about their respective duties preparing for the unknown.

Piper gathered whatever medical supplies he felt he needed just in case Sojourner and Sparks were wrong and the captain and the lieutenant needed first aid.

Sparks calculated a stealth approach vector to land near the fighter debris.

Lin and Raqmar gathered the gear they felt would be most effective in protecting everyone and the ship in case they needed to make a hasty retreat.

Captain Vee visited the empty fighter bay below the main deck. The bay, normally the berth for the fighter, sat barren, cold. She brushed off the negative feelings and thought of the good times and smiled to herself as she thought of better days. She dearly missed her friends and hoped they were not too late.

Sojourner's voice pierced the busy quiet. "I found it. I found the fighter."

"Where?" Vee asked.

"It is deep within an underground complex in the middle of what would best be described as a city. The complex appears to be a military base."

"That sucks," was Piper's disappointing response to the news.

"Where are they on the sentient scale?" Vee asked.

"On a scale of five, they appear to be level two."

"Great!" Raqmar rejoiced. His response was more gung-ho than the others. "Technologically, they're nowhere near us. We should go down there and—"

"Do nothing," was Vee's stern reply to Raqmar's outburst. "First-contact protocols are to be observed. We do not alert them to our presence until we have no choice. Do. I. Make. Myself. Clear?" She punctuated each word for emphasis. The anger in them was unmistakable.

Raqmar snapped to attention and belted out, "Yes, sir," like a first-year academy cadet.

Everyone else just sat in stunned silence.

In a calmer toner, Vee continued. "We are here to find Captain Leahcim, Lieutenant Markka, and Cora," she paused. "Alive or dead, and bring them home. If that means none of us getting home, so be it. I would much rather get everyone home in one piece. But not at the expense of a primitive civilization. Does anyone have a problem with that?"

"There was a collective "No, sir," heard through the ship's speaker system.

"Good. I'm heading back up to the bridge. Once it's dark, we'll begin our descent."

Lin elbowed Raqmar in the ribs as they continued to pack. "Way to go, Jarhead."

They did not have long to wait before the area was covered in darkness.

"Sparks, activate the cloak," Vee ordered.

They broke orbit and proceeded to the crash site. The ship was invisible to the naked eye and all planetary sensors but one. It came in low, silent, and slow on a flight path straight toward the glade. The crew of the *Infiltrator* landed and went about their business, certain they went unnoticed.

CHAPTER 37

Markka was awakened by a series of vibrations on her wrist. She rolled back the fog of sleep enough to remember she was wearing her wrist comm. She looked at the readout and saw it was Cora. She gingerly got out of bed and made her way to an adjoining room so she would not disturb her husband.

Standing in the dark, she said, "Go ahead, Cora, what is it?" in a low tone of voice just above a whisper.

"They're here," Cora said.

"Who's here?"

"The *Infiltrator.*"

Markka's heart skipped a couple of beats. After all this time they finally found her, she thought. They never stopped looking for them? It could not be them. Not after eleven years.

"Are you sure it's them?"

"Yes. I conducted a scan of the ship. It is the *Infiltrator* and her crew.

"Where are they?"

"They are currently at the crash site. I detected their entry into the atmosphere and tracked them. If they found the crash site, they will undoubtedly locate the fighter if they have not done so already."

"Count on them having already done so. They're probably deciding how to get to it. Get the crew together," she told Cora. "We're going to form a welcoming committee. We need to intercept them before they meet the locals."

"Indeed. Yes, ma'am."

"Do you think they detected you tracking them?"

"No, ma'am. Oddly. It looks like they have made no upgrades in all this time."

"That is odd," Markka agreed. "I'll let Tory know what's going on. Then I'll meet you at the staging area."

About thirty mictons later Markka was addressing the team of troops hand-picked to intercept the *Infiltrator*'s crew.

Standing before her was the most elite team of commandos in Uderra. Among them were her own children, nieces, and nephews.

"The day David and I always hoped for has arrived," she told them. "But since so much time has passed, we don't know what to expect from our would-be rescuers. I would remind you all that they are here to conduct a stealth operation. They will defend themselves if they believe they are in grave personal danger."

"Then we shall kill them where they stand."

Horrified at the ferociousness of the statement, Markka took a step back from her niece. Then looked at both of her brothers to see if they shared their sister's sentiment. They each tried to conceal smirks of pride and approval.

"No, Zora. Certainly not. That goes for all of you."

"Why should we show them mercy after they left you and father for dead?" Zora asked. "They let the two of you languish in years of hopelessness."

Markka smiled softly at her niece and placed a gentle paw on Zora's cheek.

"Zora, if we kill them outright, we'll never know what took them so long to get here."

"Then we will torture the reason out of them then kill them where they stand."

Markka sighed a heavy sigh and patted Zora's cheek. "You will not kill them or torture them. They were . . . are my friends."

Tears welled up in Markka's eyes as she removed her paw from her niece's face.

Zora Leahcim, of the House of Mahli, had become a cunning warrior. She had her mother's beauty and her father's tenacity. Her parents would have been proud of her and all their children. But the devastating loss of her parents hardened Zora's heart. The one trait missing from her psychological arsenal was compassion. It died within her when her parents died. And she always blamed herself for their deaths.

"You will pursue and subdue. Cora will assist you. She knows their strengths and weaknesses. You've all grown up hearing our stories about them. Now it's time to meet them."

"If it is them." Zora was not giving up easily.

"If it *is* them," Markka said emphatically. "Do not kill them." Then as an afterthought, Markka said, "And if it's not them, don't kill them either."

Markka's oldest child, Mook, spoke up and said, "We will do as you command, mother."

Like his three siblings, he inherited most of his father's physical attributes. Instead of paws, he had hands that concealed dagger-like claws that sprang from his fingers like hidden shivs. One physical attribute he and his siblings did inherit from Markka was a tail that could strangle an adversary as effectively as a cord around their neck.

"Good. See that you do," Markka said. Then she stared straight at Zora.

Zora tossed her cousin a disapproving look then sighed in surrender, "Yes, ma'am."

"Good. Now do us proud. May the Goddess be with you. Dismissed."

Markka turned to the person who had been standing off to the side and asked, "Are you ready for your first command?"

Cora replied, "Yes, ma'am."

"Good. By the way, your new synthetic body looks better than the last one. It's not as robotic-looking. It's more android-ish this time. You look like Leahcim and me blended into one person but more feminine. Not that it matters."

"Thank you. That is precisely the look I was going for."

"Perfect. Now keep my kids safe."

Markka turned and left as Cora and her commandos mounted up to face their queen's rescuers.

Zora turned to Cora after mounting her speeder and asked, "So what's the plan, commander?"

"I'll explain on the way."

They switched on their speeders, activated their infrared guidance systems, and sped off into the night.

The plan was to blind, misdirect, and disable Sojourner. Immobilize Sparks and Piper, then surprise and neutralize Lin and Vee. With everyone taken out of the game, Raqmar would reluctantly surrender to ensure the safety of his friends.

When they reached their destination, they got into position and waited. Cora set the plan in motion by projecting false signals of a group of soldiers approaching the ship.

The ruse worked. The signal was so convincing that Sojourner warned the crew without ever detecting the deception.

As expected, Lin and Raqmar believed they had the element of surprise on their side. They stopped guarding the ship and approached what appeared on their proximity sensors as enemy soldiers. They planned to outflank and stun the entire group. But this left Sparks, Vee, and Piper vulnerable to capture. Exactly what Cora intended.

She knew they would have scanned the planet to assess the technological capabilities and determined the inhabitants to be technologically inferior. Cora counted on them underestimating the abilities of any military force. So Cora used this knowledge to her advantage.

Wearing electronic camouflage nets of Cora's design to mask them from Sojourner's sensors, three of Markka's kids, all of whom inherited her feline ability to see in the dark, eliminating the need for night vision goggles, scanned the ship to determine the locations of its crew. Once that was done, they tossed an EMP grenade inside the ship. It was not a real grenade in the traditional sense. It was not designed to cause physical damage but to wreak havoc with unshielded electronics. Detonating it inside the ship was the only way to disable Sojourner.

The grenade worked. Sojourner and the entire electronic framework of the ship shorted out. It was just a simple matter of boarding, overpowering and tranquilizing Sparks who was working on a navigation relay in the fighter bay, and Piper who was running an inventory of supplies in the adjacent medical bay. The ambush was so swift, neither had time to be aware of what happened to them.

Captain Vee was on the bridge when she was hit with a paralysis dart. Cora designed the dart as a means of immobilizing a target without putting the subject to sleep. Cora wanted Vee immobile but conscious in case things did not go as planned. All that remained were Lin and Raqmar.

Cora jammed the comms as an insurance safeguard. Then stood ready to emulate any of the onboard crew if Lin or Raqmar called the ship for any reason. Lin was their next target.

Skilled in several forms of martial arts, Lin was a formidable fighter. Despite Raqmar's strength due to growing up on a heavy gravity planet, she bested him in one-on-one combat every time. So she ordered Zora and five others to openly confront Lin.

"Halt, stranger," Zora ordered, speaking in the Uderran language. "You are trespassing on the sovereign land of the Uderran people. You are hereby ordered to surrender your weapons and come with us."

Cora thought Zora's performance was a bit over the top, but it put Lin right where she wanted her.

Lin, on the other hand, was not about to be captured without a fight. And although she probably wouldn't kill anyone, she would most definitely dish out some serious pain. Lin slowly lowered her weapons and placed them on the ground then moved into a fighting stance and said, "I don't know what you just said, but if you want me, you're gonna have to take me down."

Cora did not want to take the chance that Lin or Zora or her team would be seriously hurt or worse. Markka would never forgive her. So Cora stepped out of her concealment and shot Lin with a tranquilizer dart that shocked her nervous system. The woman's body twitched and quivered before it dropped to the ground.

Zora turned to Cora and complained, "Hey! I could have taken her."

"I do not doubt it," Cora said, "but your aunt gave me explicit orders to allow no harm to come to you or your team."

Zora opened her mouth to respond with a retort when Cora cut her off and said, "That means not even a scratch."

Zora huffed, folded her arms, but remained silent.

"Now let's go get the strongman. Remain alert with him. He's immensely strong but mentally headstrong. He tends to act before thinking, which makes him somewhat predictable and unpredictable at the same time."

"My people and I can handle one man," Zora said confidently.

Cora and Zora watched as Raqmar detected their presence and attempted to contact Lin. When she did not respond, he attempted to contact the *Infiltrator* but was greeted with whispered static. They watched as he realized something was seriously wrong.

He was about to double back toward the ship when Cora signaled to Zora to repeat the tactic they pulled on Lin. However, Raqmar did not lower his weapons as Lin did but pointed them at Zora. Who in turn drew her weapon; her team drew theirs as well.

Would he pull the trigger? She thought. She was certain Raqmar would have no worries if he did. So she decided to disappoint Zora yet again. She ordered two of the guards with her to bring her their captives.

Sparks, Piper, and Lin were all still unconscious. Captain Vee was conscious but still immobile. They would all be that way for the return trip back to Uderra.

She ordered her team to show Raqmar they had his shipmates.

Once he realized the rest of the crew was captured, he surrendered and dropped his weapon. But when Zora stepped toward him to place restraints on his wrists, he lashed out and took a swing at her head.

To her credit, Zora anticipated he would attempt something like that and avoided a punch that would have surely done some serious damage. She ducked below his swinging arm, pivoted behind him, then kicked out at his leg behind his knee. The swiftness of her kick surprised him and brought him down to one knee. Zora pivoted again, got directly behind Raqmar and wrapped her arms around his neck in a chokehold, and squeezed with all of her strength. She barely budged him, but he was unable to break her grip.

He grasped her forearms and scratched at her hands, but he could not break her grip. The tighter she squeezed, the lighter his head felt and the weaker his arms became. He eventually dropped his arms to his sides; two members of the team ran over to help Zora hold him down while a third clamped the restraints on his wrists and feet. Once he was restrained, Zora slowly released her grip.

As Raqmar gasped for air, there was fire and fury in his eyes. His surrender was not without threats.

"You'll pay for this, bitch. You and all your sorry-ass people. You don't know who you're fucking with. Mark my words. We'll make you all pay."

"You and what army, strongman?" Zora asked in plain, unadulterated standard.

"You speak standard?" he asked surprised.

"Yes," was all Zora said as her team put the crew, the conscious and unconscious, into a prisoner transport for the trip back to Uderra.

As she secured the doors to the transport, Cora asked, "Did you enjoy yourself?"

"Yes. I did enjoy myself. I was afraid you were going to intervene."

"If you had lost control of the situation, I would have."

Cora rode alongside Zora carrying a small, hexagon box contained within a mini force field as they headed back to the city.

CHAPTER 38

When they reached the city, the commandos took their prisoners directly to the citadel and lined them up at the foot of a set of steps in a large reception hall. Sparks, Piper, and Lin regained consciousness by then. At the top of the steps were two thrones.

"You are fortunate," Zora told them. "The queen wishes to meet with you. She has been looking forward to this moment for cycles."

"Really?" Raqmar scoffed. "Cycles, my ass. We don't even know this queen of yours," he spat.

"Quite the contrary," came the voice at the top of the steps.

A robed figure stood on the top step. Her face was hidden, but Vee thought she recognized the voice. It sounded familiar. It was a bit older, and there was a weariness to it, but somehow it sounded familiar. There was no way it could belong to the person she thought it sounded like. The robed figure standing before them was a queen. The person she thought of was nowhere near royalty.

The robe the queen wore seemed oversized down to the sleeves. Not a centimeter of skin was visible. The queen gestured to a second figure wearing a robe. "Come, my husband, join us in this bittersweet reunion."

The second, more imposing figure stepped from the shadows and stood beside the queen. There was a regal air about him. His walk and stance reflected that.

"How do you know us?" Vee asked.

"I once served with you in your war with the GSE."

"Get the hell out of here," Raqmar blurted out. "This whole thing is some fucking GSE trick. You bastards won't get away with this shit."

175

Before Vee could order Raqmar to shut up, Mook stepped forward and jabbed him with a shock stick. There was a crackling sound accompanied by a pained growl from Raqmar as it sent a jolt of energy through his body. He dropped to his knees bringing Lin and Piper, who were chained on either side of him, to their knees as well.

"You will not speak to my mother with such disrespect." The anger in his voice was unmistakable. "We will not tolerate such insolence." He was about to strike Raqmar again when Vee intervened.

"No, wait!" she yelled.

Mook glanced up at the queen who raised her hand ordering him to stand down. He nodded and stepped back, but he was prepared to strike again.

Frustrated to the point of losing control of her anger and uncharacteristically insulting, Vee could stand no more of Raqmar's antics. "Raqmar," she yelled. "Shut the hell up, you imbecile! That's an order." She took a few deep breaths to get herself back under control. Then she addressed the queen in a calmer, more controlled tone of voice.

"Please forgive his stupidity, your majesty. He tends to react before he thinks."

"I know," the queen giggled. "Looks like some things never change."

Puzzled by the queen's odd reaction, Vee bowed and said, "If I may be so bold to ask again, how do you know who we are?"

"It's like I said, I once served alongside each of you."

The queen reached up and pulled back the hood to her robe and revealed herself. "It's me, Markka," she said through a wide-eyed grin with glistening incisors.

As Raqmar, Piper, and Lin returned to standing positions, Lin elbowed Raqmar and irritatedly called him a Jarhead.

Markka descended the steps, stood before Vee, and saluted. Then she turned to Mook and Zora and said, "Well, what're you waiting for? An invitation? Get those damned cuffs off our guests." They both hesitated before they complied with the order. Zora motioned to the guards to be ready to shoot anyone who made a threatening move.

Satisfied her order was being adhered to, Markka turned back to Vee. "Captain, you and your crew are my guests for as long as you are with us. I will answer all of your questions tomorrow."

Then she turned to the lone figure that was standing off to the side.

"Cora," she said, "see to all the creature comforts of our guests, please."

"Right away, ma'am."

"And stop calling me ma'am."

"Yes, your majesty."

"Oh never mind."

Vee stood staring at Cora and Markka before speaking again.

"Cora?"

"Yes, Captain?"

"What the hell happened? What the hell is going on?"

"As Queen Markka said, she'll explain everything to you—tomorrow."

"What about my ship? Sojourner?"

"I assure you, captain. They are quite safe. Your ship will soon be within the protected boundaries of the city. Sojourner is right here." She extended an artificial-looking and revealed a hexagon box. "You may take her with you to your quarters."

Vee took the box Cora handed her and looked with puzzlement at Cora. "But how—"

"Enough questions for tonight." She gestured to a couple of guards. "Please show the captain and her crew to their quarters."

CHAPTER 39

The following morning, the crew was escorted to a lavishly decorated private room in the Royal House. In the center of it sat a long banquet table adorned with a colorful assortment of foods artfully arranged with succulent fruits and vegetables, roasted and grilled meats, and a variety of sweet pastries complemented by an assortment of seductive drinks.

Having spent the last few days eating military rations, a hearty meal was a welcomed surprise. One look at the cornucopia of foods on the table was enough to make military rations look like a kids' meal.

Once they were all seated, Markka welcomed everyone to morning refreshments. "I trust everyone had a restful night?"

There were nods of affirmation around the table.

"Good. Now let us thank the Goddess for this bounty and for lost friendships renewed." Markka led them in prayer thanking the Goddess for the food and drink before them and for the good health of those in the room. Then she began the introductions as the food was served.

"Let me introduce my staff," she began. Gesturing toward the man seated next to her, she said, "This is my husband, Tory."

Tory did not say a word but nodded to their guests. He eyed each of them with fascination and suspicion.

"Next is Garath, our chief healer, Sho'khan, our lead tactical officer, and this is B'rtann, our commander of all military forces, and these two fine officers are my son, Mook, captain of the Royal Guard, and niece, Zora, head of our commandos."

When Markka finished with the introductions, she addressed Vee.

"Captain Vee, I know you're bubbling over with questions like how did we survive the crash? How did I get to be queen? And where is Captain Leahcim?" She paused and looked at the rest of the *Infiltrator* crew. "Before I answer them, I encourage everyone to eat. Tough questions are more easily discussed on a full stomach."

Most of the conversations centered around what life was like in the Alliance or on Progensha. Zora and Mook spoke sparingly and kept a wary eye on their guests.

When everyone had their fill and the small-talk started to wind down, Markka stood up and raised her arms to get everyone's attention. The room quieted down.

"Now," she said. Time to answer your questions. But before I do, I have just one question for you: How were you able to find us after all this time?"

The room grew even quieter as all eyes turned to face Vee.

Vee cleared her throat and said, "Believe it or not, but we started searching for you as soon as we reached the battlefield over Aggro Nine. Eleven days ago. We found the flight recorder and Cora's message; we followed your ion trail into the nebula."

"For us," Markka said, "that was eleven cycles, uh, years ago."

"It is what I suspected," Cora said. "There is some type of time displacement between our respective universes or realities."

"What do you mean by displacement?" Vee asked Cora. "We arrived at Aggro Nine six hours after you missed your rendezvous. Fleet received a cryptic message about a battle and our battle group was sent to assist. We weren't prepared for what we found. Between rescue and recovery efforts, discovering Cora's message, and a briefing with the Fleet commander, you had a few days' head start on us. We couldn't have been more than three days behind you. At least."

"Remarkable," Cora said. "For each day in your universe, a cycle passes in ours. While Queen Markka and I have experienced the passage of time, gotten older, and have had offspring, you have aged no more than a few days."

"Incredible," another disembodied voice said.

"Sojourner? Is that you?" Vee asked.

"Yes, captain."

"Where are you?"

"With Cora and . . . her children."

"Get the fuck outta here," Raqmar said. Regretting his outburst when all eyes landed on him—especially the withering stare he got from Vee.

"Sorry," he murmured.

"Now, I believe you have one glaring question for me," Markka said.

"Yes," Vee began. "Where is Captain Leahcim?"

Markka turned to Zora and asked her if she wanted to answer the question. Zora, in true Zora fashion, went straight for a brutally honest answer.

"My father and mother were killed two cycles ago in a battle with our sworn enemy."

This time it was Lin who could not hold her tongue. "You're shittin' me."

"I shit you not," Zora replied. She was poker-faced-serious.

"Hold up. He had a wife?" Raqmar asked with obvious disbelief. The question earned him another jab in his ribs from Lin.

"He's . . . dead?" Vee asked. She was visibly shaken by the news. "I don't believe it. He can't be dead."

"Believe it, captain. My father is as dead as my mother." The remorse and reverence in her tone were evident.

Mook spoke up in support of Zora. "Commander Leahcim and Commander T'oann were the greatest of us. They helped build the Uderran people's spirits, strengthened our resolve to take a stand against oppression and tyranny. They were the architects of the coalition; celebrated as heroes, revered as martyrs."

"We will live free or die free," Zora finished.

Vee and the others looked to Markka for confirmation.

"It's true," Markka said. She glared at both Zora and Mook, but she could not blame them. They took the deaths of their beloved parents and aunt and uncle hard. "Sorry to put a damper on the festivities."

"How did they die?" Vee asked.

"In glorious combat," Zora said with obvious pride in her voice.

"There is a visual record in our archives if you wish to view it," Cora said.

"Yes. We all wish to see it."

"Cora, please display the visual record for our guests," Markka said.

"Right away, your majesty."

Almost instantly a holograph of the arena fight flickered on in the center of the banquet table. The replay of the heroic efforts of Leahcim and T'oann in their battle with the scorb had the full attention of the crew. They watched with fascination and horror as Leahcim and T'oann fought for their lives against their unholy adversary.

When the pike impaled Leahcim and T'oann, The room was pin-drop quiet. And all eyes were on Vee and her crew.

"Did I just see what I think I saw?" Raqmar asked.

"Yes," was all Markka said.

"The cowards murdered our parents," Zora said. "And they will pay dearly for it."

The recording ended with the killing of the Disposal Unit's commander.

"So now you know," Markka said. "Within a sol, the Thourons bombarded the mountain, collapsing the top section. We lost a lot of good people in the span of three sols."

"Damn, that's fucked up." This time, Lin was the one who broke the silence with her expletive.

"This was not what any of us was expecting," Vee said. "We sort of were expecting to find you floating around in the nebula or where you crashed. Not dying in gladiatorial games or ruling nations."

"Yeah," Piper said. "We now know what happened to Captain Leahcim. But how'd you get to be queen?" Piper asked.

Tory's authoritative baritone voice filled the air. T'oann was my sister. Her death was too much for our mother to handle. She fell into a state of depression and died broken-hearted. The mantle of ruling Uderra became my responsibility as heir to the throne. And since Markka is my consort, she is naturally the queen."

"So you run things around here, then?" Piper asked.

Tory responded, "In a manner of speaking."

"What he means," Markka said, " is he could, but chooses not to because he's a stickler for tradition."

"I don't understand," Piper said.

"Uderra is a matriarchal society," Markka explained. "The job just sorta fell in my lap because I'm married to the king. And because he has a stick up his butt and adheres to tradition," she eyed him with a snarky smile, "I get to do all the heavy lifting."

"And you do an admirable job," Tory said. His response was accompanied by a sly smirk only Markka recognized as a playful jab.

Piper persisted. "I don't mean to sound insensitive, but Captain Leahcim lost his life here. Why stay? Now that we're here, you can come back with us."

"And do what? Pick up where I left off? I can't go back."

"Why not?" Raqmar asked this time.

"Because my life is here now. I have a family I love, a coalition to help run, and a war to fight. I cannot and will not, abandon all that. Besides, I owe it to David and T'oann to continue the fight so their deaths weren't in vain. You are free to go, but I'm staying."

"That goes for me as well," Cora added.

"However," Markka added, "There is something you can do for us before you go."

CHAPTER 40

After a day filled with more questions than answers, Vee sat on the side of the bed in her quarters thinking over Markka's request. Tory and Markka wanted to use the *Infiltrator* to recover David's and T'oann's bodies from the mountain. The Thouron bombardment made reaching the ancient burial grounds too treacherous for a retrieval team to attempt, but the *Infiltrator* could fly cloaked and possibly find a place to land or drop a retrieval team.

Markka and Tory wanted to recover the bodies and bring them back to Uderra for a proper burial. Vee and her team had volunteered for a possible one-way mission to do the same thing with Markka, Cora, and David. And now David was dead and Cora and Markka were staying on Progensha.

She thought about what her report to Fleet would say. Captain Leahcim, Lieutenant Markka, and Cora had lived more than a decade of their lives as members of another culture on a planet in a time-displaced universe.

They had married, raised kids, and fought a war of survival. David had died a revered military leader, Markka was a queen, and Cora was the central nervous system of an entire culture.

If they returned with nothing, Fleet would want to know why they hadn't tried harder to persuade them to return—or had not forcibly returned them. But if how easily she and her crew were captured was any indication, it seemed like nothing they did would have a positive outcome. Would Fleet and the Alliance consider them deserters?

To make matters even more confusing, she wondered what kind of world they would return to with the time displacement. Would they return to the exact time they left when they passed back through the event horizon?

Vee's head ached. So she decided to get some sleep and discuss it with the crew in the morning.

Early the next morning, Vee was up, washed and dressed, and meandering about the compound they were quartered in. She was still wrestling with many of the questions she fell asleep pondering when she made her decision. "Cora?"

"Yes, captain?"

"Can you put me in touch with Markka?"

"Right away."

With everything her crew experienced in the last couple of days, she thought they earned a little extra sack time. So she let them sleep while she spoke with Markka.

Sparks was the first to greet her. "Morning, cap."

"Morning."

"I'm telling you, that Markka thought of everything. She had an aqua bed installed in my quarters. I'm gonna get one for the *Infiltrator* when we get back."

One by one the rest of them greeted their captain and sat with her in the compound garden. Each praised the comfortable sleep they had and pretty much scarfed down the food that was provided. When everyone had their fill, Vee informed them of the request Markka made.

"Now that we're all here, I need to tell you I got a request from Markka. She and her husband want to use the *Infiltrator* to find Captain Leahcim and Commander T'oann."

"So what'd you say, cap?" Sparks asked.

"I told her we would do it."

"Good. How soon do we start?" Raqmar asked.

"As soon as our escort arrives."

As if on cue, Zora requested entry to the compound. Once she entered, she wasted no time outlining what she wanted them to do.

"My aunt says you have the means to travel undetected."

"We do," Vee confirmed."

"Then we will leave immediately." She turned and left the compound. The rest of them followed. Zora took them to where Cora had berthed their ship where they were greeted by Sojourner.

"Good morning, captain."

"Good morning, Sojourner," Vee said. "I presume Cora briefed you on our mission,"

"Yes, captain."

"Good. Let's get underway."

Once everyone was onboard, Sparks punched in the coordinates Zora gave her and Sojourner engaged the cloak.

Vee watched Zora and her retrieval team stare in amazement at the ground rapidly receding from them.

"What do you think?" Vee asked her.

Zora looked at her with childlike wonderment on her face. "Fascinating," she said, trying and failing to mask the excitement in her voice.

Moments later, Sparks announced they reached their objective. "We're here."

"Any chance the Thourons know we're here?" Vee asked Sojourner.

"No, captain."

"Good. Are we anywhere near the ancestral burial grounds?"

Zora responded. "Yes." Standing behind Sparks, she pointed to a flat portion of the mountain that miraculously survived the bombings.

"Can you safely set her down?" Vee asked.

"Depends."

"On what?"

"On whether that flatland can support the weight of the ship."

"Well, Sojourner?" Vee asked.

"We can land."

"Good. Set her down here. Zora, Lin will accompany you and your team."

"So be it," Zora said. She turned to Lin and said, "Keep up."

Lin was about to say something snarky when Sojourner interrupted.

"Captain," Sojourner said. "There is something you should know."

"What?"

"I'm detecting a chamber of some kind a few meters below the surface. I am picking up faint energy readings and nearly indiscernible heartbeats. They are weak and rhythmic."

Vee turned to Zora. "Any idea what that might be?"

"The Mountain People did have a research facility deep within the mountain. Those who survived the attack reported that the entire facility was destroyed. Your computer may be picking up signs of equipment still running."

Incensed at being called a mere computer, Sojourner responded quite indignantly, "Firstly, I am not a computer. Secondly, the signals I am getting are distinctly biological."

"Perhaps you are reading the life signs of small animals that have found their way in," Zora said. Ignoring Sojourner's indignation.

"The readings are not those of small animals," Sojourner insisted.

Determined to keep the peace on her ship, Vee said that the readings warranted investigating and asked Sojourner if she could detect a way in.

Zora was visibly irritated by the captain's insistence they investigate some biological readings from some mountain rodents.

"You disagree with my decision, commander?" Vee asked.

Zora glared at Vee. "Finding my father *and my mother* is imperative, but they have been gone for two cycles. If your . . . Sojourner feels it is vital we investigate, then a few more mictons will not make a difference in their fate," Zora angrily retorted. "We must identify these *weak* biological signals first because this is your ship, your crew, your command."

Zora gave Vee one of those if-looks-could-kill stares.

Sojourner cut through the tension when she said she detected passable crawl spaces that appeared to be stable.

"Then we shall traverse these passages to determine what it is your comp—" In the interest of diplomacy, Zora reluctantly changed direction in mid-sentence and referred to Sojourner by her name. "Sojourner has found," Zora said. She ordered her team to find a way into the facility.

As Zora and her team exited the *Infiltrator*, Vee told Lin to "Play nice." Then reluctantly added, "Take Raqmar with you."

Lin looked at Raqmar. "You heard the cap. Let's go. And don't fuck this up."

After the group left, Sojourner closed the hatch. She did not want a repeat of the other night.

CHAPTER 41

Using a pocket-sized sensor, Lin took point, sweeping the sensor out in front of her, getting directional data on the life readings as they crawled through narrow passages.

The cold weather gear they wore made some of the tighter spots along the route a bit tough to get through, but everyone was able to fit. The deeper they went, the wider the passages became.

The group eventually reached their destination. The sensor was beeping wildly. They were in what appeared to be a spacious chamber they were all able to fit in while comfortably standing. In front of them was a huge door. Next to the door was what looked like a control panel.

"We're here," Lin said. She held the sensor up to the panel. "Can you figure out how to open it?"

"Give me a moment," Sojourner said. A few seconds later Sojourner said, "Do you see the three buttons off to the side?"

"Yes," Lin replied.

"Press those three buttons simultaneously then pull the lever next to them down."

"Got it." Lin pressed the buttons, but could not budge the switch. "Raq, get your ass over here and help me with this."

Raqmar stepped up next to her and pulled on the switch. It did not budge. Lin grabbed a hold of the switch and helped him pull. It fought against both of them but eventually lost the battle with a metal scraping against metal sound followed by a thunk and a release of atmosphere from within the chamber on the other side of the door, which also refused to move.

Together with Zora and her team, they pulled and tugged and strained against the stubborn door as it screeched and creaked in protest to being forced to reveal what was locked away behind it. The door eventually surrendered. They pried it open enough for each of them to squeeze through.

Their flashlights scanned a room filled with various pieces of equipment. Much of it was crushed from falling debris. Scattered among the debris were the dead. On the farthest side of the room was another blast door. Against the door were more bodies.

Lin scanned the bodies and was shocked by what the sensor revealed. "What the hell?"

"What is it? What have you found?" Zora demanded to know.

"The source of the life readings. It's them." She pointed at the pile of bodies. All of them. "They're . . . alive."

"How is that possible?" Zora asked.

"Are you reading this, Sojourner?" Lin asked, deflecting Zora's question.

"Yes. It appears they are in a cryogenic state."

"But they're not in tubes or canisters of any kind."

"An analysis of the chamber's atmosphere reveals high levels of a cryogenic gas," Sojourner said.

"Are we in any danger?"

"No. Now that the room has been unsealed, the effects of the cryogenics will begin to wear off."

"You mean they'll start to come around?"

"Yes."

"Lin turned in Zora's direction when she heard the young officer exclaim, "By the grace of the Goddess. I need help over here," as she gestured for her team to join her while she tugged on one of the bodies.

Zora's team took each of the bodies and gently laid them next to each other. Zora knelt between two of the bodies and said a prayer of thanks.

When Lin moved closer to get a better look, she gasped, "Holy shit." The rest of the retrieval team turned to see what she saw. Lin recovered from her surprise and immediately let her captain know what they found. "Hey, cap, we got us a situation in here," she said.

"What's the situation?" Vee asked.

"Captain Leahcim is alive, and so is his wife."

"Say again?"

"Captain Leahcim and his wife are alive. As well as a bunch of other people. We need Pipe down here."

Vee looked at Piper who was just standing frozen in place.

"Well, you heard her. Get a move on, son."

"Yes, sir," he said. He grabbed his gear and headed to meet up with Lin.

As he was smaller than nearly everyone else, it did not take him long to reach the chamber. After he recovered from the shock of seeing Captain Leahcim alive, Piper conducted a hasty examination of all the cave-in survivors. "I can't tell if they'll all wake up on their own or wake up at all," he reported.

"Get them to the ship," Vee ordered. "We'll take them back to Uderra. They need to wake up in friendly surroundings with friendly faces."

"Right away, cap," Lin responded. "You heard her. Let's get these people on the ship so we can get the hell outta here. Use the fighter bay. That should be big enough."

It took a little under thirty minutes to get everyone on board and fly back to Uderra.

Zora notified Markka of their discovery and stayed with her parents and accompanied them to the healing center. Markka and Tory were waiting for them.

"Damn," Markka said. "If I hadn't seen it with my own two eyes, I probably wouldn't have believed it." She asked Piper, who walked over to her and Tory to give her his report, "How long before they're revived?"

"Your guess is as good as mine," Piper said. "According to the medical logs, the cryogenic gas was designed to suspend life functions for a maximum of thirty days, not two years."

"Cora?"

"Yes, your majesty."

"Get more healers down here to assist. And stop calling me your majesty."

"Yes, your highness."

Markka whispered to Tory standing next to her, "I swear. If she wasn't an SI, I'd kick her scrawny little butt."

"I heard that," Cora said.

Markka sighed; Tory chuckled.

Markka turned her attention back to the group of survivors in general and Leahcim and T'oann in particular and wondered aloud more to herself than to Tory, "We all thought they died two cycles ago. We saw David and T'oann die in the arena and witnessed the mountain. How are they still alive?"

"Not able to say at this time," Piper said.

She forgot Piper was standing there. "Have you identified the others?" Markka asked him.

Piper said, "As best we can tell, the others appear to be a mix of Mountain People, Uderrans, and other Progenshans."

"I believe I can be of service with that," Cora said, "but I need to speak with her majesty in private."

"In this place?" Markka asked.

"We can use the isolation chamber. It will be secure."

"Okay, give me a micton." She turned her attention back to Piper. "Pipe, you and the others are free to head back to your compound. I'll summon you when or if I need you."

"Sure thing, uh, your highness." It felt awkward for him to call Markka by her honorific title when just a few days ago, at least for him, he had called her simply Markka or lieutenant. He was glad for the chance to get away from her presence for a while.

As Piper and the others left, Markka made her way to the chamber and stepped inside while Cora ensured it would be protected from eavesdropping of any kind.

"We are now secure," Cora said.

"What is so important about the survivors that we have to take security precautions? Is one of them a Thouron spy or something?"

"No, but two of them are genetically related to T'oann and Tory."

"Who and how?"

"The two individuals wearing the hooded robes. One is Tonga."

"Tonga? You mean T'oann's sister?"

"Yes."

Markka was suspicious. "But she said her sister was dead."

"She was mistaken."

Markka visualized a variety of scenarios before asking, "So how is it she's alive?"

"Unknown at this point," was Cora's response.

Markka stared into space at something only she could see. Then, with an almost gleeful sound in her voice, she said, "You know what this means?"

"That T'oann has her sister back?" Where Markka was concerned, Cora could never quite figure out which direction her mind would go.

"Besides that."

"What else is there?" Cora asked.

"I'm no longer the queen." Markka squealed with excitement."

"I don't think the king will take the news as enthusiastically as you have."

"He'll get over it." Markka was smiling broadly like a child who had just received the best gift in the world.

"There is one more thing you should know," Cora said cautiously.

"What's that?" Markka was half-listening.

The other individual is Tonga's son. You are also familiar with him because he is the Thouron Disposal Team Commander."

"Wait. What?" Cora had Markka's undivided attention. "The Thouron who had his neck broken by the Mountain guards?"

"Yes."

"Now that you mentioned it when the retrieval team brought in the cave-in survivors, I thought he looked familiar, but I brushed it off because it couldn't have been him because I watched him die."

"Not exactly. We heard sounds out of visual range that sounded like he died."

Markka thought back to that day. "Crap! You're right. I never questioned what I saw and heard that day."

"Nor did I. We accepted what we saw as the truth. Now we know otherwise."

"Not until we get confirmation from the healers," Markka cautioned.

"Your assessment is sound," Cora said. "He is either a biological twin or we have all been deceived by an elaborate ruse."

Markka thought about the sudden turn of events when she cursed. "Damn."

"What is the problem, your majesty?"

"Uh, we got a bigger problem, Cora."

"What is bigger than Captain Leahcim and Commander T'oann being alive and discovering the return of Tonga and her son?"

"Remember?" Markka asked.

"Remember what?"

"Zora and Tory don't know about Tonga. T'oann made us promise not to tell anyone. And since we all believed she was dead, there was no reason to say anything."

"Like we all believed the Thouron commander was dead," Cora said.

"Holy shit!" Markka exclaimed.

"What is it, your majesty?"

"If Zora recognizes Tonga's son, she might kill him on the spot." Markka rushed to the chamber door as Cora unlocked it. Markka called to Zora, who was still kneeling between her unconscious parents. "Commander Zora, I need to see you. Now!" Markka made sure to say it as an authoritative command emphasizing the word now. "And bring your uncle," she added.

Moments later, Zora and Tory entered the chamber. Cora locked them in and secured the room. "You are free to speak," Cora said.

"What is going on?" Tory asked.

"Yes, what is going on?" Zora repeated.

Markka looked at Tory and told him that she was breaking an eleven-year-old promise she, Leahcim, and Cora made to T'oann. She told him that two of the survivors were his sister and nephew.

Tory was dumbfounded by the shocking revelation. And Zora just stood looking unsure and wondered if what she just heard was true.

Markka's voice cracked when she said, "I'm sorry I didn't tell you before now, but I made a promise. I'll understand if you're angry with me, and," her voice faltered, "I'll understand if you don't want to have anything to do with me." She tried to stifle a sniffle and turned her head away from Tory and Zora so they would not see her eyes tear up.

Cora interjected, "If you are angry with Markka, then you must direct your anger toward me and Commander Leahcim, as we all made the same promise."

Tory stepped toward her with a pained expression on his face as he took her face in his hands. He looked directly into her shimmering eyes. "I am shocked, to say the least, but I am not angry with you. I am sure T'oann had her reasons for making you promise not to tell me. If anything, I am proud of you for honoring her wish." He wrapped his wife in his strong arms and hugged her with every fiber of his being.

Zora, on the other hand, said nothing.

When Tory released her, Markka stepped back and said, "There's one other thing." She paused wishing she did not have to tell them more disturbing news, but she continued. "I just found out about it myself." She winced as she said it.

"What else is there to say?" Zora asked. She was noticeably flustered.

Markka knew there was no delicate way to tell them, so she decided to take the direct route. She drew in a breath, exhaled, and said, "Tonga's son is the Disposal Team Commander."

CHAPTER 42

"Cora, unlock this door now!" Zora demanded.

"I am afraid I cannot do that at this time," Cora said.

More insistent and even more belligerent, Zora said, "I order you to unlock this door." Her anger and frustration were palpable.

"I am sorry, Commander, but I cannot do that."

"I'm sorry too," Tory said. "As your king, I command you to stand down." His expression was stone-faced.

Zora was seething. "You cannot, no, will not, keep me from exacting retribution for my parents!" She said through gritted teeth.

"Zora," Markka said in a calming voice. "If you don't stand down, I will relieve you of your duties and place you under house arrest for disobeying the commands of your king and queen."

"You wouldn't dare," Zora challenged. Her eyes flared with heated anger. If looks could kill, everyone in her field of vision would be dead.

"I love you with every fiber of my being, but if you defy us, you will regret it." Tory returned Zora's look.

Zora studied Markka's and Tory's faces for any sign they were bluffing. She saw none.

"Okay," she reluctantly relented. "I will refrain from exacting revenge. For now."

"Good," Markka said. "And to make sure you don't, Cora, please activate the force field."

"Right away, your majesty."

A moment later, Zora was immobilized within an invisible barrier that surrounded her entire body and held her in place. She was not in any pain, but the more she struggled, the more restrictive the field became. Zora was forced to quickly come to terms with her situation and relaxed.

Tory watched his niece struggle against the force field. He had never seen his niece contained. "Impressive," he told Markka.

Once Zora accepted her current situation, Markka took Tory's hand and asked if he was ready to find out what happened to Leahcim and T'oann and why they were with Tonga and her son. He nodded and Cora let them out of the room. All Zora could do was watch. So she sat in a meditative position and waited.

A mos passed before her parents were revived and examined. Zora watched as an army of healers went about their work helping the remaining survivors with their recoveries. She seethed as she watched her parents talking with Markka and Tory, as well as . . . her aunt and cousin. The thought of it made her stomach churn.

Unable to stand the isolation and immobilization, she swallowed her pride and asked Cora if she could at least listen in.

Cora cheerfully replied, "Certainly, Commander."

Zora swore it sounded like Cora was having fun at her expense, but she brushed it off as a symptom of her emotional distress and listened intently to the conversation.

"How the hell are you two still alive?" Markka asked. "We all watched you both die two cycles ago."

"We did die." Leahcim began.

"But the Goddess gave us a second chance," T'oann finished.

"By the Maker, by the Goddess, I'm happy you're both alive. What happened? Come on. Fill in the blanks."

"Well," T'oann began, "when we were impaled, husband and I mind-walked. We knew we were dying; we didn't want to die alone."

"So," Leahcim continued, "through excruciating pain, we found each other one last time."

"And as our consciousness began to fade," T'oann said, "something . . . someone grabbed us and pulled us away from our bodies."

"It was Tonga's son, Marshon," Leahcim said. "He carried our life forces to the ancestral burial grounds of the Mountain People as part of an elaborate ploy to rescue us."

"Yes," Tonga interjected. She was now fully recovered and joined in the conversation. "My son and I have been working with the resistance. He was working within Shang's inner circle, I was working with the Mountain People and those of the Dark Woods. When you and my sister were captured, we devised a plan to rescue you both. We did not anticipate how swiftly Shang was going to kill you."

Markka interrupted. "Apologies for interrupting, and please don't misconstrue my next question, but how are you still alive? T'oann said you took your own life twelve cycles ago."

"Oh, that." Tonga cleared her throat. "The search party that found me was that of a Dark Woods resistance cell. When I stabbed myself, I made it look as if I pierced vital organs. In her weakened condition, my sister did not notice I had not. I feigned death so she would not linger in case the search team was truly the one Shang sent to look for us." She tossed an apologetic glance at T'oann, who stood expressionless. "After my sister headed for the Dark Woods," Tonga continued, "the resistance team administered to my wound, and cleared the area so there would be no evidence we were ever there. My Dark Woods allies also made certain my sister made it back to Uderra safely."

Satisfied with Tonga's explanation, Markka apologized again for interrupting and said, "Please continue telling us how you were able to rescue Leahcim and T'oann."

"So," a deeper third voice chimed in, "I and my operatives manipulated Shang into letting us take their bodies to the sacred burial grounds. The third voice belonged to Marshon. "We needed to stroke his ego and stoke his anger. We staged the attack on my unit.

200

Once my team was eliminated, we made a show of my death."

"Then I took your life forces from my son and placed them back into your bodies once the healers had stabilized them," Tonga finished.

"They used nanites to repair our bodies," Leahcim added.

"But the mountain? We all saw it get pulverized—" Markka suddenly registered the full weight of what Leahcim had just said. "Wait. Nanites?"

"Yep."

"But how . . . they have that level of technology?" Markka sidetracked herself and her thought process. "Never mind. How did you get frozen?" She finally decided to ask.

"We were in the process of evacuating when everything caved in on us," T'oann lamented.

"The cryogenic conduits ruptured just as the blast doors closed," Tonga said.

"And we died again," T'oann said, "and now you tell us it's two cycles later."

"Wow," Markka said. "You guys have more lives than a Terran house cat. You'll need to be briefed on what's happened since you guys got buried. Swing by my place this evening for an update—and a surprise. And don't ask me what because I'm not saying."

"Fine. We won't ask." Leahcim knew that once Markka made up her mind about something, there was no changing it. So when she said, "Don't ask," he knew not to ask. He decided to shift the focus of their conversation to something else. "So, how are our kids doing?" he asked.

Markka burst into a big grin. "You guys'll be proud of them. They're all doing well and excelling in their respective fields. Which reminds me," Markka glanced over toward the isolation chamber, "there's someone anxious to see you." Then she looked at Marshon and said, "You, however, if you value your life, you might want to disappear for a while."

"Why's that?" Marshon asked.

"Because Cora is currently holding Zora captive in the isolation chamber. And she's none too happy to see you."

Marshon took a deep breath and let it out. He crossed his arms defiantly and said, "May as well get this over with now."

Markka looked Marshon up and down before she said, "Okay, but it's your funeral." Then told Cora, "Release the scorb."

"As you wish," Cora replied.

The small group huddled together in front of Marshon watching Zora guardedly as she approached them.

The first thing Zora did was hug her parents and began apologizing for letting them get captured. "I'm so sorry. I let you down. I failed you." She did her best to keep her emotions in check but was quickly losing control.

Markka and Tory judiciously moved the rest of the group to a discreet distance to allow Zora and her parents some privacy.

"You could never let us down," T'oann said in a comforting tone. She lovingly caressed her daughter's cheek.

"But you died . . . almost died . . . whatever, on my watch."

"What happened wasn't your fault," Leahcim said. He stepped back, held his daughter by her shoulders, and told her, "What happened couldn't be helped. None of us was prepared for what happened."

"But—"

"But nothing," T'oann assured her. "As your father might say, 'Shit happens.'"

Zora looked at her mother and smiled.

"Well, what do you know," Leahcim teased, "she *can* smile." He paused before he said, "Oh, yeah. One more thing. Markka says you want to personally help Marshon meet the Goddess."

"About that," she cleared her throat, "Cora let me hear what you all were saying. I am not as inclined to kick Marshon's ass as much as I was before."

"Great!" T'oann said.

"But I reserve the right to do so if he deserves an ass-kicking."

That's my girl," Leahcim said proudly.

While Zora and her parents made the best of their reunion, Markka told Tonga she needed to speak with Tory and excused herself as she led her husband a few steps away and spoke with him in a hushed tone. "I hate to be the bearer of bad news, but with Tonga back in the picture, our little reign as king and queen is over."

He looked at her and saw both relief and remorse in her face. She was relieved that she would no longer be considered Uderra's queen, but it hurt her to know that he would no longer be king.

"Well," he sighed, "It was fun while it lasted."

"For what it's worth, I am sorry it didn't work out," Markka said. She paused then said, "Well, let's get this over with. Are we together on this?"

He assured her he was and took her paws into his hands and asked, "Shall we?" He led her back over to Tonga and Marshon where he bowed before his sister and addressed her with the respect befitting her position, "My Queen." Markka echoed the sentiment.

Of all the things Tonga was prepared for, this sudden turn of events was not something she ever envisioned. She was blindsided.

"What?" She had that look a dazed boxer has just before the fight is called.

Both Tory and Markka looked at her with uncertainty. "What do you mean, 'what?'"

Markka asked. "You're the rightful ruler of Uderra."

"I cannot accept," Tonga said. She regained some of her composure.

"But you are next in succession to the throne," Tory insisted. "It is your birthright."

"I lost that birthright when I was stolen from my home and raised to fight and kill my brethren. I do not deserve the throne. I am not worthy."

"But our traditions must be upheld," Tory said. "You must assume the throne."

"For once I agree with my stick-up-his-ass husband," Markka said.

Tonga stood quiet and pensive for a few moments before she spoke. "Very well," she began. "In compliance with our laws and traditions, and recognized as the rightful queen of Uderra, I hear-by decree that effective immediately, I ordain my brother, Tory, of the House of Mahli, heir, successor, and rightful ruler of Uderra, abdicate the throne, and officially renounce my birthright and all privileges associated with it."

Without skipping a beat, Tory seized the opportunity and accepted.

"Wait. What just happened?" Markka asked.

Marshon grinned then broke out laughing. "Looks like you're still the queen, your highness."

"Shit," was all Markka thought to say.

CHAPTER 43

Back at their bungalow, T'oann and Leahcim took some time to relax and reflect on recent events.

"I can't believe it's been two cycles," T'oann said. "For us, it was just yesterday the mountain caved in on us. Now we're supposed to go see Markka so she can catch us up on what's been going on."

"It does feel weird," Leahcim agreed. "At least the Thourons haven't overrun the place yet."

"You know what that means?" T'oann said wryly.

"What?"

"Our chances of dying again just increased."

"At least that hasn't changed," Leahcim said.

They sat cuddled together on a small bench in their garden listening to the running stream and speculating on what Markka had planned at the briefing. When their escorts arrived, T'oann and Leahcim headed for their briefing with Markka both poised and refreshed.

The trip to Markka's home was pleasantly uneventful. They disembarked from their transport and were escorted to the briefing room where they were surprised and moved to tears when they were greeted by their children. Even Markka's children were there. Hugs, kisses, and emotional platitudes were passed around and shared.

"This is a most pleasant surprise, Markka," T'oann told her. "Thank you."

"I'm not done. There's one more surprise. It's for you, David."

"Wow. This must be important for you to call me by my first name. You hardly ever call me by my first name."

"I suggest you sit down for this," Markka said.

Everyone else in the room sat down around the conference room table. No one spoke. So Leahcim and T'oann did the same.

After everyone was seated, Markka said, "Cora, please send in our guests."

"Right away, your majesty."

From behind a black curtain on one side of the room entered the crew of the *Infiltrator*.

Captain Vee was the first to speak. "Hello, Commander. Good to see you again." She then saluted him along with the rest of the crew.

Leahcim sat staring at his friends unable to move or speak. A wave of emotions ranging from happy to sad, angry and confused, to grateful and bemused flooded through him. After a few moments, he regained most of his composure, stood on shaky legs, and returned their salute. Then sat back down visibly shaken. T'oann could tell his emotions were overwhelming him. For the first couple of cycles, all he talked about was missing his friends, and how they were probably looking for them. But as time passed, he eventually came to terms with never seeing them again. And now here they were in the flesh. And he appeared to have some kind of stressful reaction upon finally seeing them. Concerned about his mental well-being, T'oann decided to mind-walk with her husband. She lightly touched his hand and entered his mind.

"I am here, husband. You are not alone. What is it that has distressed you?"

"These are my friends," he replied. "The ones I said were probably looking for us? They came. After all this time. They still came. They found us."

"I thought you would be glad to see them if you ever saw them again. So why are you so upset? Aren't you happy?"

"Yes . . . Yes, I am."

"I am happy for you. So if you are so happy, why do you appear to be so sad?"

"Because they've come all this way and I'm not so sure if I want to go back anymore. Markka and Cora and I have lives here now. We have families and new friends. We just can't drop everything and go back with them. At least I can't."

"Well, just tell them that."

"I can't."

"Why not?" T'oann felt the intense stress eating away at him.

"Because," he faltered before continuing, "I'm torn. Because part of me wants to go with them, but another part wants to stay. I have a life here now. I have a wife I love and kids I adore, friends, and commitments. I just can't give all of that up to go back to a life I haven't lived in more than ten cycles."

"I can't tell you what to do. I can only say you need to follow your heart. Whatever you decide will be the correct decision. And I will abide by it. Now, we need to get back to the others."

Leahcim and T'oann broke their link and rejoined the others in the now silent room. All eyes were trained on them. Raqmar was the first to break the silence. "What the hell just happened?"

Leahcim laughed nervously. "Oh. That. Uh, that was a mind-walk. My wife and I were discussing something of, um, great concern to us."

"Wait," Sparks said. "Did you just communicate telepathically with your wife?"

Attempting to save Leahcim from any more discomfort, T'oann spoke up. "Yes, we were speaking what you call telepathically."

The entire *Infiltrator* crew turned toward Markka who quickly said, "Hey, don't look at me. I can't do that." They all turned back to T'oann and Leahcim.

T'oann explained that she had the ability and discovered that Leahcim had the trait. So she taught him how to use it.

This time it was Captain Vee who asked, "Does anyone else have this ability?"

"Only two others," Markka replied.

"Who else knows about this?" Vee asked.

"Only those of us in this room. Their ability is classified. So if you go and spill the beans, I'll have to kill you."

Vee wasn't sure if Markka was joking, but judging from the facial expressions of everyone else in the room, she surmised Markka was serious—just maybe not about the killing part she hoped. Living on Progensha for more than a decade no doubt changed Markka, Leahcim, and Cora. The *Infiltrator* suddenly showing up did not help make things any easier. They were not the same friends she knew a week ago. Even if Markka was joking, others in the room might not have any reluctance about killing her and her crew. She decided to err on the side of caution.

"You have my word that what we witnessed here today will remain classified," Vee said. She turned to address her crew. "Does anybody have a problem with that?"

They all replied in unison, "No, sir."

"Good."

"Now that we've got that out of the way," Markka said, "I just want to say just how thankful I am to you guys for the effort you made in trying to save us, but like I said before, and I don't mean to sound ungrateful, but I will not be going back with you. Tell Fleet I stayed of my own free will."

"Ditto for me," Cora said.

Everyone turned to Leahcim.

Before I give you my answer," he said, "I have a question."

"What's your question?" Vee asked.

"What took you so long? And why do you all look so young?"

Before Vee could respond, Markka interjected. "Uh, about that. There's a bit of a snag. To them, we've only been gone a wee bit over a week."

"What?" Leahcim asked, confused.

"Sorry," Markka apologized. "In all of the excitement, I sort of forgot to mention the time displacement thing."

"What the hell are you talking about, Markka? We've been gone for eleven cycles."

"Uh, Cora? Sojourner? One of you want to explain the situation to the Commanders?"

"Certainly, your majesty," Cora said.

"The slipstream that brought us here," Cora began, "passed through some kind of event horizon or portal into another universe. It does not affect those passing through it. However, time passes differently for each universe sharing the portal."

"What was eleven days for us in our universe," Sojourner continued, "was approximately eleven years for you, Markka, and Cora in this one.

"And since Captain Vee and her crew have only been here for three sols," Cora explained, "if they were to return now, it would only be a matter of minutes if not hours for them back in their universe."

"So if we go back just for a month and return, we'll be great grandparents," Markka said.

Leahcim sat ramrod straight and stared out into space. He looked like he saw something in the room no one else could see. After a few moments of pin-drop quiet, he slowly stood up and excused himself before leaving the room.

"Well," Markka said, piercing the awkward silence. "That went better than I expected."

T'oann looked at Markka, who gave her a secretive nod. T'oann excused herself and followed after her husband. She caught up with him outside at the bottom of the palace steps where he was leaning against the transport which brought them to the briefing.

As the late evening suns blazed overhead, Leahcim stood unsteady on his feet more like he had imbibed a bit too much ambrosia and needed something—anything—to use to keep himself standing upright.

"What do you wish to do?" T'oann asked.

Leahcim looked more shell-shocked than inebriated. Without looking at her he said, "I need to get out of here."

T'oann spoke softly into her wrist comm to summon their driver. When she arrived, T'oann requested she take them home.

CHAPTER 44

Neither T'oann nor Leahcim spoke during the ride back home. When they arrived at their residence, T'oann released the driver from her duties while Leahcim simply exited the vehicle and walked straight into their compound. T'oann jogged a little to catch up. Together, they wordlessly passed through the garden to their bungalow. Once inside, he collapsed into the nearest chair and sat there until he eventually fell asleep. T'oann retired to their bedroom and laid down on the bed wondering what to do.

She knew her husband well enough to know that trying to make him talk about what preoccupied his mind would be a wasted effort. He would talk about whatever was bothering him when he was ready. She needed to give him his space to work things out. In that respect, she knew they were perfectly matched. She spread out on the bed and let its comforting softness lull her into a troubled sleep.

When she awoke, it was dark. Night had fallen upon them. She sat up in the darkness and felt around the bed for her husband. He was not next to her. Panic set in as she started visualizing images of him doing something out of character.

She called out to him through the darkness. There was no answer. "Cora?"

"Yes, Commander?" Cora said in a soothing tone.

"Where is my husband?"

"He is currently in the garden."

"Thank you."

"You're welcome."

T'oann rose from the bed, asked Cora to turn the lights on to their lowest illumination, and made her way to the garden where she found him stretched out on the ground staring up at the stars in the night sky.

"Am I intruding?" she asked, looking down on him.

"No. Not at all. I'd love it if you kept me company for a while." He leaned on an elbow, patted the grass next to him then laid back down. The distress, which had etched itself in his voice and mannerisms earlier, seemed to have disappeared. T'oann sat on the cool grass beside her husband, stretched out, and snuggled next to him. She breathed an audible sigh of relief, but the concern for her husband remained.

"Care to talk about it?" was all she thought to say.

He stared up into the onyx void, with its twinkling lights suspended above them before he spoke. "Before this morning, I thought I'd gotten over missing my old life," he said, "but seeing my friends again brought all of those feelings flooding back. Hard. And to know that I have an opportunity to go and get that life back after all this time . . . harder."

"Well, as I said," T'oann began, "whatever you decide, I will respect your decision."

"What I want is to take you with me and show you my world. But I know I can't take you away from your people, your family, your world. To ask you to give up everything you've ever known is selfish." He heaved a saddened sigh. "I look at the stars and wish I was flying among them again. I miss the thrill of jumping from star system to star system. I miss the adrenaline rush of piloting a starfighter in combat. But if I make that choice, I may never see you again. And I can't bear to lose you."

"You could never lose me," T'oann said. No matter where you are in my universe or yours, I will always be with you. But I could never live with myself knowing it was I who kept you from fulfilling your destiny. "

"And I couldn't live with myself knowing I made the worst decision of my life." He remained pensive for a moment before he resumed speaking. "All my life I've believed we make our own choices, decide our own destinies. Now I'm not so sure."

Intrigued, T'oann asked, "What do you mean?"

"Have you ever stopped to wonder if we truly make our own decisions or whether what we choose has already been decided for us by God, the Goddess, the Maker, the universe, or fate? That our lives have been predestined and we are simply actors performing predetermined roles with predetermined outcomes?"

T'oann thought for a moment. "I've never truly thought about it in that way before," she said. "I have always believed that we make our own choices, and the consequences of those choices determine any future choices we make. I do believe there is a guiding hand, an intelligence, helping us decide which choices to make, but I do not believe our choices are not our own to make."

Leahcim stopped looking at the stars and rolled slightly to face his wife. "Good. Because I've made *my* decision."

T'oann looked at him straight in his brown eyes. She had a sad expression on her face. T'oann's voice cracked slightly as she snuggled closer and said, "I will miss you dearly, my husband."

"As I, you," he said. "Which is why I'm staying." He felt the tension immediately flow from her as her body nervously vibrated against his.

He wrapped his arm around her trembling form and drew her closer to him. He kissed her lightly on her quivering lips and waited for her to slip into his mind. T'oann reciprocated without hesitation; together they spent an intensely intimate night below the blanket of the stars.

CHAPTER 45

The following morning, they awoke to the warming air as the twin suns began their rise in the morning sky. They greeted each other with equally warm hugs and kisses before they left the serenity of the garden and went into the house to begin their day.

After a quick, invigorating shower, they sat down in the garden and ate a light breakfast, and discussed their plans for the day.

"You know, we still have to be debriefed," T'oann began. "We have no idea what's happened during our absence."

"Sorry about that," he said, as he stabbed a slice of boar meat with his fork. "I shouldn't have lost my shit yesterday." He shoved the forkful into his mouth and thoughtfully chewed.

"All things considered, I'm surprised it didn't happen sooner," T'oann said. She took a couple of sips of her glass of nectar. "After everything we've been through."

"After everything we've been through," he bit off another bit of meat and chewed before he said, "I'm surprised you haven't had a meltdown of your own."

T'oann put her glass down and reached for his hand. "You have no idea," she said. "You are my support. My rock. My foundation," she said. "I had no one before you fell from the sky. I accepted my status in life and all of the responsibilities that came along with it. I never allowed myself the luxury of thinking that I needed anyone. Ever. Even when I was captured by Shang. I accepted it as my obligation to my people."

"And then you were rescued by your sister," he said.

"Yes. Without her intervention, I wouldn't have gotten the chance for you to come into my life."

Leahcim reached for his glass of nectar and sipped. "But if my memory serves me correctly, you wanted me, Markka, and Cora dead."

She let go of his hand and looked down at the table. "Until I laid eyes on you, I didn't know just how much I needed someone in my life. And then, boom, there you were. I was drawn to you immediately. And I was revolted by my own longing. It disgusted me." When she looked at him again, her eyes were moist. "So I tried to deny those feelings and convince myself that you were a threat and not a savior."

"But why would you be disgusted by something you longed for?" She had his full attention.

"I guess my reaction to you was a form of a breakdown. I was drawn to you . . . because you were an outsider, and I felt like one among my people."

He reached for her other hand. "Call it fate or whatever, but I'm glad I fell from the sky."

Their conversation was interrupted by Cora's voice. "Ahem."

They both looked at each other and suddenly realized they spent the night in the garden. They forgot that Cora surveilled all public spaces.

"Sorry, Cora, we forgot where we were," Leahcim said.

"I assure you I was discreet and accorded you both total privacy."

"Thank you. We appreciate your discretion," T'oann said.

"You are welcome, but the time has come for you to meet with your queen. She's been trying to reach you both since you left the briefing room yesterday."

"Sorry about that," Leahcim apologized."

"And you, Commander Leahcim, have a question to answer. Captain Vee and her crew deserve an answer."

"Okay, fine," he said. "We'll head over to the briefing room when we're finished breakfast."

"I will inform the queen, commander."

"Thanks." Then he had an epiphany. "Cora? Are you permitted to brief us on the current state of affairs?"

"Yes, commander."

"Well then, lay it on us."

CHAPTER 46

They ate breakfast while Cora caught them up on everything that happened during the two cycles they spent in frozen suspension. Halfway through, Leahchim remarked, "Holy shit. Things took a turn for the worse?"

"That is correct," Cora confirmed. "With the loss of both of you, Tonga and Marshon, and the massive attack on the Mountain People, the coalition was thrown into chaos. The coalition started to fall apart. Markka and Tory were able to fill the void and hold things together, but the coalition exists in a tenuous balance."

"And Shang has taken advantage of the disarray he instigated," T'oann added.

"Yes, but now that you are back, and have decided to stay, I am certain the prevailing hope will be you can provide the leadership and stability the coalition desperately needs."

Leahcim swirled his drink before he said, "Well, what are we waiting for? Let's not keep our friends waiting." He rose from the table and reached for T'oann's hand. She took it and they left the compound. "I'm driving," he said.

"I will inform the queen you are on your way," Cora said.

"You do that," T'oann called out as the door to their compound closed behind them. She turned to Leahcim and asked, "Are you sure you want to drive?"

"Yep," he grinned.

As they took their seats, Leahcim noticed T'oann reached for her seatbelt and buckled up. "She turned to look at him and said, "It's been a while so go easy on the turns."

"What?" he asked. He buckled himself up, threw her a wink, and punched it. If the transport had tires, they would have screeched and left their mark on the ground.

They got to the palace in what T'oann thought was record time.

"See?" he said, "We're here in one piece. You can let go of the grip now."

"I'll let go when we stop."

"We've stopped."

"Oh," she teased. "It feels like we're still moving."

"Oh shut up."

They got out of the transport and proceeded up the steps to the briefing room where Markka was waiting for them.

"It's about time you brought your skinny butts back here," she playfully admonished.

"Tell me, Markka, does everyone you know have a skinny butt?" T'oann asked.

"Bite me," Markka retorted. In a more serious tone, Markka asked, "Are you okay, David? You gave everyone a scare yesterday."

"Yeah, I'm fine now." He gave her one of his signature winks for assurance. "So where is everybody?"

"I asked Vee if she and the crew were up for a clandestine mission."

"What the hell did you do? You know they can't get involved with the geopolitics of this world—even if it is in another universe."

"We did," she challenged.

"We didn't have a choice; they do. They can leave anytime they want. We couldn't."

"Relax. They're just doing a stealth reconnaissance run. Since the *Infiltrator* is the most advanced thing on the planet, I just asked Vee if she and the gang would do a cloaked survey run of the planet—especially the Land of No Return. Since air travel is practically nonexistent, Cora and I thought it would be a good idea to use the *Infiltrator* to our advantage since her drones have a limited range."

"Drones?" T'oann asked. "What are they?"

"Oh yeah. You guys still have some catching up to do. We sorta have an air force now," Markka beamed with pride. She quickly explained to T'oann what drones are. When she finished, Leahcim expressed his displeasure at not being informed of the existence of the drones.

"Cora briefed us before we came over here; she said nothing about drones." The irritation in Leahcim's voice was noticeable. He crossed his arms and demanded an explanation. "Cora, you need to come clean with us."

"Very well," Cora said. "The drones are experimental prototypes. We use them for nighttime reconnaissance only. We are concerned that if we use them during daylight, the Thourons will become aware of them and attempt to acquire one. According to our intelligence reports, they are unaware of their existence."

"And we'd like to keep it that way for as long as we can," Markka said. "That's all we need. Thouron drones flying overhead. We'd lose our edge. We rarely deploy them. So if Cora neglected to mention them, it's because they are so seldom used. They're considered more of a liability than an asset. A great idea that might not be so great. So I thought, why not take advantage of the *Infiltrator*'s cloaking technology?"

Markka's explanation visibly calmed Leahcim's concerns. He stroked his chin as he considered what Markka told him. "Okay. There's no harm in using Vee and her crew to learn more about the planet. A little extra knowledge might come in handy."

"Exactly!" Markka agreed. "A cloaked ship might give *us* an edge over the Thourons for a change." She eyed Leahcim warily to gauge his mood. Satisfied he had calmed down enough to reason with, she moved on to her next concern. "Now," she said, "have you decided on whether you're staying or not?"

Without any hesitation, and maybe a bit too enthusiastically, he said, "Yes, I have. I'm staying."

"You sure? Yesterday, you seemed to have had a near emotional meltdown."

"I'm good. I just needed to sleep on it." He put an arm around T'oann. "My wife here helped me get through it."

Markka suspiciously eyed them both trying to decide whether to believe him or not.

T'oann satisfied Markka's concern by telling her she trusted Leahcim's commitment to his decision implicitly. "As your people say, 'I would bet my life on it.'"

"Whew! That's a relief. Saved me and Cora the energy."

"The energy for what?" Leahcim and T'oann asked.

"If you had said you were leaving, we were going to kidnap your ass and tell Vee you changed your mind."

Leahcim was genuinely surprised that they planned to kidnap him and lie to Vee and her crew. "Really? You two were going to do that?"

She gave him a long stare before she said, "No. I just said that to see how you would react."

"You are so lucky you're the queen."

"I know, right?" she said with a big, silly grin plastered on her face. Then more seriously, she told them how much they were missed and how glad she was now they were back.

"We're glad to be back," T'oann said.

CHAPTER 47

"So," Markka said, "aside from the drones, Cora's caught you up on what's happened in your absence."

"Yeah, she filled us in," Leahcim confirmed.

"Good. So you know things went to shit after you died, uh, disappeared. Whatever."

"Cora said you and Tory filled the vacuum in our absence," T'oann said.

"Fat lotta good that did. We've barely been able to keep the coalition together. We just don't have the charisma you two have."

T'oann approached Markka and put a hand on her shoulder being careful not to mind-walk with her. "Don't sell yourself short," she told Markka. "All things considered, you two have done an admirable job. If it had been anyone else, Uderra and the coalition would have collapsed and been under the control of Shang and his people."

"You think so?"

"I believe so."

"Sorry to interrupt, your highness," Cora said, "but you asked to be informed when the *Infiltrator* returned. They are waiting for you at the staging area.

"Oh good. Let's go see what the gang has to report. Cora, have a transport ready in five."

"It will be ready, your highness."

Markka tossed Leahcim and T'oann a woeful glance, "One of these days," she muttered."

T'oann was always amused by how much Cora's use of honorific handles irked Markka so she decided to try something, but she needed to get Markka's permission.

"My queen," T'oann began.

"Not you too," Markka lamented. She sighed a heavy exhausted sigh. "You know, since your sister doesn't want this job, it should rightfully be yours. All you have to do is say you want your birthright and I'll abdicate in a heartbeat."

"And how would the king feel? Hmmm?"

"The *king*," Markka made a point of emphasizing the word, "would be happy not to have to perform kingly duties, and you would be queen. Hell, I've only had the job two cycles, and look at me. I'm a wreck."

"You're a natural," T'oann assured her. "I don't want the position. I am happy where I am. But I believe I can solve a problem you have. All I need is your permission."

"Okay, but if you change your mind, the job is yours. Now, what do you want my permission for?"

"A mind-walk."

Markka nearly choked. "Come again?"

"I would like your permission to mind-walk with you."

Markka became as giddy as a school kid. "Say no more. Mind-walk away."

T'oann turned to Leahcim and said, "I'll be right back." Then took Markka's hand and entered her mind.

"Wow! This is so cool. So this is what it feels like. I'm jealous. Are we floating? It feels like we're floating." Markka marveled at the mental representation of her physical body. "I think I could get used to this. Whoa. I'm sensing feelings that aren't mine." She studied the emotional recreation of T'oann at the same moment she realized she was experiencing T'oann's amusement. "Whoops. Sorry. So, what's so important that we have to mind-walk?"

"It's about Cora."

"What about her?"

"If you want her to call you by your name instead of by your title, just command her as her queen to address you by your name."

She frowned slightly before exclaiming, "Damn! The solution was as plain as the whiskers on my face." The realization that she could do that never occurred to her. "Why didn't I think of that?"

"Because you're the queen. You have others to think of those things for you. Now if you don't mind, I want to get back to my husband."

"Oh yeah. Sure, sure."

T'oann broke the connection and looked at Leahcim.

"What was that about?" he asked.

"Oh, just helping a friend in need."

"That's it?"

"Yep."

Markka's wrist comm beeped. Their ride had arrived. "Our ride is here."

The three of them left the briefing room and headed to the transport. Markka was humming a Felidian song. The mind-walk made her giddy.

They arrived at the staging area where the *Infiltrator* was resting. T'oann stared in wonder at the ship. The mind-walks with Leahcim were wonderful, but they were no substitute for seeing the real thing. "It's enormous." T'oann was in total awe. Her face was pressed against the transport window.

"Are you going to sit there drooling or are you going to join us?" Leahcim asked.

"I think she wants to drool," Markka said.

T'oann caught herself and pretended they were seeing things. "I wasn't drooling."

"I love it when you use contractions," Leahcim teased. He flashed her a wink and offered his hand.

"I can get out on my own," she playfully huffed.

Captain Vee and Sparks were waiting to receive Markka, Leahcim, and T'oann at the bottom of the ship's loading ramp.

Vee exchanged pleasantries with Markka and T'oann before addressing Leahcim.

"Good to see you, David. I trust you're doing well?"

"Much better than yesterday. Thanks."

"Great. Good to hear it."

"Before we get started, I believe I owe you an answer to your question." Leahcim looked at his wife and gave her a reassuring smile. "I'm staying. My life is here now. And I'm not going to leave it."

"I thought that might be your answer. I've seen the life you have here and, considering the circumstances, I agree with your decision." Vee looked at Markka and said, "That goes for you and Cora."

"Cool. Now that we got that out of the way, what news have you got for me?" Markka asked.

"We surveyed the planet and we found something intriguing. First, there are three continents. The one we're on is the largest and the only one that's inhabited. The oceans are full of what can best be described as sea monsters, there are no birds—or anything else that flies—and the part of the desert you guys call the Land of No Return contains lethal levels of radiation. And on the other side of that are what can best be described as mutated life forms. The radiation zone protects your side from being overrun."

Markka let out a long whistle. "Now aren't you glad we didn't crash land there?"

Leahcim rubbed his chin in thought. "That might explain that *thing* T'oann and I fought in

Shang's arena. They somehow managed to capture one." He stopped rubbing his chin and asked, "Any idea what the source of the radiation field is?"

"Sparks? You want to run with this one?"

"Sure thing, cap." Sparks' excitement was most apparent when her hue transitioned to lime green as she explained what they found. "There's a lot of residual background radiation that interfered with our sensors. Needless to say, Sojourner wasn't too happy about that. And as you know she tends to get testy when—"

"Ahem, lieutenant?" Vee saw Sparks was about to go off on a tangent so she stepped in to put her navigator back on track. "Can you get back to the report?"

Sparks turned an even lighter shade of green before she returned to the point.

"Uh, sorry about that."

Leahcim gave her a wink and said, "No problem, lieutenant. Please continue."

Relieved he wasn't as annoyed with her as her captain was, she continued. "Anyway, we were on the clock so we just took preliminary readings with a cursory flyby. However, what we were able to determine is that it looks like the remains of a crashed starship buried deep below the surface. If we had more time, we would have done a more thorough investigation."

Intrigued, Markka asked if they could identify the ship. Sparks said they could not, but that Sojourner detected traces of an element in the radiation field that was unique to Alliance starships.

"That's odd. What would an Alliance starship be doing here in this universe?" Leahcim wondered aloud more to himself than to the group. No one said a word while he stood there muttering to himself until he asked Sparks, "Any idea how long it's been there?"

"Well, based on the half-life of atomic decay, approximately five hundred years."

"That would mean the ship disappeared from Alliance space about, what?" Leahcim ran through a series of calculations in his mind. "Geez. That would mean the ship disappeared over a year ago in your universe."

"Not possible," Vee said. "There haven't been any reports of missing Alliance starships."

"At least none you're aware of," Markka said. "Cora?"

"Yes, your majesty."

"Two things. First, as your queen, I command you to no longer use an honorific title when addressing me. You are to call me by my given name, Markka, from this moment forward. And secondly, check your records and let me know whether any Alliance ships were deployed on stealth missions in the two years before you, me, and Commander Leahcim crashed here."

"Right away, uh, Markka."

Markka fist-pumped and triumphantly hissed, "Yesssss!" Then she looked at T'oann and smiled. T'oann returned the gesture.

Moments later, Cora said her records indicated two Alliance starships were deployed on classified missions a year before the battle over Aggro Nine. One was an Alliance battle cruiser. The other was a science vessel.

"Do the records indicate where they were deployed?" Leahcim asked.

"The records are heavily redacted, but it appears the *Zulu* was dispatched to protect a diplomatic conference in the Omega sector."

"And the other one?"

"The *Michael P Anderson*. She was sent to study the Gihon Nebula near the Aggro Nine star system."

CHAPTER 48

"No shit!" Markka blurted out, saying what the others were thinking—except for T'oann. "Does the record say whether the ship was lost?"

"Their last transmission said they were monitoring GSE activity in the area and were going to use the nebula to mask their presence. That was the last time they heard from the *Anderson*. It is believed the ship was destroyed by the GSE. All hands lost. No ships or probes were deployed to the area to investigate the disappearance. The starfighters of Delta Squadron were the first Alliance ships dispatched to the area following the disappearance."

"Bastards," Leahcim angrily spat. All heads turned in his direction. His fists were tightly balled and his eyes narrowed. "Fleet knew there was enemy movement in the area and didn't tell us. We went to Aggro Nine believing the area was clear. Relief mission, my ass."

Markka was struck with the same realization. "The shitheads sent us on a fucking suicide mission? Had they told us what they suspected, we would have been prepared." Having nowhere else to sit, Markka plopped down on the ground and stared into nothingness, and softly cried. She whispered through her tears, "All those lives. Wasted. And for what?"

Leahcim joined Markka on the ground next to her. He lowered his head and heaved an angry sigh. "We were expendable," he said. "We were sacrificial lambs. We were—"

"Fodder," Markka finished.

"There's got to be some other explanation," Vee said. Not wanting to believe Fleet would set up an entire squadron to see what the GSE would do.

"Believe what you want, Vee. It doesn't negate the fact that we were sent to Aggro Nine and weren't told the cold-bloods were in the area," Markka said.

"Or the fact that help arrived too late to be effective," Leahcim said. "They used us to gauge their strength and tactics after letting them run around out there unchecked for nearly a year."

Still hesitant to believe it, Vee said when she got back, she would find out for herself if their suspicions were true.

"Knock yourself out," Leahcim said. "But if the decision came from the top, the only things you're going to find are roadblocks and trouble for yourself."

"I'll be prepared for that eventuality if it comes to that," Vee insisted.

"Suit yourself."

"You know," Markka said, "If they did that to us, there's no telling who else they've done it to. Hell, for all we know, they probably sent the *Michael Anderson* to her demise."

"At this point, I wouldn't be surprised." Leahcim shook his head in disbelief.

"Speaking of which," Markka said, "how about we do a flyover of the crash site? I'd love to get back in the air again. How about it, commanders, care to take a little ride?"

Grinning like the fabled Cheshire Cat, Leahcim said, "I thought you'd never ask?" Thankful for the change in mood, he was vibrating with excitement. "Would you like to accompany us, wife?"

T'oann was a bubbling cauldron of excitement. "Yes!" She nearly squealed when she accepted Leahcim's offer. This was better than a dream come true for her.

"How about it, Vee?" Leahcim jerked a thumb at the *Infiltrator* and asked, "You got room in there for one more?"

"Certainly. Sparks, tell the crew we're taking guests aboard."

"Aye, cap." Sparks saluted her captain and headed up the ramp.

Leahcim and Markka helped each other get up from the ground and followed Vee into the ship. They left T'oann standing at the bottom of the ramp dumbfounded. "Well?" Leahcim asked her. "Are you coming or did you change your mind?" T'oann nearly sprinted up the ramp to join the others.

When everyone was aboard, Vee gave the order to cloak and head out to the desert. T'oann stared out the nearest window transfixed.

"Well, what do you think?" Leahcim asked her.

"This is . . . incredible," was all she could think to say.

"Hey, Vee, think you could make a detour and put us in orbit?"

"Sure thing, commander." They were still in the fighter bay so Vee asked Sparks to make orbit then gestured for her guests to follow her up to the bridge. It was a quick ride from the bay to the bridge. The lift doors swished open revealing a brightly lit room the full width of the ship.

T'oann stood in total awe at the size of the ship's bridge. It was larger than the observation deck at the healing center. She gawked with childlike amazement through the enormous windows to space on the other side of them. "Is that Progensha down there?" She stared at the peach-colored sphere illuminated by its twin suns outside the bridge windows.

"Yep," Leahcim said. "But when we last saw it this way, Markka and I were a little busy fighting to stay alive and not crash on it."

"So the commander and I didn't have time to take in its splendor," Markka added. She paused to let T'oann soak in the view before she changed the subject. "Sorry to have to bust your bubble, but we need to get back to the mission."

"Uh-huh," was all T'oann said. She was only half-listening.

Markka looked at Leahcim and shrugged. Leahcim just smiled.

Moments later, Sparks announced, "We're over the coordinates, cap."

"Very good. Take us down."

The ship, invisible to the naked eye and most of the technology on the planet, hovered kilometers above the desert. It was then that the cautious and alert T'oann returned.

"You said there's radiation here. Aren't we too close?"

Sparks answered. "Nah, we're good. The ship has shielding that protects us from the effects of all types of radiation. We could land if we wanted to and suffer no ill effects."

"Wow," was all T'oann said.

"So what can you tell us, Sojourner?" Leahcim asked.

"As Lieutenant Sparks said, we were under orders to do a quick mapping of the planet so we did not have adequate time to take precise readings and do an in-depth survey. However, I can perform a more detailed spectral analysis now that we are here. I have adjusted the sensors to compensate for the radiation interference."

"Do it," Markka ordered. Then remembered she was a guest on Vee's ship. "Sorry, Vee, Sojourner, I forgot where I was."

"No apology is necessary," Vee replied. We were carrying out your orders so basically, this op is yours."

"Well, it isn't exactly an op. I sort of just asked you to do me a favor. That's all.

"Well, since the request came from the Uderran queen, the mapping run was an op performed at the behest of a head of state, and a ranking member of the Alliance military," Vee reminded Markka."

"Whoa. Ranking member? A former member is more accurate," Markka reminded Vee.

"Technically, you're MIA. You're both MIA. That makes you both still active-duty officers in the Alliance military."

"Oh, yeah," was all Markka said.

"So, Sojourner, you may begin your analysis as Queen Markka requested."

While Sojourner and the crew ran tests and analyzed the data, Vee took the others to her conference room adjacent to the bridge to discuss their options. When the doors slid open to let them in, T'oann thought it was worthy of a military leader. The walls were painted some sort of cream color, the mahogany-colored conference table in the center of the room, with matching cushioned chairs, rivaled the briefing room furniture in the palace. She took a seat in a chair across from a room-length window so she could see her planet's horizon.

The rest seated themselves around her and wasted little time discussing their plans for the future. The consensus was they would all go back to their lives, but nothing would be the same for any of them ever again. Markka and Leahcim decided to return to Uderra, rebuild the coalition, and continue their fight against the Thourons with T'oann, Tory, Cora, and their children by their side.

Vee and her crew decided to return to their universe and try to pick up where they left off. Their time on Progensha would only be measured in hours, not the days they spent there. Upon their return, they would begin an undercover investigation for the truth behind the disaster at Aggro Nine.

"I wish you would come back with us," Vee said. "We could use your skills and knowledge."

"Sorry, Vee, but our destinies are here in this universe now. Our choice," Leahcim told her.

"You do realize Fleet will consider you AWOL when they get my report."

"So," Markka said. "What are they going to do? Come through the portal and arrest us?" She snorted a laugh. "By the time they get around to that, we'll be long gone. Our kids'll be running things. Maybe our grandkids. Besides," she sneered, "what the hell do they care? They tried to kill us."

"That's still an unproven assumption."

"Oh come on, Vee, wake up and smell the coffee. They sent us on a suicide mission," Leahcim insisted.

"Well, I'm having difficulty believing that. I need more proof." Vee spoke more forcefully than she intended.

As if on cue, before things looked like they were about to become heated, Sojourner announced she and Sparks finished the survey.

"What does your analysis reveal?" Vee asked. Thankful for the interruption.

There was a momentary pause before Sojourner spoke again. It was completely out of character for her not to respond immediately. "Our analysis has determined the vessel buried in the ground below is the *Michael P Anderson*."

A shroud of silence descended over the table before Markka pierced it with, "Is that sound I hear a roach pissing on the carpet?"

"Looks like you got your smoking gun, Vee. What do you think of Fleet now?" Leahcim asked.

Vee let out a long breath and nervously cleared her throat. "Looks like your suspicions are . . . probable."

"Probable?" Markka asked. There was a harshness in her voice. "Probable my ass. This is what we know: they sent the *Anderson* on an intelligence-gathering mission and something went wrong. Instead of following up and finding out what happened, they sat on their asses for a year and did nothing. Then some shithead thought it was a great idea to send us on, what, a relief mission to a sector crawling with cold-bloods? The brass either underestimated the GSE's military capabilities or overestimated Delta Squadron's. It's like we were meant to get wiped out."

Leahcim picked up where Markka left off. "Whatever the case, we ended up paying the price. I feel like we were sold out by Fleet. If I had wanted to go back, I sure as hell don't want to now. And if we're right with what we suspect, what we know makes us targets."

"We all knew the risks when we signed up," Vee said.

"And we were willing to pay the price, but not have our lives simply thrown away at someone's whim."

"What are you going to do now, Captain?" T'oann crossed her arms and waited for an answer to her question.

"I must file my report. I can't lie."

"No one's asking you too, Vee. What my wife is asking is what will you do if you're ordered to forcibly bring us back?"

"Or sent to silence them about what they suspect," T'oann added.

Normally, Vee thought three steps ahead, but in this instance, she was uncertain of what her options were. "Honestly? I don't know."

"Then my people will fight your Fleet if we must." T'oann scowled at Vee. The pleasantness of her soft features hardened.

Vee immediately became defensive. "It won't come to that. You have my word."

"Don't make promises you won't keep," T'oann shot back.

"Believe me, T'oann, when I say, it won't come to that." Vee gambled that addressing T'oann by her name rather than rank would seem more personable. All T'oann did was sit in silent protest.

Leahcim reached over and rubbed his wife's shoulder to help calm her.

The room grew quiet again.

Sparks' voice sang out through the second wave of quiet in the room.

"Captain, the age of the *Anderson* is correct. Based on our metallurgical analysis, radioactive decay, and carbon dating, the ship crashed here approximately five hundred years ago. Give or take a decade."

CHAPTER 49

When the *Infiltrator* returned to Uderra, Leahcim, Markka, and T'oann disembarked.

"You sure we can't change your mind?" Leahcim asked Vee.

"I've talked it over with the crew. We're all in agreement."

"Even Raqmar?" Markka asked.

"Vee smiled an assuring smile. "Yes, even him."

"You're always welcome to join us," Markka said. "Just remember, the offer won't last long. If you wait too long, you'll be working with our grandkids." She let out a loud belly laugh that made everyone smile.

"I'll remember that," Vee said. "Take care of yourselves, you two." Vee saluted them then bowed to T'oann and wished her the same. "Take good care of yourself and my friends."

"I will," T'oann said. Then saluted the captain in the Uderran tradition.

Vee returned the Uderran salute, turned and strolled up the ramp to the fighter bay, and closed the ramp. Within seconds the ship cloaked and rose through the open hangar-like structure and silently headed to space.

"So, do you think we'll ever see them again?" Markka asked.

"It's hard to say," Leahcim said. "Part of me believes we'll never see them again, but part of me says, they'll be back."

"Me too," Markka agreed.

"I think you both are victims of subconscious want and loss," T'oann said.

Leahcim took hold of her hand and looked up at the now-closed hanger ceiling. "You're probably right, but I can't shake the feeling."

Markka cleared her throat. "I think we should get back to the palace and plan our next moves. You two need to get the coalition back on track and we need to include Tonga and Marshon. Their work with the resistance will be invaluable."

Leahcim and T'oann nodded in agreement.

Markka spoke into her wrist comm and summoned a ride; they rode back to the palace exchanging ideas and playful insults.

Back in the briefing room, Markka started talking about what they discovered. "You know, it all makes sense when you factor in the *Anderson*."

"What do you mean?" T'oann had no idea what a ship that was five hundred years old had to do with anything.

The usual lighthearted look that normally framed Markka'a face was replaced by a serious frown that displayed no humor. "Remember when you gave us that vial of Tonga's blood to analyze? And Cora said there were genetic markers we shared?"

"Yes." Markka had T'oann's full, undivided attention.

"And that there was genetic evidence of other species that showed up that belonged to known cultures in the Alliance?"

"Holy shit!" Leahcim cursed. "The Uderrans and all the other cultures on this continent are descendants of those who survived the crash."

Markka slammed her paws on the table and excitedly exclaimed, "Exactly! The longest-lived species in the Alliance are the Selemites. They can live to one hundred and fifty Earth years. So not even the youngest of them who survived would still be alive to remember what happened back then. It's always intrigued me that despite the many varied differences amongst the tribes, there are similarities in appearance, language, and technology. And a collective fuzzy memory." She paused long enough for Leahcim and T'oann to grasp the magnitude of the realization. "Over the centuries, everyone sorta blended together and then separated by choosing which culture they identified with. There were probably so few who survived the crash, and during the days following, that banding together was the safest course of action."

Leahcim snapped his fingers as a thought occurred to him. "The survivors maintained their cultural identities while still upholding the principles and ideals of the Alliance—and they also let nature take its course."

"Offspring?" T'oann asked.

"Bingo! Like us," Markka grinned. "And after centuries of mixing it up, everyone sort of started looking humanoid-ish, but with subtle differences. Hair, feathers, lungs, gills, varied coloring, and hues."

"Like our children," T'oann said.

"Now you got it," Markka agreed.

T'oann considered the theory and was hit with a startling thought and chimed in. "So that might explain why many of the Dark Woods inhabitants resemble your people, Markka, why Uderrans resemble Terrans, and why the Mountain People resemble Raqmar.

"Damn, you're right. His people are Selemites. Okay," Leahcim said, "I can wrap my head around that, but what brought about the schism between them and the Thourons?"

"Best guess?" Markka thought for a moment. "The Thourons were probably the indigenous species native to Progensha and felt threatened by the sudden influx of the strange beings they felt had encroached upon their lands."

"There are stories, mostly legends," T'oann said, "that have been passed down about a Great War that nearly destroyed the world. But since nothing has ever been found to corroborate the stories, they have remained just that. Stories."

"If the stories are true," Leahcim wondered, "then the records and recollections have been lost to the passage of time."

"All the more reason to patch up the coalition," Markka said.

Leahcim banged a clenched fist on the table. "We need to dig into those histories and legends of each coalition member, discover the commonalities, and use that as a foundation to build upon," he finished.

"I suggest we start with the Selemites," Leahcim suggested.

Markka thought it was odd he suggested starting with the Mountain People. "Why them? Why not just have Cora begin digging through Uderran records?"

"Because they're the most technologically advanced members of the coalition." He looked at T'oann. "No offense."

"None was taken," she replied.

He continued to press home his point. "They might have an archive we could look at that might give us an idea of what happened. Besides, if the Uderrans had data, buried somewhere, Cora would have found it by now," he concluded.

T'oann snapped her fingers after remembering something. "There is an old repository of ancient knowledge stored in a vault in the lowest levels of the Royal Palace. It has languished there for generations."

"What's in them?" Markka asked.

"I don't know. As children, we were forbidden to go down there. We were told it was guarded by spirits that would steal our souls if we did. So we never did. We eventually forgot about it."

Her curiosity piqued, Markka asked Cora for assistance on a scheme. "Hey, Cora?"

"Yes, Markka?"

"Would you be willing to help me find those old records and go through them?"

"I would welcome the change in pace."

"Great! I'll get back to you with the details." Markka heaved an exasperated sigh, "Too bad we can't breach the *Anderson* and see what survived the crash and time. It would certainly help fill in any gaps when we start digging into the Uderran and Solemite archives."

"Yeah," Leahcim agreed. "Too bad we didn't think about that before the *Infiltrator* left."

"Why?" T'oann asked. "What difference would it have made?"

Leahcim and Markka both grinned. Knowing she was bursting to tell her, Leahcim let Markka explain.

"The *Infiltrator* has equipment onboard that would allow us to safely go inside the *Anderson* for a short time without danger of long-term radiation poisoning."

"Could not Cora come up with something?" T'oann asked. "She did create those drone things and a body for herself."

"Maybe, maybe not." Markka twitched her whiskers and squinted her eyes as she mulled over T'oann's question. Then she snorted a chuckle. "Hell, if she can create a body for herself, have kids, and make drones, she should be able to come up with something."

"That's it!" Leahcim shouted. He startled both Markka and T'oann. Then he kissed his wife and said, "You're a genius."

Confused, T'oann asked, "What did I say?"

"Drones. We can use them to explore the ship. He planted a kiss square on his wife's lips. "I love you."

"Good call, T'oann," Markka said. "I love you too, but don't expect a kiss from me."

"Cora?" Leahcim asked.

"Yes, commander?"

"How long would your prosthetic body last exposed to the radiation inside the *Anderson*?"

"Based on the readings from the *Infiltrator*, approximately half a mos at best."

"Could you design drones that could fly their way through the *Anderson*?"

"I believe I could. I would need to produce shielding that would protect them from long-term exposure. But, theoretically, yes."

"Good. Would you mind getting right on that?"

"Consider it done, commander."

Then he had another thought. "Also, can you make us something to protect us from the radiation?"

"Not with the current technology we have available."

"The Mountain People might be able to help with that," Leahcim said hopefully. I've seen their technology. It's pretty sophisticated. T'oann and I are alive because of their nanites.

"Indeed. I had not considered what you proposed. The nanites still reside in each of you. They survived the freezing process."

Leahcim snapped his fingers. "That's right. They never got the chance to remove them before we were frozen."

"I might be able to negotiate a mutually beneficial accord with them," Cora said.

"Great. I'll set up a meeting with the leader of the Mountain People and—"

"Sorry to interrupt you, commander, but I was not referring to the Mountain People. I was referring to the nanites."

239

Leahcim, T'oann, and Markka all exchanged questioning stares.

T'oann asked the question begging to be asked. "What do you mean? How?"

"The nanites are highly intelligent life forms capable of independent thought. They are not simply sophisticated microscopic robots. They are a community unto themselves and work with the Mountain People to their mutual benefit."

"And how do you know this?" T'oann asked.

"They told me."

"The Mountain People?"

"No, the nanites."

"Oh great," Leahcim moaned, "Our bodies, our very lives, are being held hostage by beings who could potentially kill us?"

"They assure me they would never do that. Their very existence depends on them keeping you alive. If you were to die, they would eventually cease to exist as well."

Leahcim thought about what this meant for him and T'oann. "Symbiosis," he finally said softly. More to himself than to the others.

"What?" T'oann asked.

"Symbiosis," he repeated. "You and I have a symbiotic relationship with the nanites. If we could learn how to communicate with them, it might prove beneficial to the coalition."

"I have an idea," T'oann said. "Mind-walk with me, husband." She reached out a hand to Leahcim who clasped hers with his. An instant later, they were standing in their incorporeal world and were having a conversation with a chorus of melodic, almost childlike voices speaking as one.

"Greetings," the voices said. "How may we be of service?"

Leahcim and T'oann began their negotiations with the nanites.

Moments later, Leahcim and T'oann were back in the corporeal world.

"Well?!?" Markka asked. She was practically straining like someone trying to eavesdrop on a conversation they were not privy to.

"We have established a way to communicate with them, and they are willing to help us," Leahcim said.

"Great! So what are we waiting for?" Markka asked. "Let's get to work, people. Cora?"

"Yes, Markka?"

Hearing her name rather than her title, was music to Markka's ears. "Contact Tonga and Marshon. Tell them we need to see them ASAP. We got a coalition to rebuild, new allies, a mystery to solve, some butt to kick, and a war to win."

"Will that butt be a skinny one?" Cora asked.

"Bite me."

About the Author

Michael D. Brooks is a fiction and nonfiction writer.

His work has appeared in a variety of literary magazines and national and international publications.

He is the author of three books of short fiction, has a B.A. in Communications, and an M.A. in Writing Studies.

You can also find him on Twitter where he can be found flitting about.

Destined: By Choice or Circumstance is his first science fiction adventure.

Other Books by the Author

Conversations with Pop: the musings of an Average Guy

More Conversations with Pop

Even more Conversations with Pop

Starfighter pilot Captain David Leahcim and his young gunner, Lieutenant Markka, are left to die in the cold of space after their squadron is wiped out.

They are found barely alive by T'oann, a distrustful military commander who will stop at nothing to learn their secrets while hiding one of her own.

Trapped on a world unlike anything they've ever known, in a universe they never knew existed, David and Markka must choose to stay alive long enough to be rescued or sacrifice their lives to save a world at war with itself.

In a bid to end a generations-long conflict her people are desperate not to lose, T'oann must choose to protect her people from certain genocide or trust her feelings and put the fate of her world into the hands of strangers.

Can they gain each other's trust and alter their futures before destiny does it for them?

Made in the USA
Las Vegas, NV
23 October 2021